CW00835727

THE PALETTI NOTEBOOK

Darren Priest Mysteries Book 3

DICK ROSANO

Published 2022 by Next Chapter

Edited by Fading Street Services

Cover art by CoverMint

FLORENCE 1553

SAN MARCO MONASTERY

August 13, 1553

MOST OF THE LAMPS AND TORCHES IN THE NARROW HALLWAYS of the monastery had been extinguished by the time Pietro Paletti made his way toward his cell on the second floor. Head bowed, hands folded at the rope belt around his waist, he padded softly across the stone tiles to the small chamber he had been assigned by Abbot Cisone upon his recent arrival at San Marco.

It was late in the evening and the few lamps still burning left only a disquieting semi-darkness in the hallways and small chapels along his path. At the monastery, night prayers – *compline* – had just ended and the monks were retreating to their private quarters to pray in silence and beg forgiveness for past sins and forbearance for future weaknesses.

Pietro reached his cell, gently swung the wooden door closed, and fell to his knees beside the rope and canvas cot. He addressed his Lord and tried to focus on his confessions, but he was also conscious of every sound beyond the door of his chamber. He had found no peace since coming to San Marco, whether on his knees or curled beneath the thin blanket on his cot. He had not mastered the monk's habit of praying in silence, and as he murmured his entreaty to God, he occasionally silenced his voice to focus on a creak or murmur in the corridor.

Instead of a being absorbed in a communion with the Lord, Pietro's mind kept coming back to his sins and the real reason he found himself in a cold cell in San Marco instead of walking the streets of Florence as a free man, as he had done so recently. Flashes of memory interrupted his concentration – a knife, the furious look on the face of a man engaged in hand-to-hand battle, the shrieks of a woman standing nearby, and the red sticky blood that dripped onto the sidewalk.

Pietro's sub-conscious had dimmed a clear memory of that evening, but the mind that played this trick on him had more deception in store: While hiding the actual retelling of the murder, it still disturbed him with a series of ghostly images of the fight that he had instigated.

"He's not serious about marriage," Pietro had thought of Luca, his rival for the attentions of Isabella, a beautiful daughter of a rich merchant. Pietro had wooed the woman for months with serious intentions, only to see Luca step in with ungentlemanly promises that turned Isabella's head and brought the blood into her cheeks.

"But I won't let Isabella fall under the spell of his charms," he muttered. And yet, he feared that Luca's methods might still seduce the woman and cause her to foreswear the oath she had made to Pietro.

"A woman's pleasure," Pietro muttered in his prayer. He knew that a visual image of his lost love was a sinful diversion from his meditation as a novice monk, but he was too recently a man of the city and had not yet shed his worldly desires. Luca might win the woman over and take her to his bed, and Pietro knew he had to do something. He had to stop him. So, on a dark night weeks before, using a long knife stolen from the kitchen of his father's restaurant, Pietro had gutted Luca like a pig. Right in the street. Right in front of Isabella.

Her primal screams at first sounded like a gleeful spectator's approval, and so Pietro pushed the knife in farther, spilling the man's blood on the stone tiles of the street and yanking the cord of his intestines out after it. But when the deed had been done, Pietro had a moment to consider his action and, suddenly, Isabella's cries sounded different to his ears – more plaintive, more terrified.

He turned toward the woman he loved and saw her face twisted in horror at what she had seen. He saw her eyes bulging from their sockets, tears fully wetting her cheeks, and her mouth gaping open as if in the midst of some silent, voiceless scream.

Isabella met Pietro's eyes and looked at him as if not comprehending what had happened. It didn't come from her love of Luca; no, it emerged from a deep terror in her soul, an unfathomable horror that life and death could meet so quickly, exchange their destiny in a single moment, and then move on.

She ran from thc scene, which was fine with Pietro at first.

Once Isabella was gone, he looked at the knife in his hand, the bloody stones at his feet, and the once-was-man lying prostrate on the street. He had ended Luca's life – with cause, he was sure, but only by his own measure – and now he would face the consequences of judgment by someone else's measure.

The knife simply slipped from his hand as if Pietro was willing it away from him. He turned north onto the street beside the piazza and began walking, then running in the direction of the monastery of San Marco. He had no plan and hadn't considered what he would do if this deed came to pass, but he knew one thing.

If he was caught, he would be hung from the Palazzo Vecchio as a murderer.

Better to retreat to the monastery, confess his sins, and take the vows of a monk. Then he stopped and turned suddenly as he remembered a moral obligation, a family edict, a directive from his long-dead grandfather, Sandro. He bolted back toward the restaurant on the Piazza Gran Duca that his family had run for four generations, dashed into the back room where simple tools of the trade were kept, and retrieved a leather-bound satchel. He tucked it under his arm and then resumed his flight toward the monastery.

That was weeks ago. Every night he feared that his guilt would be recalled and he would face judgment. Not yesterday, tonight, or tomorrow. But any night.

And, as he did each night since, he prayed, consumed by guilt. Tonight would be no exception.

He knelt beside his cot, praying to God to forgive his sins, preparing himself for what he already knew would be another sleepless night. He had only recently taken his vows as a novice and was still plagued with anxiety about his actions in confronting the man flirting with Isabella. She had promised herself to him, Pietro, when he was still a free man in Florence. But the smiles and laughter she shared with Luca enraged him, and the soft touch of her fingers on Luca's arm angered Pietro. So he had taken his revenge on the man and the woman.

Now, on this night as over the weeks in San Marco, every rasp or tap that echoed in the darkened cells of the monastery sounded like whispers of his impending judgment, punishment for murdering his rival in the streets of Florence. Isabella's screams when the broad blade of the knife sank into Luca's belly still haunted Pietro in every moment – during prayers, meals, and especially when he was alone.

It was quiet in the monastery. The monks had all returned to their cells to engage in their own communication with the Lord. No sound came from the hallway; if any did, it wasn't anticipated or planned.

His ears were primed and caught every creak of timbers or whistle of a breeze. Suddenly, there was a sound that was out of place. A faint sound of leather shoes sliding across stone steps outside his cell seemed to be coming closer. Pietro lifted his head from prayer and held his breath, trying to discern where the sound was coming from. A soft pad of leather on stone, then another, and he heard the breath of someone outside the wooden door to his room. Pietro's eyes went wide and his ears were alert, but then there was nothing – for a moment.

A subtle squeak of the hinges sounded as the door opened. Pietro turned his head away from his folded hands and to the opening at the doorway, where he saw a tall figure. It was hooded like so many of the monks with whom he lived, but the face was in darkness. There was only the dim light of the hallway candles coming from behind casting an eerie aura around the man.

With a sudden swift movement, the hooded figure moved forward, raised a long knife above his head and brought it down swiftly on the back of the kneeling Pietro. The novice monk's face displayed both guilt and resignation; even in youth he seemed tired of life. The assailant's knife penetrated the monk's robes and went directly into the center of his back as brilliant red blood spurted out and Pietro slumped to the stone floor.

The hooded man finished the job by grabbing Pietro's hair, yanking his head upward, and pulling the knife blade across his neck from ear to ear.

The intruder then pushed the limp body aside. Without pausing, he turned his attention to the floor of the cell, peering intently at the tiles at his feet as if he already knew where to look. He turned the knife point to the mortared edge of the stones in the floor of the cell. Scraping and digging, he wedged the blade beneath a stone and pried it up. There he found a leather satchel which the intruder lifted out from its hiding place. He quickly glanced at the contents, then closed the straps once again around the satchel and returned the stone to its original position over the now empty cavity in the floor.

The intruder withdrew a piece of parchment from his cloak and slipped it into the robes of the dead monk at his feet. It read "*Ego sum ira Dei,*" – "I am the wrath of God."

Tucking the folder under his arm, the hooded intruder stepped quietly through the portal, pulling the wooden door closed and hastening from the monastery with his treasure.

Pietro, novice monk, recent murderer, pursuer of the elegant lady Isabella, and grandson of Sandro Paletti, was dead. And the treasure that his grandfather had given him on his deathbed in 1546 was gone.

WASHINGTON 2021

APRIL 4, 2021

Dulles Airport

Darren Priest tipped the paper cup to his lips and inhaled the steam from the tiny spout in the plastic lid. Coffee was always welcome, even if he had to settle for the airport version from the kiosk near the international gate. After a brief moment to check the temperature of the liquid, he took a tentative sip and lowered his hand to rest the cup on the edge of the "Information" desk where he awaited the next plane's arrival.

Being early was a habit for him, especially when he reflected on how much he hated making someone wait. But while he stood sipping coffee and watching one stream after another of people push through the security doors, people with a range of skin colors and clothing styles representing every region of the world, he thought back to the many times he had used this airport to complete missions abroad.

It was a relatively brief tour of active duty – four years in all – that started him on this path. Now, thirteen years after discharge from the intelligence service, he was still being dispatched to all continents at the request of flag officers in the military establishment, sometimes even the U.S. President himself.

"Some things you can't unvolunteer for," Mike Pendleton had reminded him in the Oval Office. There had been a series of

recent assignments to mountainous hideouts in Iraq, Afghanistan, and Pakistan and Priest was considering calling a halt to his continued covert operations. He was no longer a member of the six-man team from the war – three of his companions had died by suicide, the other two had changed their identities and couldn't be found, not even by Priest himself – but he carried the emotional scars that came with operating in close contact with sworn enemies of America.

Even he had changed his identity, from Armando Listrani he became Darren Priest. Due to his highly classified assignments and numerous contacts with dangerous men and their long memories, the U.S. government recommended that he consider a change of identity after the war. That step was particularly hard on his family. With both mother and father deceased, he had only to break it to siblings. But they could only know that he was no longer Armando; not that he had become Darren Priest, since they were not allowed to know where he had gone. Priest softened it a bit by maintaining regular communication, even occasional in-person visits, but generally had to divorce himself from his earlier life to remain safe.

"Some things you can't unvolunteer for."

President Pendleton's words rang in his ears as he lifted the cup and took another sip of coffee. He was not on his way out of Dulles this time; instead, he was waiting for a friend to arrive from Vienna.

In the Air Force during that four-year hitch, Priest had been a member of a select team called Operation Best Guess. At the outset of the conflict in Afghanistan, he was moved from his original assignment to this select team of interrogators. Commanders in the field were having little luck breaking anti-American Islamic fighters, unable to get into their minds and harvest the secrets they protected. When he signed up in 2008, the scandals of torture and abusive interrogation at Abu Ghraib and other dark sites were still fresh, and the reaction of the American public pushed the military to come up with more acceptable means of getting *humintel*, military speak for human intelligence gathered from interviews and interrogations.

Sergeant Abraham Randal was the first to remind the brass of a successful project during the Vietnam War. A small handful of recruits had been identified as unusually able to detect truth and lies when interrogating subjects. Not the usual "oh, yeah, I know you're lying." Their talents were much more intricate. Body language, facial expression, a subtle rise in temperature of the target that caused his skin color to take on a tinge of pink. The faintest movement of his eyeball, the tightening of certain muscles around his eyes, nose, or mouth. The cadence of the target's words was easy to interpret; the muscular twitches of his exposed forearms were more complicated and elusive.

Sergeant Randal was given permission to pursue his idea and recruit men for a new detail. Women were excluded because in the Afghanistan theatre it would have been impossible to put a woman in tight quarters with murderous fighters and still get reliable information. Randal didn't interview anyone as much as he talked to officers and non-coms in the field. He was looking for specific traits that were invisible to most people but, he hoped, would reveal themselves to him.

When he had found six men, including the former Armando Listrani, who fit his model, he had a high-ranking contact at DoD cut classified orders to reassign the men to him. They were taken to an undisclosed site in Texas, then they were drilled and tested. After achieving a successful level of assurance, they were moved to a dark site in Eastern Europe to put their theories into practice.

Sergeant Randal drilled them not to think. He raged at the men when they tried to understand what was happening in each interrogation session instead of unconsciously reacting to the signals. "If you think about it," he bellowed, "you'll lose it. It's got to be below your skin, outside your mind, unthinking reaction to a host of non-verbal signals."

Operation Best Guess was about understanding what the

target was thinking, or what he was trying not to think, even if he didn't fully understand it himself. If the men in Sergeant Randal's command could get past the surface and decode the intent of his actions, they could steer the subject toward revealing far more than he would to people who tortured him with rubber hoses and electric prods.

Priest's thoughts were interrupted by the chirp of his phone. He looked to see that it was Bao Chinh, a friend in Vienna.

"You gotta few minutes?" Chinh asked.

"Sure, but just a few. What's up?"

Bao Chinh was the bank manager at DFR Wien. They had met two years earlier and he was instrumental in solving a connection that implicated American politicians and Viennese bankers. But why was he calling? And why so late? It was about midnight in Vienna.

"Something squirrelly here at the bank," Bao continued.

Priest had to smile but held back on making a smart remark. His trip to Vienna two years ago dealt with DFR Wien, and the bank had a number of squirrelly things going on, not least of which was a corrupt previous bank manager, Gerhardt Eichner. When the scandal was revealed, involving not only the U.S. Ambassador to Austria and the U.S. Senate Majority Leader, DFR barely escaped total fiscal collapse. Eichner's involvement in the money laundering scheme also came to light, prompting him to kill himself and resulting in Bao rising to the position of bank manager at DFR Wien.

"Like what?" Priest wanted to get only the basics for the moment.

"It's kinda complicated," he said – of course, Priest thought to himself – "and it deals with stolen art."

"Well, that definitely isn't my field of expertise."

"I know, but I can explain," Bao responded. "And we have other experts involved."

"Tell you what, unless it's a matter of the oil paint not drying on a painting, can this wait till later?"

"Sure, just put this in your head. It seems that we have found a long-lost collection of art that has been rumored to exist for over five hundred years."

Oh, great, Priest thought. Just drop a bomb on me.

"Well, then. You have my interest. Give me a name to research when I get back home and I'll call tomorrow."

"The Paletti Notebook."

"Okay." It didn't mean anything to Priest, but he promised to look at it later when he had returned to his condo.

When Priest met Chinh in Vienna, he came to know the man's anti-American streak. He was the son of a Vietnamese woman and an American G.I., born during the Vietnam War and, frankly, abandoned by the G.I. father when it was time for the soldier to rotate back to the States. Bao Chinh's's mother, Le Do, had to fend for herself after the Americans surrendered Saigon and left the region, and Chinh grew up with a strong distrust of Americans.

When Priest and Chinh met, that distrust was evident but it subsided over the course of their dealings. Priest was thankful for that, because Chinh's help was significant in solving the case that exonerated the U.S. President and cleared up the Vienna connection with Washington, D.C.

"Take a look at it when you have time," Chinh said, but added as a warning, "but I don't think we have much time."

"If this treasure has been the subject of rumors for five hundred years, what's the hurry?"

"It seems that people are dying."

APRIL 4, 2021

Washington, D.C.

PRIEST STARED AT THE SECURITY DOORS THROUGH WHICH THE arriving passengers were coming, then turned his attention back to Bao.

Bao said he didn't want to talk about too much on the phone, but he described records uncovered in a safe deposit box at his bank, DFR Wien, that concerned an ancient collection of art and letters dating to the year 1500 in Florence.

"What's this about people dying?" Priest asked.

"I'm not sure yet and I want to dig a little deeper. But some notes found in the box along with photographs of art..."

"Wait," Priest interrupted. "Photographs? If it's from 1500, there couldn't be any photos."

"Yeah. Well, we didn't find any real art. Or even any real letters. Just photos of these things on old paper..."

"How do you know it's old?"

"First of all, they're in black and white, and we got a professor of history involved who thinks the photos are from the World War II era. Anyway, the photos are there, but none of the things that they depict. Kind of like a photo journal of the contents of the box."

"How does this involve me?" Priest asked. He heard the

sound of another crowd of arriving passengers push through the security doors and looked up to see who was arriving.

"Not directly, of course," Bao offered. "But I don't know anyone with your investigative skills. Well, actually, that's not entirely true. I called Alana but she's not available. They said she's on vacation."

The friend Priest was waiting for was Alana Weber, a woman with whom he had become very involved over the last two years. Although Bao knew of their relationship, he wouldn't have known that she was arriving at Dulles just at that moment.

"Well, in fact," Priest said, turning toward the arrival portal to watch for Alana, "she's deplaning right now here at Dulles. That's who I'm waiting for."

"Oh, great!" Bao replied. "Maybe I can get both of you to help me."

"What exactly do you want me to do?" Just then, Priest saw Alana push through the swinging security doors with her eight-year-old daughter Kia beside her. He waved to them and directed them to his side of the crowd, trying to end the conversation with Bao.

"Let me do this," he said into the phone. "Alana and Kia just arrived so I'd like to get them through the airport and out of here. How about if I focus on them first, then look up Paletti Notebook when I get home. We can talk later tonight...oh, sorry, tomorrow. I forgot that it's late night at your end."

"Sounds great, Darren. Look over whatever you can find and let's talk tomorrow."

Hurrying to end the call, Priest asked Bao if he wanted to email anything on this Paletti thing.

"No, I really don't. You'll know more later but I'd like to keep this off the grid for now. For all of us."

Alana Weber was a Federal police officer in Vienna. She met Darren Priest under anything but propitious circumstances. She had come across him sprawled out on the lawn of Stadtpark in Vienna and, when she roused him to say that sleeping wasn't allowed there, he seemed groggy and out of sorts. Over several days of treating him like a suspect in a series of crimes, Alana came to realize that Priest had been set up. She also came to find out that he was an agent of the U.S. government and was in Vienna to solve a mystery involving his government and the Austrian banking industry.

She was a year older than Priest and had a daughter, Kia, from a former marriage. "My husband was police," she explained at the time. "I met him and fell in love with his work." When Priest asked what happened then, she huffed and smiled, "Some loves last longer than others."

Priest and Alana had navigated a long-distance relationship for two years and were coming closer to finding a more convenient arrangement. She loved Austria and he was committed to the country of his birth, so a solution was hard to come by. Flying back and forth between Washington and Vienna was not the answer. Alana was serious about her career and loved her role as an investigator; Priest was closer to abandoning his service to the government but still cherished his homeland.

Her trip to Washington that week – with a secret objective of introducing her daughter to the United States capital – might offer a chance for them to make some decisions.

"Let me get that," he offered as Alana and Kia dragged their matching bags through the throng of people in the international terminal. Kia had her mother's good looks, long legs, brown hair that tumbled in curls over her shoulders, and a dimpled smile that warmed Priest's heart whenever he got to see the little girl. She also possessed Alana sharp intellect, picking up on details and cues about her environment that caused Priest to tease her about going into police work when she grew up.

"Momma tells me we already have a cop in the family, and we

don't need another one." Kia said she was leaning toward a life in music, but she still had many years to tempt the vagaries of career choices ahead of her. Her comment about a cop in the family – noticeably a single noun – reminded Priest that the divorce Alana had endured with her husband did not go smoothly. The father's service on the police force in Vienna didn't seem to register in Kia's count of "cops in the family."

They rolled the bags to the car Priest had parked in the short-term lot just across from the taxi line. Kia had napped on the plane and so, by now, she was her usual talkative self. Alana was awake too but stayed quiet with a smile on her lips as her daughter told stories of the aircraft, the passengers, and how the flight attendant brought her a meal tray left unused by the sparsely populated First Class section.

"Momma didn't get one," she said, "but I shared mine with her."

It was no surprise that Kia had ingratiated herself with the flight crew. She was smart, pretty, and friendly, and most of the people working United flights were the same, so they responded quickly to Kia's effervescent nature.

After a long running narrative about the flight from Kia, they arrived at Priest's condo in Rockville, Maryland. He knew enough to put the two ladies up in the guest room to avoid difficult questions from the eight-year-old, then he rolled their luggage in behind them. Priest retired to the master bedroom to change his shirt and consider what they should do with the afternoon. It was only about five o'clock on a sunny afternoon and he thought they could take advantage of the day before it cooled off.

"Darren," he heard Alana call. "Can we just set up our girl things in this hallway bathroom?"

"Sure. I have my own and you can commandeer that one for the two of you."

Kia was the first to emerge from the guest quarters of the condo. Her energy and vivacious personality would not let her remain still for long. It was her first visit to Washington, D.C., and although they were in the suburbs of the city, she was sure they were only minutes from the great monuments of this citadel of democracy. And she wanted to see them all that very afternoon.

"Dear," Alana warned her, stroking the long brown hair on Kia's head, "we have time. Besides, the city is so large and so beautiful, we couldn't possibly do it in one day."

Alana's assessment was spot-on although she herself had never been to the American capital.

"It's true," Priest said, "but we can make a start. How about a driving tour of the city so you can see the Capitol building, the White House, and some of the classic buildings of the Smithsonian Institution? I'll even drive us past some of the famous monuments for a drive-by viewing to start us out. By the time that's over, you'll have the lay of the land, and probably begin to tire from your long trip."

Kia nodded, but had to suppress her excitement to go along with a plan that didn't include going into the buildings.

"Then we'll come back to my neighborhood, get dinner at a restaurant I've been going to for years, and come back to the condo."

"That sounds perfect," Alana chimed in, wanting to get her stamp on the plan before Kia pushed the effort further.

"Okay," the girl replied gleefully.

They spent about two hours driving through and around the city, taking in the glorious sights of Washington, D.C. Priest was justly proud of his native city and maintained a running monologue of the features along the way.

"As we work through the heart of the city, here on Constitution Avenue, you can see the Washington Monument to the right, the Lincoln Memorial behind us..."

"I want to see that!" exclaimed Kia.

"Yes, you will. Meanwhile, you can see the Capitol building ahead of us."

He swung past several of the Smithsonian Institution's museums, calling out their names as they drove by to "ahhs" and "oohs" and "look at that!" from Kia. Passing by the National Museum of African American History and Culture, then the National Museum of American History, they approached the National Museum of Natural History when Kia pointed out the window with bright eyes and excitement ringing in her voice.

"That's where the dinosaurs are!" she shouted.

Alana was equally impressed with this parade of unparalleled museums but kept calm and only smiled.

"And here is the National Gallery of Art," Priest said, to which Kia responded, "Yeah, okay, but where's Air and Space? I heard that's the best!"

"Yeah, probably is," Priest replied. "Certainly the most popular. We'll get to all of these later in the week."

"Well, most of them," admonished Alana. She had read guidebooks about the city and its museums and knew that they could spend their entire lives here and not cover all that Washington had to offer.

From Constitution Avenue, Priest turned right then right again and joined the traffic heading west on Independence Avenue.

"There's Air and Space," he said.

"Yay! Can we go in?" Kia asked excitedly.

"Sorry, but not now," he responded. "We'll get to it but have to head out of town now for dinner."

He drove past the round façade of the Hirshhorn Museum, pointed out the old Smithsonian Castle, the first building of this sprawling campus, then hooked the car slightly to the left to join the traffic heading toward the Tidal Basin and out of town.

"There's a lot to see here!" Kia said happily. As they proceeded along the Tidal Basin that was flanked by blossoming cherry trees, she kept looking over her shoulder at the sights that receded in the background.

The path out of town became less interesting as they joined

late evening rush hour to escape the city and get out to Bethesda.

"Bao called me," he told Alana when Kia had dropped into a silent mode.

"What about?"

"We only spoke for a few minutes – you were arriving. But he said something about an old notebook; something about art and letters from five hundred years ago."

"And...?" she pried.

"And nothing. I asked why or how I could be of help, then mentioned that you were visiting. He laughed. He said that he had called you first but found that you were on vacation."

Priest turned to look at Alana and smiled. She smiled back and patted his hand.

"Yes, and I do expect this to be a vacation," she said, turning her eyes back to the twisting road that led them through Rock Creek Park and out of the city.

They reached Bethesda in a little over a half hour. Priest parked the car on the street then escorted the ladies into the Pines of Rome, an Italian restaurant he had supped at countless times. Marco the proprietor was usually there in the evenings but Priest was met at the door by the head waiter.

"Darren Priest," he said to him. The Pines didn't take reservations, but he wanted to announce their arrival to let Marco know that they were there so they could see him during the meal.

They were seated and given menus, although Priest had long-since memorized the offerings. While Alana and Kia considered what they would have, he ordered a white pizza with cheese for the table, a carafe of the house red wine, and a plate of sautéed peppers for appetizer.

"I want spaghetti," said Kia quickly, closing the menu and lowering it to the table.

"Well, they have many kinds," Priest commented. He talked her into spaghetti carbonara, one of his favorites, while Alana chose flounder. He opted for *osso buco*, long-roasted veal shank. The wine came with two short tumblers – common glassware for the Pines – and a pitcher of water and three more glasses. In just moments, the white pizza arrived, its surface covered with melted cheese, dappled in olive oil, and spotted with garlic and red pepper flakes. Then a platter of peppers was delivered and they were ready for the meal.

———

Later that evening, Priest typed "Paleti notebook" into his laptop and got no returns in Google. The girls were asleep as expected and it was only nine p.m. by his clock, so he knew he'd have time to look into this.

Then he typed "Palleti notebook," doubling the "l" but this returned nothing either.

Next, he tried "Palletti notebook." Double "l" and double "t." Still nothing.

His Italian was pretty strong, but double consonants were always a guess. So he tried the only other combination he could think of.

"Paletti notebook."

After watching the loading icon spin on the screen of his computer, a long list of hits popped up.

"Paletti notebook. A long-sought collection of art," said one. The brief description suggested that the artworks included in the notebook dated from around 1500, but little else was told. The final sentence suggested that the story was more about a mystical non-thing – a Yeti of the art world – than a real collection.

"Paletti notebook," said another, but it was a link to a website selling pens and leather-bound journals for aspiring writers.

"Paletti notebook. Ruminations from a philosopher in the 14th century." The narrative revealed the background of its subject, but the focus on philosophy didn't jibe with Chinh's introduction.

Priest checked three more hits on "Paletti notebook" and "paletti notebook," considering all the spellings and upper case and lower-case initials.

Then he saw, "Paletti Notebook," all cap initials, and he clicked on it.

"Rumors of an extraordinary collection of draft pieces from Renaissance artists, philosophers, and politicians. All from Florence circa 1500 CE. Considered to have been collected by a restaurant owner named Sandro Paletti in that period. Legend has it that even the lost Gospel of Matthias is captured in the Paletti Notebook."

Priest skimmed the paragraphs below the entry and became intrigued by the supposed contents of the notebook. Then he read this.

"There has been no real evidence of such a notebook; in fact, even records of the existence of such a person as Sandro Paletti seem unreliable, at best. More likely, he was a fictional character created to give 'life' to the story. Like rumors of unfound Dead Sea scrolls and the discovery of great works of art from Botticelli to Picasso in grandma's attic, the Paletti Notebook seems to be the product of wishful thinking."

Priest scrolled back up the page to see what items were supposedly in the notebook and his eyes went wide. This guy, if he ever existed, this Paletti guy, collected sketches, designs, and draft letters from some of the great men of Florence in that era. And if he had also found the Gospel of Matthias – something Priest had heard stories of over the years – then this Notebook could be the most incredible discovery of all time.

Reading further about the art, he saw that the collection included pieces from Michelangelo, Leonardo da Vinci, Raphael, and Brunelleschi, as well as letters from politicians like Niccolò Machiavelli, Cesare Borgia, and members of the Medici family – all indicative of their anti-Pope and anti-Church beliefs. Even religious personalities like Girolamo Savonarola and his fellow friars from San Marco monastery in Florence appeared in the brief list of contents of the Paletti Notebook. Some were devout; some were heretical.

"It couldn't be," Priest muttered aloud, just as he felt a touch on his shoulder.

"What couldn't be?" Alana asked, standing behind him wearing only a t-shirt.

"Uh, I..." Priest was momentarily speechless at the sight of her. She had great legs and the shirt barely reached her thighs. Without a bra underneath, her breasts pushed against the fabric of the shirt, just about eye level for him.

"Paletti Notebook," he said, then spun the chair around to embrace her and bury his nose between her breasts.

"Oh, okay," she said, not concealing her smile.

Changing the subject, he said, "So, I thought..." he began.

"No," she responded without waiting for him to finish his statement.

"Seriously, I wasn't thinking..." he tried to extricate himself from what began as an embarrassing start. "I meant...well, I'm not sure what I meant."

"You meant that, perhaps, maybe, possibly, if only, after Kia was asleep..."

"Yeah, that's it."

"No." Her voice was firm, but she smiled, stroked his hair, and pulled his face back into the cleavage of her chest.

"Okay," he responded. "Got it." Although he only slowly removed his face from the thin fabric of her t-shirt.

"We talked about this," Alana added.

"Yeah, I know. It's worth it to have you visit. We can always..."

"No." Firm, but without the smile.

"Tell me what you're researching," she continued, grabbing a chair and sitting beside him. Alana pulled the front of the t-shirt down between her legs, leaving her long legs exposed but hiding the rest from him.

After a moment to refocus, Priest responded.

"The Paletti Notebook. Apparently a collection of art and letters from about the year 1500. In Florence."

"What's special about it?" she asked.

"You mean other than that the Notebook also supposedly contains a first century gospel, the lost Gospel of Matthias, the earliest gospel in history and written by a man who personally knew Jesus?"

"Jesus!" she said, more an exclamation than a correction. "What else?"

"Not sure yet, but it seems like it's just a legend, a rumor. Some of the websites suggest contents that are not believable, everything from da Vinci to Machiavelli."

"Wait," Alana said, holding up her hand. "That's an artist and a politician. What's the connection?"

"That's just the point, the core of the mystery. How could anyone collect records from both the worlds of art and politics... not to mention Cesare Borgia."

"Why him?" Alana asked.

"He's suggested in the mythology of this Paletti Notebook, too. How could anyone collect thoughts, letters, records, drawings, sketches of all these people in one place?"

"Well," Alana speculated with a finger to her chin, "Florence in 1500 was a pretty interesting place. I mean, nowadays, we consider it the birth of the Renaissance. In addition to the art, the Medici ruled the city..."

"Not so," Priest interjected, and Alana's brow furrowed. "The Medici family had left Florence by 1500...," he continued.

"Exiled," she corrected.

"Whatever. They were gone and didn't return until later."

"About 1510 or 1513," she said, but she patted his shoulder as if to compliment him on his European history.

"The point is that the Medici had ruled the city until just

before 1500," he added, "and brought a bunch of artists to their studios before their..."

"Exile," she inserted.

"Yeah, exile. They brought a bunch of artists who continued to work in the city for a decade or more."

"I remember an art history class," she offered, still resting her hand lightly on his shoulder, "in which they told of these artists, and more..."

"And Botticelli, Raphael..."

"Right," she said, "them. These artists all living in Florence in the years before and immediately after 1500. It must have been quite an Algonquin Round Table," she added.

Priest looked over his shoulder and had to smile. The Algonquin Round Table referred to a small dining room of New York's Algonquin Hotel during the early 20th Century at which artists, actors, critics, and writers gathered to share lunch, critique the politics of the day, and challenge each other to a battle of wits.

"That is precisely what this sounds like," he admitted, very impressed with Alana's mastery of American cultural history. "But it didn't exist," he concluded.

"What, the Algonquin Round Table?"

"No, the Paletti Notebook. I've read through dozens of entries here. Some talk about the fantastic entries in the notebook, the drawings, letters, even complete – though small – paintings, but all conclude that it is a mirage. Like Sasquatch."

"Who?" she asked with a quizzical look.

"Sasquatch. Yeti. The abominable snowman."

"Sounds like so much American fantasy," she replied with a wink.

"Yeah, just so. But that's probably what the Paletti Notebook is."

Alana rose from the chair, kissed him on the cheek, and walked into the guest room. He could see the backs of her naked thighs and the slight bulge of her butt cheeks below the t-shirt, and for a moment, he wished fervently that Kia wasn't visiting also.

Later that night after Alana and Kia had gone to bed, Priest's phone rang.

"What's up, Bao?" It was only dawn in Vienna and Bao was already calling. Priest figured this was something that couldn't wait.

"I took a chance that you'd still be awake and..." Bao began.

"And alone at night?" Priest quipped. "You know Alana's here," he added with a laugh.

"Yeah, well, I also happen to know that Kia's with her and you, well, you being the gentleman that you are..."

"Okay, okay," Priest replied. "Quit the saintly stuff," and laughing again, "this is hard enough as it is."

"Anyway, I didn't want to wait till morning and I'm anxious to share what we have."

"Paletti Notebook," Priest said, to get the conversation going.

"What do you know about it?" Chinh asked.

"Only that it's a myth, a legend of uncertain origin."

"So, you researched it?"

"Of course," Priest admitted without pause.

"What if I told you that it wasn't a myth?"

"I wouldn't believe you."

"Well," Chinh continued, "I'm not sure I believe it myself, but let me tell you what I have."

He backtracked for a moment in his narrative to set the stage, telling Priest some of history of Florence around the year 1500. Then he included a long story about Matthias, how he was a contemporary of Jesus, had known him in his lifetime, and wrote the earliest gospel known in the record. As Chinh ran from one topic to the next, Priest had to admit that Europeans –

even Vietnamese ex-pats in Europe – knew more about history than most Americans did.

Chinh talked about the guy Paletti as if he really existed, a statement of fact that Priest challenged with his own research.

"Be that as it may..." Chinh repeated several times, as if to put off Priest's doubts until a later discussion.

Chinh talked about the amazing confluence of life stories in Florence at that time. That Leonardo da Vinci was born near the city and spent most of his productive life there. That Michelangelo did the same, and that they were both living in Florence from the late-1400s to the early-1500s. That Botticelli lived and worked in Florence his entire life, including that same period. That the Vespucci family – famous for, among other things, producing Amerigo Vespucci, after whom America was named – lived on a street that paralleled the Arno River in Florence. That Niccolò Machiavelli lived in the city his entire life, rising to prominence in the same period that these artists were there. And that Cesare Borgia, of the Borgia house that produced kings, princes, and popes, was in and out of Florence that entire time and solicited drawings and designs from artists like da Vinci to produce his war machines.

"Yeah," was all Priest could say at first. "There aren't many periods in human history that enjoyed so much talent packed into such a concentrated area. So, what does this mean for us?"

"The accident of history that brought all these people together is either the reason for the Paletti rumor," Chinh replied, "or the substance of the real Paletti Notebook. Not to mention the Gospel."

"If it existed," Priest said, continuing his Doubting Thomas routine.

"How much do you know about the contents of the Notebook?" he asked.

"You mean, the rumored Notebook."

"Well, actually, I mean the real Notebook."

Priest was momentarily speechless as Chinh continued.

He described Sandro Paletti as a real person, as if he had read a biography of him. Chinh knew about Paletti owning a restaurant in Florence around 1500. He knew a little about the things the guy saw and learned – as if Paletti left behind notes of his life experience – and he knew more about piles of papers and drawings that comprised the Paletti collection of artifacts. He also knew, or seemed to know, about how Paletti came into possession of the ancient gospel.

"I've read a good bit about the man," Priest offered, "and about some of the things supposedly included in his Notebook. But I have not found any proof that he actually existed, or any proof that such a collection could have been held by any one person."

"Exactly. I spoke to an art historian here..."

"Who?" Priest didn't know why he asked that; he wouldn't recognize the name.

"Andres Leitner. He's an art professor at the University of Vienna. I told him what I found and he said it's a fake. At least, that it can't be – isn't – true."

"What have you found? You haven't told me yet."

"I had trouble convincing Dr. Leitner at first because he has a bias against the existence of the Paletti Notebook. Like you. So I needed to convince him first – and you – that it's possible."

"Again," Priest repeated, "what have you found? Maybe that will convince me."

"Photos of artwork, letters, a yellowed parchment-and-paper notebook, and a stack of papyrus written in Coptic. That's an ancient language attributed to Egypt and the Arabic states. With the name Sandro Paletti on the first pages."

"Photos?" Priest asked. "I can't tell what that shows us. Clearly, there was no photography in the first century A.D. Or back in 1500 in Florence. Or anywhere else for that matter."

"No, of course not," Chinh continued. "That's why I know that the Paletti Notebook exists and someone from a more modern era took pictures of its the contents – pictures that couldn't be taken if the Notebook didn't really exist – and stored them in a vault in my bank."

Priest wondered how all this had begun and now he had some clues. Chinh explained that at DFR Wien, they maintain many safe deposit boxes. Any boxes that show no record of activity are subject to a decennial audit. His predecessor, Eichner, was lax on this practice, so many of the boxes remained locked and out of view for many years, decades at least. When Chinh took over as bank manager, he initiated a clean sweep of the boxes, checking off all those that had been opened in the previous ten years and highlighting those with no record of an audit. Some were barely outside of the ten-year period; some were many years out of date. One particular box had not been audited for a little over seventy years, in the period just following World War II.

Chinh went straight for that box and opened it to survey the contents. He found prints made from a number of old photographs, the prints themselves showing their age. As he described them to Priest, he could see that they had to have been taken decades ago when photographic technology still required development through use of chemicals and dark room equipment.

"What were the photos of?" Priest asked.

"I'm getting to that," he replied.

Chinh continued to describe what the photographs were, much like the list of things he talked about earlier. Priest was especially intrigued by one he described as a machine to move water and he couldn't help but think about the Walter Isaacson biography of Leonardo da Vinci and his engineering designs. Another photograph captured the face of a woman, just a charcoal rendering, but one that bore a clear resemblance to the face of Mary, the mother of Jesus, as depicted in Michelangelo's sculpture *Pieta* in Saint Peter's Basilica in Rome.

"There are more," he went on, "including something that looks like a letter and signed 'Ces. Borgia.'"

"Could that be Cesare Borgia, the son of the pope?"

"Yep."

Priest was falling under the spell and couldn't wait to hear more.

"And there's a note I found," Chinh said. "It read: 'These scraps of art and the letters belong to me, and the journal is mine.' The note has no signature, but the first leaf of the journal indicates that it belonged to Sandro Paletti.

"Then I found another note, on newer paper, but still old by our reckoning."

"Define old," Priest said.

"Nineteen forty-three," Bao replied.

"How can you be so sure of the age?"

"There's a signature and a date."

"Whose signature, and what date?"

"Emil Gutman, March 8, 1943."

"What does it say?"

He read it to Priest.

" 'I was forced to surrender the things that Fra Nizza had given me,' he said, 'giving them to Ira Hillyer, who assures me that they will be safe.'"

Thinking through his list of questions Priest realized that he had been swept up in the story and couldn't shake the feeling that the Paletti Notebook was real.

"And you think the photos are real?" Priest asked.

"Of course they are," Chinh replied. "The question is whether the images depicted in them are real also."

"And where they are right now," Priest said.

FLORENCE 1501

PALETTI OSTERIA, FLORENCE

Saturday, May 18, 1501

"AND JESUS SAID, 'HERE IS MY WIFE.'"

The brittle fragment of papyrus lay upon the table as his finger traced the words written in Coptic, the ancient language of Egypt which had long held the secrets of early Christianity. Leonardo da Vinci – artist, engineer, scientist – looked up from the scrap as his left index finger tapped the last word.

"*Tasoni*," he whispered with a smile. Then he elongated the pronunciation for those at the table to hear. "Tay-SOH-nee," Leonardo said slowly. "It is the Coptic word for wife." He sat back and smiled but remained momentarily silent. Leonardo reveled in drama, and he was as much a master of performance as he was of art.

Sandro Paletti stood quietly by the side. It was in his restaurant where Leonardo and the great men of Florence had gathered. Sitting with the artist was Cesare Borgia, a warmonger and illegitimate son of Pope Alexander VI, and Raphael, a nervously devout follower of Jesus Christ. At the next table was Niccolò Machiavelli, a politician skeptical of most things – except the power of power. In the shadows a few feet away stood Leonardo's nemesis, Michelangelo.

The small dining area of Paletti was lit by candles on each table and small torches hung from black iron brackets on the walls. The flickering light provided by these sources danced upon the faces of the men as well as the yellowed parchment under Leonardo's fingers. The surface of red wine in the goblets in front of each man shimmered in the reflected light.

Paletti was a modest restaurant. Like many of the city's *osterie* serving food and wine to patrons from across Florence, it was known more for the quality of the food than any luxurious trappings. And yet it was a successful enterprise, successful enough to pay the bills and fill the tables with a range of patrons from across the city, from peasant farmers, petty bureaucrats, and artisans to renowned artists and ruling patrons, to the priests and soothsayers of the day.

Sandro Paletti had inherited a struggling business from his father, Alessandro Paletti, a man who took pride in his chosen profession but who served out his sunset years tending to a public who seldom even acknowledged that he was there. With his strong work ethic, Sandro built upon Paletti's reputation and, under his care, he ran a restaurant that guaranteed the best beef in Tuscany, the brightest vegetables that could be grown in the region, the freshest fish that could be brought in through Pisa from the Mediterranean, and the finest wines from the hills of Tuscany.

"Why is that important?" asked Borgia, pointing to the parchment at Leonardo's fingertips. He cared more for the artist's military machines than a shard of ancient writing.

Leonardo tapped the fragment again and smiled. Throughout his life the great artist had carefully hidden his disdain for Church orthodoxy behind a parade of religious paintings – all for handsome commissions – but he was amused by this papyrus that had come to him recently.

"It's sacrilegious," muttered Raphael, who sat across the table. He pulled his hands away to keep a safe distance from the scroll as if by mere touch it might send a devout man to eternal damnation. Raphael was the youngest of the group, with a clean-shaven face, soft feminine features, and long, curly brown hair. He was an apprentice under Pietro Vannucci, known even then as Perugino from the city of his birth, whose students continued Perugino's tradition of paintings glorifying the saints of early Christianity.

Raphael's paintings of religious icons were drawn from his early studies and the influence of Perugino, not to mention from his deep devotion to Jesus and the New Testament teachings. Although he would occasionally dine with Leonardo, whom he suspected of heresy, he wanted to maintain a safe distance for the sake of his eternal soul.

Paletti stood by the side stroking his long dark beard, occasionally adjusting his round skullcap to hide the expanding bald spot on the crown of his head. He enjoyed Leonardo's theatrics, on this day as on others when the famous man graced his dining room. But this time was different.

"It is described to me as the lost Gospel of Matthias," the artist said, one eyebrow raised as if to convey his amazement at his own luck of commandeering this precious artifact. "This man, Matthias, was with Jesus when Our Lord was alive, and he wrote the story of Jesus's life as he witnessed it."

"Where did you get it?"

The voice was small though not tentative, and it came from the corner of the dining room where the men had gathered. Leonardo looked up and allowed a sneer to pass his lips. The question came from his nemesis, Michelangelo, a man that Leonardo publicly dismissed as unworthy but an artist whom da Vinci also knew had won the approval of the Medici family and the leading men of Florence. A man who had contrived to win work that Leonardo coveted.

"Where did you get it?" Michelangelo repeated.

He wasn't seated at the table occupied by Leonardo, Borgia, and Raphael. Instead, the tall, sinewy man of the tattered cloak and serious gaze stood apart from them. Michelangelo had rugged features, deep set eyes strong hands, and a nose flattened in an earlier fight with Pietro Torrigiano, a jealous artist, features that marked him as much as a stone mason as a sculptor. His inelegant cloak hung loosely about his frame, and his homespun clothes offered no clue to his background or artistic prominence.

Leonardo and Michelangelo did not get along. They vied for sponsors' commissions but, otherwise, differed in every respect. Michelangelo – from a family of financial success – dressed poorly, lived in the shadow of guilt for his homosexuality, and perpetually feared that he would be condemned by God for sins of the flesh. Leonardo – the illegitimate son of a merchant and banned from formal schooling due to his birth – dressed in flowing purple robes and jewelry, enjoyed the favors of both men and women, and didn't believe in God.

Machiavelli listened in, gripping a gleaming goblet of wine but focused on the conversation going on nearby. When Leonardo pointed again at the papyrus he pinned to the table with his forefinger, Machiavelli rose from the stiff wooden chair to stand alongside the artist and stare down at the object of their attention. He took it upon himself to repeat Michelangelo's question.

"Where did you get it?"

Leonardo raised his left index finger a centimeter above the paper and traced it across the page.

"It's written in Coptic," he said again, more to boast of his ability to translate the archaic language than to attest to its origin. "It is a message from a disciple of Jesus, this man known as Matthias. Some bishops say it is a gospel of Jesus, the only one written by a man who lived during the time of the Teacher, and who knew him."

Unlike the New Testament gospels of other followers of Jesus – Matthew, Mark, Luke, and John – one written by a contemporary of the Man-God could be trusted to be most accurate. The men who crowded around the table at Paletti knew this – even Raphael could overcome his superstitions as he leaned in closer to get a look at the fragment that Leonardo had laid on the table. They had all heard the legend of Matthias, a man who had written of Jesus not as a god, but as a man married like other Jewish men of his time, a man who fathered children who, themselves, may sometimes have wandered far from his reputed saintly ways.

"I see only a single sheet," Michelangelo said. Borgia, Raphael, and Machiavelli looked up at the tall man in the corner of the room.

"How is that a gospel?" he asked. Then he repeated his question.

"Where did you get it?"

Leonardo enjoyed theatrics; it suited his way of performing for the society around him.

"Yes, it is only a single piece of the gospel," Leonardo conceded, "but it is a piece that I thought you would most like to see. I have the rest in my room at the studio."

The men waited for more of an explanation but Leonardo paused, enjoying the suspense of his own making.

"It came to me by way of an old merchant who sailed from Cairo to Messina and now here, through Pisa to Florence. One by the name of Aegyptius."

Leonardo was loquacious when speeches suited his purpose, which was usually to impress the local people with his genius. But at a table with these great men of Florence, he won their attention by being brief with his words.

Paletti stood by the side in a portal that joined the dining area with the kitchen. From that position, he could keep an eye on his laborers at the stove and oven while insinuating himself into the conversation of these men. When he salvaged their scraps of drawings and letters – some of them heretical, some of them threatening to royal powers – he would take on the role of loyal servant.

"I'll make sure this is burned now," Paletti remembered telling Borgia one evening after the military man had penned an obscene letter to the French king. Borgia nodded in thanks, belatedly repentant and thankful that the proprietor would destroy the draft epistle and save him after a dangerous fit of pique.

And yet, Paletti did not burn Borgia's rants.

Paletti had kept scraps of paper from Michelangelo's note-book, sketches that carried hidden images of a union of God and man, some that bore remarkable resemblance to ongoing art projects in the city. Engineering designs of Leonardo, hidden images in Raphael's doodling, and other draft works that captured the genius of the men who frequented Paletti's tables all found their way into the collection that the restauranteur was compiling. He also saved pieces of paper on which Machiavelli would string words together, short phrases only, but thoughtful ruminations about an unnamed prince in a narrative that seemed more political treatise than biography.

Paletti's collection of these tidbits and cast-offs of the great men made interesting reading, but he might not have been inspired to keep them had it not been for a small prayer letter that was thrust upon him three years earlier.

When the prophet, seer, and heretic Girolamo Savonarola was being dragged to the gallows May 23, 1498, a drunken man in the crowd had pushed a scrap of paper into Sandro's hands. It was a prayer letter from the condemned friar that Sandro initially kept out of reverence, but then kept longer out of curiosity.

In 1498, Osteria Paletti was right on the Piazza del Gran Duca where the execution was to take place. The square was already crowded with people anxious to see what they hoped would be bloodshed and burning; all to witness the execution of the condemned friar Savonarola that they had followed for these recent years. Sandro elbowed his way into the crowd and was immediately pulled along by the tide of humanity.

"He's a beast among men," blurted a man with foul-smelling breath who pushed his way through the crowd and ran into Sandro. Their faces came so close that the man's breath and odor of onion and bad wine filled the air between them. His filthy clothes, dirt-smudged hands, and wild eyes made he seem demented.

"He will rot in hell," the man said, bringing his face up close to Sandro's, "but we'll arrange the burning here...now!"

The man thrust a paper into Sandro's hands.

"His prayers," he said abruptly. "Hee-yah," he blurted. "Burn in hell!" And with that the wretch pushed away and was lost in the crowd, disappearing from Sandro's view.

Sandro looked at the paper and read the first few lines.

"Al nostro Padre celeste, perdona i peccati di queste persone..." – *"Heavenly Father, forgive the sins of these people..."*

"Fra Sav." *was etched at the bottom of the page.*

The signature must have been from Friar Savonarola – the prayer letter from the condemned man. Sandro folded it up and pushed it roughly into the pocket of his leather pants to save and read later. It might be a thing to keep, a souvenir from the day's execution.

The crowd was noisy and rough. Sandro saw some men raise flagons above their heads, spilling the purple wine over the lips of the vessels, something to rouse the mood of the people to new heights. He saw only a few women and no children and was thankful for that. Such a gathering was not right to be attended by gentle people.

"There will be a hanging," he heard people in the crowd say. In reply others said, "and a burning of the false prophet, Savonarola."

"What would a man of God look like," he thought, "when he is hanging by the neck above a blazing inferno?"

Sandro had never been to a festival this big, and by any measure this would qualify as a festival. Killing a man seemed like an odd reason for celebration, but there was a certain bloodthirst in the air, and it transformed the spirit of the people around him.

The crowd ringed the contours of the area, leaving a broad empty space in the middle. At the very center of this void in the crowd was a long wooden walkway, connecting the broad open doors of the Palazzo Vecchio to the rounded platform on which the gallows stood.

Wood and timbers had been piled around the circular platform, sized and splintered well to kindle the fire that would soon be lit. Upon the platform were two vertical beams that supported a horizontal cross-beam with a span of about three meters. From the crossbeam, three ropes dangled loosely, spaced evenly apart, each bearing a noose at their end. A ladder was leaning against the crossbeam and held in place at its foot by a skinny man in a leather tunic.

As a hush settled over the assembled masses, Sandro's eyes were drawn to the corner of the piazza where everyone now looked. Even with his height, he couldn't see everything, but he was able to pick out three pairs of black-hooded men, the campagni di neri *– "companions in black" – executioners who hid their faces beneath heavy woolen cowls. The peak of their head-covering raised their height above the crowd and made them easy to spot, but their gait suggested that they didn't walk alone.*

Sandro stood on his toes to see more and could make out two lonely figures, one each between the first two pairs of executioners, hunched over and trembling in fear of the fate that awaited them. Between the third pair of compagni di neri *was a short man but one who held his head high.*

Sandro recognized the face of this proud man; it was the preacher Savonarola, the friar who had defied the city's rules, the Signoria, and even the Pope himself. The friar's short stature, beaked nose, and ruddy complexion made him look like a common laborer, not an angel from God. People in the crowd shouted rude curses at him, even those whom Sandro knew had until recently been fervent believers in the friar's teachings.

Savonarola's reign of religious domination had come to an end.

The first man to reach the gallows was quickly led up the ladder where the executioner looped a noose around his neck. After only a minor tug on the rope to tighten it, the campagno *pushed the man off the ladder and watched as the body swung from the crossbeam. The noose was not tight enough to quickly strangle the man, and his legs kicked and his body twisted in agony while enduring a slow death.*

The second was brought to the ladder and subjected to the same treatment. As he gagged for breath he was heard to mutter "Jesu" *several times in a final plea for his savior's mercy.*

Savonarola was brought to the ladder in the same way, pulled up the rungs to the crossbeam, and fitted with a noose around his neck. The campagno *grabbed onto the man's tunic and yanked his feet from the ladder, watching as his body pitched forward and downward while the rope pulled taut.*

Sandro knew that for a hanging to be done properly, the noose must be secured and tightened around the neck. Otherwise there would be painful delays in strangulation or even decapitation. Ropes that were fitted in this way would kill the men slowly, sucking the air from their lungs and squeezing the blood from their necks over many minutes.

By the time the executioner had descended the ladder all three bodies were writhing and twisting in the air above him, and several men on the ground were lighting the firewood at the base of the gallows. There was enough kindling in the mix that the flames licked higher and quickly reached the soles of the men still twisting in the air above, gagging for breath. Before long, the breeze carried the smell of sizzling flesh as the flames worked up from the condemned men's feet to their knees and torsos, boiling the fat that seeped from their muscles, until the men melted into the fire below them.

Sandro pulled the crumpled prayer letter from his pocket and read the words, "Santo, santo Dio, salvami." *"Holy, holy God, save me." He looked back at the flames that now consumed the entire gallows, then folded the letter neatly and put it back into his pocket.*

Sandro stood in the doorway of the *osteria,* listening to Leonardo and his companions argue about the ancient gospel, and he recalled the afternoon that he had held a holy man's last prayer in his hands. Since then, he had collected writings, sketches, and draft letters of other great men of Florence and, now, he planned to add the Gospel of Matthias to his notebook. It would be the crown jewel of his collection.

He had only to send the right thief to relieve Leonardo da Vinci of the prize.

LEONARDO'S STUDIO, FLORENCE

Monday Night, May 20, 1501

Gian Giacomo Caprotti – known as Salai, "little devil" to many – won Leonardo's attention as a young boy of ten, showcasing his slightly feminine features and lean musculature for the pleasure of the forty-year-old artist who was always seduced by the human form. While learning the art of painting as an apprentice, Salai also modeled for the other artists – assuming the identity of male and female forms depending on the subject of the composition.

Salai's artistic abilities were not the reason for his twenty-year association with Leonardo. The great man tolerated the boy's ambitions as a painter while he admired Salai's physical form, often enduring behavior that he would not excuse from other apprentices in his studio. Salai would frequently be absent from the workshop without explanation, and his forays into the busy streets of Florence nightlife had become the subject of rumor and conjecture among the young artists-in-training. Leonardo dismissed these misbehaviors either because he was too busy to monitor Salai's whereabouts or because he expected the little devil to sample the city's favors without remorse.

It was also known that Salai stole money from Leonardo, a minor sin that the older man could forgive, but a fact that the apprentices were aware of – a fact that was revealed to Sandro Paletti during one of the evenings that Leonardo dined at his *osteria.*

Knowing that Salai valued coins over honor, Sandro decided to exploit that weakness to get what he wanted. The restauranteur also intended to use Salai's immorality as a weapon against him – if the young man was still capable of feelings of guilt – and then would capitalize on Salai's unscrupulous temptations to force him into a theft to serve Sandro's own objective.

In the end, a handful of coins was all that was necessary to convince the little devil to remove the gospel from Leonardo's studio and deliver it to Sandro.

"*Salve, Signor Caprotti,*" Sandro said, greeting Salai on the curb of a cobblestoned street. He was leaning against a table set with two chairs in front of *Da Quinto*, a small bar on Via Tavolina, away from the bustle of the city center and hidden a bit from random passersby.

Sandro could not have risked telling Salai in advance the reason he wanted to see him, not wanting to count on any as-yet unsettled confidence. That would have to wait for their meeting. Still, Sandro assumed that a promise of money would bring Salai to the meeting while he maintained his guard considering the unstated reason for seeing him.

"*Salve, Signor Paletti,*" Salai said cautiously. A man who frequently dared to engage in dishonorable behavior would not be cowed by Sandro, but he knew that the restauranteur was in routine contact with his benefactor, so Salai needed to remain wary of Sandro's intentions.

Standing up from his leaning position and pointing to the chairs, Sandro invited Salai to sit.

"It is so nice of you to join me," he began. "I understand from the Master that your performance in his studio is coming along wonderfully."

Salai knew this was a lie; he had aspirations of great art but he knew his relationship with Leonardo was of a more carnal nature.

"*Sì*," he replied, to maintain the positive tone.

A waiter appeared from the dimly lit doorway of *Da Quinto* carrying a carafe of wine and two goblets. Sandro thanked him but raised his hand dismissively when the waiter asked if there would be anything more.

"*No, grazie*," he said, handing the man a few florins to pay for the wine. Sandro filled Salai's goblet then his own, took a long draft of the wine, then set the cup down on the rough-hewn table.

"You could do me a favor," Sandro began without prologue. "One that would reward both of us."

Salai remained silent but drank from his cup of wine while keeping his eyes on Sandro. His first thought was irreverent, and a bit flirtatious, thinking that he could provide this middle-aged man the same pleasure he bartered for his living expenses. Sandro saw the roguish smile spread slowly on his visitor's face and understood immediately how the conversation had taken an unexpected turn.

"*No, grazie*," he said to the young man. "That is not what I meant."

Salai's expression changed, the smile drooped, and his eyes narrowed as he realized that he was unprepared for the next chapter of this engagement.

"I want you to get something for me," said Sandro. "A book. A parchment."

Salai remained silent but sipped from the wine again and stared intently at his companion.

Sandro had thought through this conversation many times already, but he was wavering in the right way to bring it about.

"Your Master introduced me to a parchment that he has come into possession of. An old manuscript. Do you know of it?"

Salai shrugged to indicate that he didn't know of such a thing. Sandro hoped that wasn't completely true because no knowledge would impede the completion of this deal. So he proceeded.

"It is a parchment that your Master says is a lost gospel, the writings of a man named Matthias. Do you know of it?"

Again, a shrug.

Sandro stared back at the young man, took a sip of his wine, and changed tactics. Reaching into his purse, he withdrew a handful of coins. Earlier, Sandro had carefully counted the coins he would bring with him to set a limit on the negotiation, but as he held the shiny coins in his left hand, he pulled three of the florins out with his right, returning them to his purse. He wanted to portray himself as thoughtful about the price, but also show a willingness to raise the price.

He cupped his hand around the coins, tipped it, then let the florins fall to the table with a light clatter.

Salai still didn't know what he would be expected to do for this money, but the pile of coins on the table made his mouth gape slightly.

"I'll ask again," Sandro began, "do you know of this parchment that the Master has?" Although he asked the question, he knew that Salai's greed would produce an affirmative answer, even if he didn't know the whereabouts of the gospel. So Sandro swept up the coins and returned them to his purse, eliciting a mumbled wail from his guest.

"If you can get that parchment to me, I will give these florins to you. Now you know how much I'm willing to pay. Can you do it?"

Salai nodded yes, then drank thirstily from the wine cup.

"Remember, it is a very old parchment," Sandro advised, "written in Coptic, the ancient language of Egypt. You won't be able to read it but I will be able to," he lied. "Remember, it is this and only this that I want you to bring to me – if you want to be paid."

Rising, Salai shook Sandro's hand and promised that he would retrieve the parchment that very night.

"Good," the restauranteur replied. "And if you do, we will meet again here, tomorrow evening, so that you can give it to me and receive your payment."

Twilight had passed and the sky had darkened when Salai approached the broad stone entrance to the Basilica della Santissima Annunziata on Via Cesare Battisti. He had not come to pray so he avoided the grand doors that admitted visitors into the nave of the church, choosing instead to swing left around the stone steps leading up to the entrance and toward the cloisters that served as residence for the monks of the basilica.

He was a regular on this site and he didn't fear drawing any attention. His destination was in the workrooms behind the church, the tall-ceilinged rooms of the studio used by Leonardo and his apprentices. Arriving after nightfall might seem a little unusual, especially for Salai who couldn't be counted on for habitual attendance even during the day. But he also knew that the Master was out for the evening and would not return until mid-morning when he had slept off his drunken indulgences of the night.

Salai pushed open the heavy wooden door secured by five-pronged iron hinges and entered the cavernous workspace. The added advantage of knowing that Leonardo was otherwise occupied for the evening guaranteed that his apprentices would also take the night off, so Salai knew he would be alone.

Spread across the center of the dimly lit room and around its perimeter were half-completed paintings and blocks of Travertine marble with only cursory chips taken off thus far. Toward the back, under the sole stained-glass window of the chamber were two easels on which the Master's work stood. One was a charcoal sketch on a hardwood panel, sweeping lines and hashmarks defining the flat space and creating the outline of a future work. On the other easel stood an oil rendering of a lush landscape of distant hills cut through by a meandering stream. In the center of the unfinished work were a few tentative strokes of black lines rounded at the top and flowing below it. Salai admired the work as he had many times in the past, shaking his head at the ability of Leonardo to capture an entire composition with only several strokes of charcoal.

He pulled a flask from the table beside him, a flask that he knew the Master always kept on his worktable. Lifting the mouth of the bottle to his lips, Salai let the cool wine slip down his throat.

Setting the flask back on the table and offering one last nod of appreciation for the half-completed painting, Salai swung to the left and walked past several other works that belonged to the apprentices. He knew the room where Leonardo slept when he worked late at night – Salai had been admitted to the rough bed in the room on nights past – and he assumed that this gospel that Paletti had mentioned would be there.

The back room was separated from the studio only by a heavy drape hanging over the arched stone portal between them. Salai pushed aside the red cloth and step inside Leonardo's private chamber. There was no candle or torch lit and he preferred not to draw attention by lighting one, so Salai chose to remain still for a moment while his eyes adjusted to the faint light managing to enter through the high windows on the wall behind the Master's bed.

While waiting for his vision to return, Salai considered the various places where Leonardo might keep the gospel. The Master was not much of a collector, but he did possess valuable things, including an assortment of jewels bestowed on him by his admirers, a trunk of coins that was left unsecured, and other personal artifacts of less interest to the thief.

When the dim light of the moon brought back his ability to see, Salai moved promptly to the closet where he expected to find the gospel. Reaching for the braided rope handles, he pulled open the wooden doors to peer inside. Leonardo's cloaks hung there, and his britches were folded on a shelf below. There were four drawers at the bottom of the closet which Salai opened carefully, slowly, to avoid creating too much sound. On his first occasion of stealing money from Leonardo, he remembered being too hasty and allowing the drawer to the coin trunk to squeal as he pulled it open. It was a grievous mistake; he was caught before he could even get out of the room with his handful of florins.

This time, he was better prepared – and more handsomely rewarded. Just as he hoped, he found a clothbound bundle tied with a string in the lowest of the four drawers. Lifting it from its hiding place, he placed the bundle on top of one of the fancy trousers on the shelf and pulled the string. Unfolding the cloth he saw a stack of ancient papers. The dim light made reading difficult but even without a lantern Salai could tell that the language on this parchment was indecipherable to him. It was line after line of swirls, tiny pictographs, and angles, nothing like the local language he had come to know, nor the official Latin language that he failed to learn.

This seemed in every respect to be the papyrus that Paletti was seeking, and for which he would pay handsomely. Salai rewrapped the cloth around it and tied the strings once again, then pushed the drawer shut and closed the doors to the closet. He tucked the bundle under his arm and turned to leave the Master's chamber.

As he re-entered the vast room of the studio, he sensed a presence. Stopping to listen for signals, Salai caught sight of movement to his left. As he spun in that direction a clatter occurred behind him, and he swirled on his heels to face in that direction. If he was going to be attacked by two people his best strategy would be to flee immediately. A man appeared from the shadow on one side and approached him. Rather than a stranger, it turned out to be the merchant Salai had met in the studio a few days earlier. A man named Aegyptius.

"*Salve*," the merchant said tentatively, keeping his distance.

He too remembered Salai but he had kept his distance from the young apprentice while dealing with Leonardo.

"I was hoping to see the Master," the merchant said, although Salai doubted that alibi since who would approach the studio in the darkness of night to see Leonardo.

"He is not here." Salai kept the wrapped parchment under his arm and secured it with his other hand. Aegyptius moved his eyes in the direction of the package, smiling as he recognized it.

"I had hoped to see the Master so that I can perhaps interest him in some other purchases," Aegyptius said, pointing to the gospel under Salai's arm, clearly indicating that he knew what the man held.

Another noise from the other side of the studio brought both men to attention as they shifted their gaze from one another to the location of the disturbance. Salai darted behind a large block of marble but Aegyptius remained exposed in the space between the artworks. A man emerged from the shadows, hooded and dressed in a flowing black cloak, carrying a long dagger as he moved forward toward the merchant.

"Who are you?" Aegyptius said, the fear showing in his quavering voice.

The hooded figure didn't reply but continued approaching the man. Luckily for Salai, the merchant took a step to the side, away from Salai's hiding place, drawing the man in black in that direction. The apprentice knew that he would have little opportunity to escape so he would have to plan carefully. Behind the block of marble were some chips that lay on the floor, detritus from the work earlier in the day. He carefully bent over to retrieve the largest of these, then stood to peer around the stone shielding him.

The hooded figure was turned toward Aegyptius and, just then, Salai executed his hasty plan. He threw the marble chips in an arc which would fall to the floor just behind the merchant. He hoped the noise would draw the armed assailant closer to

Aegyptius and allow Salai to dart out of cover and toward the door.

The plan worked. The clatter of stone chips was enough to convince the hooded figure that Aegyptius was planning retaliation so he lunged at him with his knife. Just as quickly, Salai dashed out of cover and ran toward the door of the cloister and out into the street, running free and not turning back to assess the situation that he had escaped. He was alive and the gospel was still tucked under his arm. That was all he was hoping for.

Behind him, in the studio, the dark figure had lunged forward and driven his knife deep into Aegyptius's chest. A brief struggle ensued but the merchant's life force ebbed quickly. The figure let the knife blade slip out as the dead body fell to the floor. He looked over his shoulder at the place where Salai had run but did not bother much with him.

Instead, the intruder went into Leonardo's chamber, ransacking the room, the closet, and the drawers in search of something that he never found.

Retreating from the room, he surveyed the lifeless body of Aegyptius on the stone floor, his eyes wide open and mouth agape in death. The pool of blood that was spreading around the body made the hooded man laugh, then he dipped his finger in the blood and drew his hand across the stone tiles above the merchant's head.

In still warm crimson blood, he wrote *Ego sum ira Dei.*

The next evening, Salai arranged to meet with Sandro Paletti at *Da Quinto*. There was little conversation and a flagon of wine was not shared. Just the exchange of money for valuables.

The restaurant owner had what he paid for, a fistful of brittle sheets of papyrus with the pictographs scored in Coptic. Sandro couldn't read the ancient language but he believed da Vinci's claim and, besides, he only needed to offer Salai a paltry sum for the thievery.

Sandro Paletti kept his collection of artifacts and cast-off drawings and letters to himself, never showing it to others and never even mentioning it in conversation. He knew that some of the things he had saved were heretical and banned by the pope, some of them were lascivious renderings of the human body, and some of them entreaties to others to perform royal assassinations. All were very interesting, but this gospel of Matthias, if it was what Leonardo had described, would suggest that Jesus was not a god but only a rabbi, someone whose teaching was revered. Nothing more.

WASHINGTON 2021

APRIL 5, 2021

5:00am

"We need to talk," was the first thing Priest heard when he answered the phone. He recognized the slightly gravelly voice of Dr. Matthew Bordrick, a psychologist whose job is to screen people before they take up assignments directed by the White House. Priest was interviewed by him just before he flew to Vienna a couple years back for the case involving DFR Wien.

Bordrick knew that Priest had been called about the Paletti Notebook. Whether he got that intel from tapping his phone or poking around in his computer searches, Priest wasn't sure. But he seemed well versed in Priest's conversations with Bao. At first, Priest thought the back-and-forth he had on the telephone with Vienna would be the subject of this call with Bordrick, until he opened up about Paletti himself and the contents of the man's folio.

"This Paletti Notebook," Bordrick began, "how much do you know about it?"

"A fair amount."

"Not enough detail," Bordrick fired back.

"It's a folio of art and letters, and possibly an ancient gospel rumored to be written by a friend of Jesus himself."

"Yeah, sure. Anything else?"

Priest remained silent.

"The Notebook has much more than that," Bordrick added.

"So, you speak of it as if it's real."

Bordrick ignored the comment.

"Your country could suffer greatly if the Notebook is exposed."

"Why 'my country?' Why do you say that?"

Bordrick didn't say anything.

"What's in it that the U.S. would care about?" Priest asked. "Of the things I've mentioned, even the lost gospel, why would my country care so much if it is exposed, as you say?"

"There's more," the shrink said, breaking his silence. "There are things that directly concern the United States."

"Okay, I'll bite. Do you want me to destroy it?"

"I want you to find it and return it to me," Bordrick said.

Priest didn't trust Bordrick and would rather hand over the Notebook to the President. But that's a detail to be considered later.

"I'm heading to Vienna soon..."

"Yes, I know," he replied.

After all these years, Priest was still not comfortable living in a fishbowl.

"Yeah, well, anyway, I'm going to Vienna to talk to my friend at DFR Wien. He's on to something that I think may help in finding the Paletti Notebook."

Priest paused for a moment, then added, "Is there something specific you want me to look for?"

Bordrick exhaled into the phone but otherwise said nothing. At first.

"You just need to get the Notebook and bring it back," he said. "Intact. With all its parts."

"Can I read some of 'its parts'," Priest said with a smile evident in his voice.

"Frankly, Priest, no. You carry the highest clearance the U.S. sponsors, but you're not read into this project. Which means..."

"Which means that I am not allowed to see the content of the assignment I've been given. How does that work?"

"Priest, don't play this like an amateur. You're a trusted source and agent of the White House. You're being sent on this mission because the President trusts that you will live up to your oath. And do what I say."

"I'm not being sent on a mission. I agreed to help a friend in Vienna who called for my help."

"As of now," Bordrick said with finality, "you are on a mission for the U.S. Government."

Then the call went dead.

APRIL 5, 2021

6:15am

THE CHIRP ON ALANA'S PHONE WOKE HER UP. IT WAS PAST dawn but she had been in a deep sleep. Although her internal clock was still set on Vienna time, about noon to her, because of the previous day's flight and tour of Washington, not to mention the meal at the Pines of Rome and the copious wine, she fell to sleep quickly and stayed that way till the sun shone through the curtains of Priest's condo.

"Hello," she answered slowly.

"Alana. It's Stefan Haber."

She had to clear the cobwebs of sleep but knew the name. He was her subordinate at the police precinct on Leopoldsgasse. Haber was working his way up to a role as an inspector and was pleased to understudy with someone of Alana's reputation.

"What's up?"

"It's Bao Chinh," he said.

Alana didn't immediately respond, still trying to shake the sleep from her head.

"What about Bao?"

"He's dead."

What the fuck came to her mind, as did *that's impossible,* but she held her tongue. Although she was shocked and upset by the news, years in police work had convinced her that surprises like this were not only feared but sometimes expected.

She turned to her side, away from Kia, and rose from the bed. It was early and she wanted to let the girl catch up on her sleep. Jetlag was a new thing to her daughter, something that would still have to be learned.

Alana was sitting on the edge of the bed and heard Kia stir. Propping up on her elbow, the young girl turned to hug her mom around the waist and Alana returned the gesture.

"Stay with me, Stefan," she said, rising from the bed. "I need more information."

With that, she kissed Kia on the forehead and walked out of the room to find Priest.

"Darren," she said, finding him at the breakfast counter. "It's Stefan Haber. My precinct. Bao is dead." She clicked the speaker button to let Priest in on the conversation, introduced him to Haber, then told her assistant to continue.

"We don't know much yet, but he was found in a warehouse on the north side of the city. He was tied to a chair and his throat was cut," Haber explained. "He had other marks of torture, as if someone was trying to get him to talk or turn something over. We're not sure yet. The neck was the fatal wound, done I'm sure once they had decided Bao would have nothing more to give them."

"Was there anything else in the area?" Priest asked. "Any papers, tools, markings or otherwise?"

"No," Haber replied. "We're still collecting evidence, prints and such, but nothing obvious. Hold on," he said, and from the transmission it appeared he had brought his phone down from his mouth.

"Yeah," Alana and Priest could hear his voice. "Thanks. Got it."

Haber's voice returned to the phone and he added this: "We've found a note on Bao's chest. It was tucked into the folds of his shirt and since we didn't want to disturb the blood spatter until the coroner got here..."

"Okay, okay," Alana said impatiently. "What does the note say?"

"Not something I can understand," Haber replied. "Maybe Latin. It says, '*Ego sum ira Dei.*' Do you know what that is?"

"Never heard of it," replied Alana, watching as Priest shook his head.

They finished the brief conversation with Haber asking Alana when she would be returning home. The *Gruppeninspektor* had asked for and would probably want Alana to take over the investigation. She said she'd get back to him, then clicked off. Turning toward Priest, Alana shared his stunned look.

"We've got a problem, Alana," Priest began. "I spoke with Bao last night, twice, and he was fine. He was looking into that thing, the Paletti Notebook. When he called me the first time, in the afternoon while I was waiting for you at Dulles, I asked what the urgency was for a collection that's five hundred years old. He said people were dying. It sounded a bit alarming at first, but then I figured he's not a cop or anything. He didn't sound nervous or threatened. More like he was getting that from reading the photos and things that he found at the bank."

"And now he's dead," she responded.

"I have to find out what happened. He was talking to me and then, out of the blue, he's murdered. I don't believe in coincidences," Priest concluded, although Alana already knew this about him.

"And what, then?" she asked.

"I could catch a plane to Vienna this afternoon. You and Kia..."

"We're not staying here without you," she said firmly. "First of all, I liked Bao and I can't believe this has happened. But even if I didn't know the man – even if I wasn't a cop in the city where he was murdered – I couldn't stay here in Washington when you're flying back to Vienna."

"But Kia was so looking forward to..."

"Yes. I know. So was I," Alana said with grim determination. "And this is not how we expected to spend our first visit to D.C. But I don't think there's any other choice."

Kia came out of the bedroom rubbing her eyes.

"Hi, Darren," Kia said. "What's for breakfast? When do we leave? And what are we going to do today?"

Priest looked at Alana and tried to decide how to answer Kia's battery of questions. Alana stooped down next to her, took Kia's hands in hers, and looked directly into her eyes.

"Honey, I have some news. Some very sad news."

Kia looked at Priest. He remained tight-lipped and serious.

"Do you remember Mr. Chinh, honey? From the bank?"

Kia looked at her mother very seriously and could sense that something wasn't right. Her eyes were wide open and she only nodded her head.

"We just found out that he has died. Suddenly," she told the girl.

"Why?"

"We don't know, but it was sudden," Alana repeated. "And we have to find out why. And how."

"Does that mean we have to go back home, mommy?"

Alana sighed slowly but kept her eyes on Kia.

"Yes, darling. I think we do. I'm so sorry."

Kia looked from her mother to Priest, as if the news might somehow change. When their expressions made it clear that they were going to have to go home, she switched her focus – much as young people often can.

"Can we have pancakes before we go?"

FLORENCE 1546

PIAZZA DEL GRAN DUCA

June 3, 1546

PIETRO SLIPPED PAST THE LITTLE WOODEN DOOR INTO THE darkened room, ducking his head to avoid bumping it against the low beam across the top of the opening. He turned and, spreading the palms of his hands against the edge of the door, he pushed it closed more slowly than he had opened it after noticing the creak that the old hinges sounded when made to work.

"*Nonno*," he called softly. "*Nonno, sei sveglio?*" "Grandfather, are you awake?"

He got no reply to his whispered question, so he stood still in the darkness to let his eyes adjust to the dim light of the little room. Even in darkness, he knew that the roof beams were only inches above his head, big broad timbers that held up the rough-hewn ceiling. As the darkness thinned and his sense of sight slowly returned, Pietro scanned the little space. Small flames licked the dying embers in the stone fireplace beside which stood a meager stack of wood. The wooden floor was bare except for a small woven rug spread haphazardly at the side of the bed, a bed that looked more like a loose pile of bedding and cloaks but which Pietro knew sheltered his grandfather, the aging Sandro.

There was the bed and only one chair standing next to a small table – minimal furnishings necessary for a man who lived alone. The old man didn't cook here in his room and he counted on the fire only for warmth, the bed for sleep, and the single chair to sit at the table and enjoy some wine in solitude and privacy.

The little room was butted up against the rear of the restaurant that Sandro owned, called simply Paletti, an informal eating place, an *osteria,* using his surname without embellishment to indicate its provenance. In the years since his wife died, Sandro knew he could rely on food from his restaurant kitchen – an establishment in favor with everyone from local tradesmen to members of the ruling *Signoria*, the great artists, and the politicians and *maestri* of Florence – to satisfy his lonely nutritional needs.

Paletti's kitchen and dining area occupied the street-level rooms above an old cellar once owned by the Pazzi family. It faced the Piazza del Gran Duca. Across the expanse of the plaza, the stately Palazzo della Signoria, the home of Florence's elected rulers for many years, cast its shadow on Sandro's *osteria*.

What happened to the Pazzi – a noble Florentine family – and why did Sandro Paletti now own their building?

Jacopo de' Pazzi, the leader of the family in those times, had staged various plots to overthrow the Medici family – sometimes by politics and sometimes by violence. The conspiracy that he drew up in April 1478 would be his undoing. The plan was to murder the men of the Medici family during holy services in the church. It was successful against Giuliano de' Medici, a man brutally stabbed to death under the silent gaze of the crucified Christ above the altar. But his brother and *padre famiglia*, Lorenzo *Il Magnifico* survived and took revenge. With ropes around their necks, Jacoppo and his nephews were tossed out the windows of the Palazzo Vecchio to dance in the air until their bodies went limp.

While the Pazzi conspiracy had failed to oust the Medici

from control of the city, death by hanging wasn't good enough for these traitors. To avenge Giuliano's death and to dissuade others from seeking similar ends against them, Lorenzo de' Medici commissioned the artist Sandro Botticelli to paint the images of the executed men on the exterior wall of the palazzo, the rendered images hanging in full view of the Piazza del Gran Duca and the Florentines who frequented the square daily, surviving on the walls for years as a reminder of the dire consequences awaiting anyone who would challenge the Medici dynasty.

As the darkness abated, Pietro began to focus his attention on the slowly brightening images in the room. The dying embers on the hearth helped, but even without this he could see the clapboard cabinet, the door ajar on the cabinet that kept his *nonno's* minor wardrobe, and the unspent candles that topped the lantern set aside on the table nearby. Once recognizing the visual signals, Pietro began to realize the scents around him, from within his reach as well as from the restaurant astride this little room.

He caught the smells from the kitchen at Paletti that leaked through the old wall struts and plaster panels separating Sandro's street-level room on the alley from the restaurant that fronted the plaza.

Pietro closed his eyes, pausing to breathe in slowly and partake of the aromas from the kitchen next door. First, he recognized oregano and garlic, the most common accents in any Florentine kitchen. There was the scent of roasted meat with a thread of rosemary, then grilled fennel and onion. He smiled again as the scent of wine sifted through and among the other fragrances. "A fine *sangiovese,*" he whispered to himself, recalling the flavors of the great wines of Tuscany made from the grape named after the "blood of Jove."

He stepped closer to the bed and carefully pulled back the covers near Sandro's face. As Pietro's eyes continued to adjust to the light level in the room, he had to smile as he saw his grandfather's face. Sandro, too, was smiling, a tired, old-age kind of smile, but one of peace as he looked up at the face of his grandson.

"*Come stai, mi'amore?*" "How are you?" the old man asked.

"*Sto bene*," Pietro replied, although he thought it was a juxtaposition for his ailing grandfather to ask about his health.

"*Come stai?*" he asked back.

"*Bene*," Sandro said, but his smile failed briefly before struggling to regain itself.

"*Vuoi l'acqua?*" Pietro asked.

"*Sì.*"

Pietro stood and poured a cup of water from the metal pitcher on the nearby table. Bringing it to Sandro, he knelt on the floor to present it.

Sandro made an effort to sit up in bed to sip from the cup. The little movement caused him pain, so he compromised with Pietro's help to reach only a slight crunch forward, then lay down again against the thin pillow that supported his head.

"Pietro," he said after wetting his dry lips and swallowing several gulps of water, "I want to give you something, something that is very important to me, and will be to you."

Sandro pointed to the foot of the bed. At first, Pietro couldn't get his meaning. He looked at the pile of bed coverings, poked at and raised the crumpled cloak that his grandfather wore in cold weather but which now was spread across his lower body in bed for warmth.

"*No, lì,*" Sandro said, waving his arthritic right finger to a spot beyond the foot post of the bed itself. "There."

"*Nel bagaglio*," he said, shaking his finger to a vague place beyond his own vision. "In the trunk."

Pietro rose from his kneeling position and went to the trunk at the base of the bed. It was small, befitting the confined space of this little room, its width no more than the length of a man's arm. He pulled on the metal latch in the front and raised the lid of the trunk to peer inside. The space was mostly empty, except for a bulging leather folder with a cloth string tied around its midsection.

"*Portarlo a me*," Sandro said in a creaky voice that seemed to have mimicked the wail of the trunk's hinges. "Bring it to me."

Pietro obeyed his grandfather, lifting the thick folio out of the trunk and resting it on his grandfather's stomach. The old man still couldn't sit up so he motioned for Pietro to untie the string. Having done so, Sandro pulled back the leather cover to see what was bound in this notebook.

The contents were neatly organized, despite the varying sizes of the paper and parchment in the stack. Parchment had been the most common surface for writing and sketching for centuries, but Pietro knew that recent improvements in paper production had allowed writers, artists, and the educated masses to use hand-crafted paper as the medium instead. So the two media, parchment and paper, were jumbled together in this pile.

He laid the notebook open for Sandro to see. The old man's fingers pushed through the stack, separating the entries as he might have separated the herbs in his restaurant. Some had the slightly grainy, yellowish tint of parchment; some had a whiter appearance on a smoother surface, evidence of the new hand-crafted paper.

Sandro lifted one fragment of parchment and the left edge of his mouth curled up in a slight smile. Pietro remembered the sudden attack that his grandfather suffered in the Paletti kitchen one year ago, an attack which weakened his right arm and leg and left his face divided in half, one part alive and one part dead.

Sandro turned his half-smile toward Pietro and shook the little piece of parchment slightly.

"*Leonardo*," was all he said at first. After a pause, he added, "He thought he could tell God what to do!"

Pietro looked at the parchment. It was only a corner of a

larger sheet, a quick sketch torn off of something larger. But he recognized a short phrase labeling the Arno River that ran through Florence, then a line, then a dot to the side marked "Pisa." If this was a map by the master Leonardo da Vinci, Pietro was struck by the fact that it contained a clear error in depicting Tuscany. The drawing of the river bent around Pisa – contrary to the fact as Pietro knew that the Arno flowed through Pisa – as it did through Florence. Anyone with knowledge of Tuscany would know this.

"*Quest'è di Leonardo*," Sandro whispered.

Pietro looked at the drawing again. His grandfather was saying this was made by Leonardo, no doubt the brilliant artist from Vinci, a man known not only for his art but also for his engineering and scientific skills. In fact, Pietro knew that Leonardo had also been a military advisor to Cesare Borgia and the ruling elite of Florence, the *Signoria*. That man, now long dead, could not have made such a foolish mistake in drawing a map such as this.

"*Perche?*" Pietro asked Sandro, holding the scrap of paper to the light. "Why?"

"He thought he could tell God what to do."

That answer made no more sense than it did the first time he heard it, so Pietro pressed his grandfather.

"*È una mappa non di ciò che era, ma sarebbe*," Sandro told his grandson. "It is a map not of what was, but what would be."

Pietro knew that the Arno flowed from east to west, through Florence and thence through Pisa before emptying into the sea. And he knew that the Florentines had warred with the Pisans for generations, trying to control access to the sea without Pisa's interference on the waterway.

He looked again at the sketch and realized that this was not a map, but a plan. Leonardo was drawing up a manner of redirecting the Arno around Pisa so that Florence would no longer have to rely on treaties or conquests of that city to bring its products to market, and to receive the bounty of their sales from beyond Tuscany.

"*E Machiavelli, il mostro*," Sandro whispered. "And Machiavelli, the monster."

Pietro knew of the Florence-Pisa battles over the years but not of any plan to re-channel the river around Pisa. He knew nothing of Leonardo's interest in this and, of course, had never heard of Niccolò Machiavelli having a hand in such a plot to challenge God's way.

"He, Machiavelli, paid Leonardo to devise a plan such as this," Sandro explained. "I heard it with my own ears, and I watched them at the table in my restaurant draw a way to do it."

Sandro talked Pietro through the story as he knew it, the meetings with Cesare Borgia in Imola where they first hatched the plan to circumvent Pisa. How Machiavelli brought Giuliano Lapi in to manage the diversion of the Arno. How they used the fortress at La Verruca to support the project and, finally, how God intervened with a deluge of rain that collapsed the channels being dug by the Florentines to send the Arno River around Pisa. An act of divine condemnation that finally ended the plan of Leonardo and Machiavelli.

Sandro was growing weak from his description of that venture, but he lifted other slips of paper and parchment to show his grandson.

"*Una testa*," he said at one point, pointing to a drawing on a piece of paper among many others. "A head."

"*Di Michelangelo*," he explained, tapping the drawing.

Pietro studied the little sketch and was stunned when he realized that it resembled the head portion of the most famous sculpture in his world, the one of the liberator, David, the symbol of all that is Florence. The statue was carved by Michelangelo Buonarotti in 1504 from a massive hunk of Carrara marble and had stood at the portal of the Palazzo della Signoria since that time.

"*È di Michelangelo?*" Pietro asked in amazement. "The drawing is from Michelangelo?"

"*Sì, è vero,*" Sandro replied. "Yes, truly."

From his grandfather's declaration, Pietro realized that this sketch was an early rendition of Michelangelo's plan to turn the hunk of nondescript Carrara marble into the larger-than-life sculpture of David, the man who slayed Goliath and saved his people.

Pietro spread more of the sheets out on the bed to see the entire collection. He lifted one that seemed to be a letter, addressed and signed with obscure marks and codes instead of full names.

"*Questo,*" Sandro said poking the paper with his finger, "*quest'è una lettera da Borgia*" – "This is a letter from Borgia."

"Rodrigo?" Pietro asked, referring to Rodrigo Borgia who became Pope Alexander VI.

"*No,*" was the reply, "*Cesare. Suo figlio.*"

Pietro nodded. A letter from a pope would be an amazing artifact to be found in his grandfather's humble collection. Still, finding a letter from Cesare, the pope's son by one of the pontiff's many mistresses, was also of great importance. He skimmed through the letter and realized that Cesare was appealing for military assistance from the King of Naples, among the many shifting alliances that the Borgia family plotted to control sections of the Italian peninsula for decades. Pietro knew about the Borgia plans from local historical accounts, but thought they mattered little to his everyday life.

Over an hour's time, Sandro introduced his grandson to the contents of his notebook, including sketches from artists like Leonardo, Michelangelo, Botticelli, and Raphael, and notes and letters written by the city power brokers like Machiavelli, Borgia, and Piero Soderini – Florence's *gonfaloniere,* leader of the *Signoria.* A prayer letter from Girolamo Savonarola, the religious savant who paid for his preaching with his life, was also in the stack of papers.

Sandro grew tired over the time with Pietro and begged for some time to sleep. The young man tied the bundle of documents back together and placed it once more in the trunk at the foot of the bed. By the time he completed this minor task, the old man was asleep again, so he stood and walked toward the door, taking care to open and close it slowly to avoid the metallic cry of the hinges.

The daylight had faded by the time Pietro returned later that day. The kitchen at Paletti was coming alive with the expectation of diners for the evening, and he could hear the sounds of pots and pans through the thin wall that separated the restaurant from his grandfather's room in the back.

He pushed the door open slowly, slipped through it and into the room, then turned back toward the wooden door to close it as silently as he could.

"*Pietro*," came the call from his grandfather. "*Vieni qua.*" "Come here."

Despite what he may have lost in strength and stamina, Sandro still had keen eyesight and smell, so he had no problem recognizing his grandson nor the scent of cooking from next door.

"*Formaggio*," the old man whispered with a smile, "*e riso*."

"Cheese and rice."

Then "*e l'odore agli spinaci.*" The "and the smell of spinach," a mainstay of any Florentine cooking for centuries.

Pietro brought the lone chair in the room over to the bed. Before settling into it, he stirred the embers of the fire and lifted one more stubby log onto it.

"*Il folio*," Sandro said, pointing to the trunk at the base of the bed.

Pietro retrieved the folio with its collection of art sketches, letters, and odd memorabilia from the great men of Florence.

He pulled at the string and opened the folder on the bed space next to his grandfather.

"*Voglio che tu abbia questo*," he said, peering into Pietro's eyes. "I want you to have this." And as he said that, he sifted through the contents of the collection, then lay back in the bed.

"*Sarebbe dovuto morire*," he whispered in a tone so low that Pietro couldn't understand his words. It sounded like "he should have died," but what would Sandro have meant? Pietro knew that his grandfather had been lonely and unhappy since he lost his wife, but if he meant that he, Sandro, should have died, he would have said, "*Avrei dovuto morire*."

"*Que?*" Pietro asked.

"*Sarebbe dovuto morire*."

"*Chi?*" Pietro asked, knowing that Sandro was referring to someone else. "Who?"

"*Savonarola*."

Sandro's eyes glistened with the first signs of tears and he looked up at the low ceiling above his bed. Shadows cast by the flickering light of the fireplace danced across the room. He told Pietro about the sermons of Girolamo Savonarola, the ascetic preacher who turned the people of Florence against themselves. How the preacher told everyone that Florence was doomed if it didn't plead for mercy from God. How the leaders of the city would be doomed, how the pope himself would die, as would the kings who supported him.

"*Falò delle vanità*," Sandro whispered. "Bonfire of the vanities."

Pietro had heard the phrase before from the time of Savonarola who beseeched the Florentines to give up their luxuries – their books, their jewelry, their paintings – and consign them to a great bonfire in the Piazza del Gran Duca. The monk's white-cloaked youths would wander the streets of the city collecting these "vanities" from the penitent – or those who feared divine retribution even if they were not truly penitent –

and the boys would throw the things they had collected onto a pile in the center of the piazza.

There was not one fire, but many, all directed by Savonarola at the height of his power. The greatest of these was on the seventh day of February 1497, when the friar built a mountain of vanities, all to be consumed by the flames in a grand tribute to God Almighty and his powers over the earth and its people. He lit the flame himself after singing a hymn in a voice so low that only the front row of people crowded into the square could hear.

"*A Dio*," was heard multiple times by those within earshot. "To God."

The flames grew quickly and wide-eyed Florentines gazed as the oil in paintings that had been consigned to fire dripped down the canvas. As gold jewelry glowed bright and slumped down into the mass of congealed embers below them. As books burst into flame when their pages fanned out and caught the heat of the fire below, lifting as if by magic into the light wind in the square.

"*La follia del falò*," said Sandro with a failing breath. "The folly of the bonfire."

Sandro reached into the pile of papers on the bed and produced one that was lined and arranged as if it was a poem, or a prayer.

"*Da Savonarola*," he said. "From Savonarola."

"*Si legge...*" the old man said through whispered breath – "it reads..." – "*Si legge, al nostro Padre celeste, perdona i peccati di queste persone...*" – "Heavenly Father, forgive the sins of these people..."

"*Fra Sav.*" was etched at the bottom of the page. Pietro assumed that it was the same as the friar Savonarola that his grandfather was talking about. Perhaps even written by him.

It seemed to be a prayer beseeching the author to live a good life without sin, and then beseeching God to guide the people of Florence in the "right way," a phrase repeated several times in successive lines as if in a poem.

Sandro explained to Pietro that this was from the monk,

received just on the day of his execution. He, Sandro, had received it from a beggar in the piazza on that day and he had saved it all these years.

"Let me explain this to you," he said, "so that you will know what I witnessed."

Of the seer who had been tortured, hung, and burned to death.

PIAZZA DEL GRAN DUCA

June 3, 1546

PIETRO SAT BESIDE HIS GRANDFATHER, SANDRO, WHILE THE old man described the scene of Savonarola's death. When Sandro drifted off to sleep, Pietro remained sitting on the chair at the bedside, conjuring visual images of what had taken place on that day so long ago.

Many stories were still told of the friar's teaching, his prophesies, and his death by fire. There were Florentines who still believed in Savonarola's divine connection while others scoffed at the idea. True, he had led the *Signoria* to expel the Medici family from the city. Their power had declined once Lorenzo de' Medici had passed away in 1492, leaving their banking empire in the hands of his weaker son, Piero. Without the forceful Lorenzo in charge, the anti-Medici contingent could force Piero and the rest of the Medici clan out.

And, Pietro had to admit, the little friar took more than satisfaction from the expulsion; he took power from it too. Maybe Savonarola's lust for power outraged the republican-minded *Signoria* enough to take him prisoner, then torture false confessions out of him to justify his execution three years later.

Pietro also knew that the Medici exile didn't last very long.

Led by Giuliano de' Medici, the family was restored to Florence as power brokers in 1512.

Picking up some of the scraps and memorabilia that *nonno* Sandro had in his collection and were now scattered on the bed coverings, Pietro lifted the bound journal of yellowing paper. The first inside leaf read, "*Questo è il diario di Sandro Paletti.*" Turning that page over, he read the following: "*Il passato è il nostro tesoro, quindi è nostro dovere preservarlo,*" with his grandfather's name and the year, 1498, at the bottom. "The past is our treasure, so it is our duty to preserve it."

"*Tra i Medici*" was inscribed at the top of the following page, "between the Medici." There were several paragraphs recounting how Lorenzo de' Medici had used his money and power to bring great artists to the city of Florence, great thinkers and great writers too, and how this grand assembly of talent and genius had planted the seed of enlightenment, making Florence the center of the world. And the entry concluded with Sandro's own prophesy, that by the time the Medici returned to the city – something that Pietro knew occurred under Giuliano de' Medici– "the world would know of the greatness of Florence."

Sandro stirred in the bed and rolled toward Pietro sitting beside him. When his eyes opened, he smiled at his grandson and reached his weathered hand to rest on the knee of the young man.

"That is my journal, my diary," he wheezed through sleepy breaths. "I collected shards of work from all of the great men of the city. But I also collected my thoughts, my memories of them." Sandro paused for a moment and a little smile formed on his lips.

"And even some of the secrets that they had," he added. "You see, the man who makes and serves your food often hears stories at the table that no one else would know."

"Especially if there's wine," Pietro said with a grin.

"*Veramente,*" Sandro replied, "especially if there's wine."

In all, there were crisp chalk and charcoal drawings, carefully penned letters, designs for irrigation canals and flying machines, and other bits of paper and parchment. Sandro would point to each in turn and call out names like Raphael, Michelangelo, Leonardo, Machiavelli, and Borgia as Pietro lifted the pieces one by one.

"This is a prayer letter by Fra Girolamo Savonarola, was written on the day the friar was executed. Right there," he added, pointing his wrinkled hand in the general direction of the Piazza del Gran Duca, "in the piazza. They hung him then burned the body.

"I watched," he said. "Some drunken beggar thrust this prayer in my face on the morning of the execution, and I thought I might like to keep it. That was 1498. Then, the next year, my father, Alessandro, died, leaving me as the proprietor of Paletti, the *osteria*. Over the years, many of the great men that Lorenzo *Il Magnifico* had attracted to Florence began coming to Paletti for meals and wine. Most were not married, like the artists, so they needed someone to feed them. Others were married, like Signor Machiavelli – a very important man! – but even he needed the bars of Florence as a respite from his sainted wife, Signora Marietta Corsini.

"So, they came to Paletti. And I fed them, poured them wine, and listened to their stories. And I kept the rough sketches they made at the table when they argued about plans for art, bridges, a great palazzo, and fantastic machines that could fly through the air or plunge down into the sea."

Sandro tapped some of the papers spread across his bed, as a tear showed at the corner of his eye.

"And these...these..." he began with halting speech, "these are the remnants of these great men that I saved for our history. For our city. Our people.

"The Medici believed that connections to royal families in Rome and to Popes would ensure a durable family line. The Pitti, Orsini, and Pazzi families believed that sheer power, sometimes exhibited in ruthless suppression, would accomplish the same thing," Sandro said between coughs and through whispy breaths. "Savonarola saw eternity in religious teaching, and the artists saw it in their paintings and sculpture."

Here he paused for a rest.

"But I saw power in connections." Sandro added. "My connection. To each and all of them."

Sandro's breath was failing and Pietro decided to leave his grandfather alone, allowing him to fall into a nap, and gather what strength he still possessed.

Pietro returned the next morning to check on his *nonno* and straighten up the little room behind Paletti. The sounds of the workers in the *osteria* were already coming alive, pans banging and the sound of sharp knives meeting heavy oak cutting tables.

When he pushed the door open he noticed that the smell inside had changed from the night before. He could still detect a bit of aromas from the kitchen that crept through the openings between the two rooms, but there something more ominous. Pietro had never been close enough to death to recognize the smell, but knowing Sandro's failing health, he feared that death was the odor that filled the room.

The fire had gone out in the little hearth, and the light was dim despite the morning sun.

"*Nonno*," he whispered, but he got no response.

He crossed to the side of the low bed and touched the pile of bedding that he knew was his grandfather. Pushing gently on what he perceived would be the old man's hip, he repeated his whispered call. Still no reaction.

Pietro slid his hand up the pile of cloth toward where Sandro's shoulder would be. Resting it lightly on the bony protrusion from the blanket, he pulled it toward him.

Sandro's lifeless body rolled over toward Pietro and the young man could see the lifeless eyes staring back at him. His grandfather had passed during the night, and Pietro made the sign of the cross on his chest and uttered a prayer of thanks, not for the death but because it seemed to have come to his beloved *nonno* peacefully.

Pietro pulled the covers up over his grandfather's face, mulling what actions he would be expected to take now. The restaurant would be in good hands; his own father would see to that. Besides, Pietro was not drawn to the business of food.

And he knew that he had an important assignment. Sandro's collection of drawings and letters, plus his own diary, formed a contemporaneous record of the great men of Florence. Now, in the 1540s, the world recognized how important were the contributions made by them, with talk of that period – and this very city – being at the heart of a new surge of intellectualism and a revolution in styles of painting and sculpture.

Pietro understood the importance of his grandfather's collection, and he understood the urgency of his protecting all of the Paletti notebook.

He sat on the chair next to Sandro's bed and considered the other matters before him. Sandro would have passed this on to his own son, Pietro's father, if he thought that would have worked. But he didn't. He passed on his great treasure to Pietro, his son's son, and the young man took that as a signal that he shouldn't share the existence of the collection even with his own father.

He opened the chest at the foot of the bed and retrieved the Paletti notebook and its folder of drawings. Tucking it under his arm, he left the room and pulled the door closed quietly behind him. He would call the doctors about his grandfather's passing and tell his father about it. But first, he had to put the notebook and drawings somewhere where they could not be found.

VIENNA 2021

VIENNA

April 6, 2021

PRIEST ARRANGED FOR A FLIGHT BACK TO VIENNA THAT afternoon. Alana called United Airlines using her police credentials to get priority seating with no wait list.

There was too little time to actually get any sightseeing done in D.C. The flight was scheduled to depart Dulles in early evening and Priest had some things to take care of before the trip. Among other steps, he decided he wanted to get a friend, Arnold "Aggie" Darwin involved. Aggie was not an investigator but he was a good sidekick, had a good sense of impending danger, and was well versed in European history and Church doctrine – knowledge that Priest thought would come in handy.

Aggie was an ex-drone pilot from the American war in Afghanistan whom Priest had met at Tall Cedars, a commune in rural Virginia. The place and the people there offered solace, patience, and tranquility for war-torn veterans and other victims of 21st century American society. Aggie wore his hair in a long braid down his back, a salt-and-pepper beard covering most of his jaw, and the rag-tag shirt and jeans of a hippie from the '60s.

"Killing from a distance is worse than killing up close," he told Priest one afternoon at Tall Cedars. "You can't pay your respects to an enemy you never see." That pretty much summed up Aggie's discomfort with the U.S. government's use of military might. Priest understood his feelings and could sympathize with him, so they grew close while at Tall Cedars. Priest also recognized Aggie's keen and perceptive mind, one that was educated in the elite schools of America and could pick out both Biblical and historical references like a living Wikipedia. So Aggie was an easy match for Priest and they hung out together at Tall Cedars and in various other countries afterward.

Alana had done a fair amount of traveling in her lifetime but couldn't compare to Priest's long list of travels. They boarded the flight to Vienna, but she tossed and turned in the plane overnight, squeezing her eyes closed as if the effort would summon sleep. Priest had made numerous international flights and traveled to dozens of countries in the relative luxury of commercial planes and not-very luxurious accommodations in the cramped space of military aircraft. Through the years, he conditioned himself to find sleep whenever and wherever it was offered.

The plane touched down at the Vienna International Airport just after dawn. Priest and Alana stood to collect their carry-ons from the overhead while Kia shoved her few books into the backpack that she had brought on the plane with her. Now standing, they had to wait as the line slowly began its exit from the front of the plane.

"Why do they get to go first?" Kia asked, pointing to the First Class section ahead.

"Because they paid more for their tickets," her mother replied.

"You mean you have to pay to leave the plane?"

Alana chuckled and looked at Priest. He smiled and shrugged his shoulders.

"She's got a point," he said.

"Are you sure you're ready for this?" Alana asked.

Priest looked at her quizzically, trying to put that question in the right context. Sure, the two of them were considering formalizing their relationship, but Alana's question seemed so random that he wasn't sure if that was her meaning. Was she referring to the arrival in Vienna or the prospect of being a stepfather?

She raised one eyebrow and smiled broadly back at him.

They deplaned and wove their way through the maze of corridors leading to Customs. Alana and Kia proceeded through the EU passport lanes while Priest stood in line with the other Americans in the non-EU line for passport check. As he emerged on the other side having convinced the Customs agent that he was not a threat – big surprise there – Priest saw Alana and Kia waiting for him at the bag check carousel.

They had to stand only a few minutes at the carousel before their luggage disgorged from the trolley, appearing through the thick rubber flaps that partitioned the bag claim area from the tarmac. Then they turned toward the exit and, as they passed through the wide portal into the airport concourse, Priest looked for Aggie. A tap on his shoulder caused him to turn around.

"Hey, man," Aggie said with a smile. "Thought I'd find you here."

Aggie explained that his plane from Rome arrived just minutes before Priest's from Washington. Alana already knew him so they exchanged a hug, but Kia had not yet had the introductions.

"This is my daughter, Kia," Alana said and Aggie stooped down to shake the girl's hand.

"Your mom's very lucky," he said.

A quizzical look from Kia and then the question, "Why lucky?"

"Because she has such a cute little girl to call her own."

Kia's broad smile then turned up to Alana and was greeted with a return hug. Priest was loath to interrupt the love fest but had to return to his primary mission.

Over the phone the previous day, Priest had caught Aggie up

on what he knew so far, beginning with Bao's discovery of the old photos in the bank, the research he had done on the Paletti Notebook, and the report that Bao had been taken, tortured, and then murdered.

"I'll call Stefan Haber at the office and ask him to come pick us up. He can drop you and Aggie at the Marriott Parkring – that's where you're staying, right? – then take me and Kia home. I'll check in with the office and we'll see when we can connect."

They stood around talking mostly about the Paletti Notebook while waiting for Haber to arrive. Priest compared notes on the lost treasure with Aggie and found out that he had also done a bit of research. Alana held Kia's hand as throngs of people shouldered by toward the taxi stand, keeping physical contact with her daughter as they compared thoughts on the project at hand.

"This thing," Aggie began, "this Notebook. I found mostly references to it as a myth."

"I think that's because of the historic importance that would attach to its contents, if it was real," Priest replied. "Anti-Church writings and art, a lost Gospel that suggests – so to say – that Jesus wasn't God, after hearing quite the opposite for two thousand years from the Christian clergy."

"Well, actually it wasn't until the First Council of Nicaea in 325," Alana corrected, "that he was promoted to a god."

Priest couldn't resist a smile.

"His early followers, possibly also this man Matthias," she continued, "thought he was a teacher, a rabbi. Some thought he was a prophet as taught in Islam and by some in Judaism. But Emperor Constantine wanted to settle the dispute. So the Emperor called the bishops together in Nicaea and they voted on it."

"Wait," Aggie said, holding up his hand to pause Alana's narrative. "They voted? Seems like news of being declared a deity is important enough to have arrived on the wings of doves, or as a lightning bolt."

"No. That's the way it happened," she concluded.

"Okay," Priest interrupted, "let's go back. What we care about is the impact of this Paletti Notebook having on the billions of people who consider themselves Christian and the immense power of the Catholic Church in political, diplomatic, and legislature matters. If the Gospel of Matthias actually exists..."

"And it is what the rumors say," Alana suggested, "a contemporaneous life story of Jesus..."

"Yes, and that. If the Gospel of Matthias exists and if the other things that Paletti collected are the anti-Church diatribes – and art – of some of the greatest thinkers of the Renaissance..."

Priest couldn't complete the sentence. There was too much to think about. That didn't stop Aggie.

"If all that's true, and someone finds it and publicizes the Notebook, the foundations of Western theology, the entire Christian community – Roman Catholic and Protestant – would be exposed as based on a fraud."

"Or, at best, wishful thinking," Alana added, "based on a vote that took place nearly two thousand years ago..."

"And for the sole purpose of centralizing power in the clergy," Priest said to complete her statement.

Just then, Haber walked through the door and hailed Alana.

"*Guten morgen*," she said, shaking hands with him. "This is Herr Stefan Haber," she said introducing the plain clothes officer to them. "Stefan, we are four. Do you have room in the van?"

"*Ya*, I do. No problem."

"Okay, if you wouldn't mind, Darren and Aggie are staying at the Marriott Parkring, please drop them there and then take me and Kia home. My parents are there and they can watch Kia while you and I go to the office. I assume the crime scene has been cleaned up."

"*Ya*," he said, grabbing a handle on one of Alana's bags.

Alana and Stefan walked side by side ahead of Priest and Aggie toward the exit, she still gripping Kia's hand.

They loaded the bags into Stefan's van and got in. There wasn't much to talk about and Priest knew from his time in investigations that you didn't want to overthink something. They had next to no information at this point so any discussion of it would create false leads and steer them farther from the actual pattern of events. They had to be patient and wait for Alana to get to the scene and report back.

Stefan dropped Aggie and Priest at the Marriott first then sped off to bring Kia home.

At the Marriott, Priest and Aggie checked in and got their passes to the concierge lounge. It was still early in the day and, from past experience, they knew that this particular hotel on Parkring didn't always get their check-in guests quickly into their rooms. Thankfully, the desk clerk arranged entrance to the concierge lounge for the two men so they could kill some time until their rooms were released for occupancy.

They walked to the elevator lobby, pushed the up button and then Priest slid his keycard through the swipe pad, pressing the button for the concierge level as he did so. They emerged from the lift on the top level of the hotel, into a small lobby that only served the lounge, and proceeded through another keycard-controlled door that Priest had used many times before. Up a few steps and into the comfort of a sunlit lounge, they found a small table in the corner to relax.

The late-morning food in the concierge lounge was substantial, including cheese platters, crackers and fresh bread, fruit, and bowls of nuts. The lounge was past breakfast time when they could have gotten eggs, sausage, bacon, and rolls, but the present offering was enough to keep them going. They each filled a small plate with nibbles, pushed the knobs on the espresso machine to deliver a wake-up drink, and moved to a table by the fan-light window at the end of the room.

"What the hell happened?" Aggie asked when they sat down.

"I have no idea. I spoke to Bao twice the night before he was discovered in the warehouse. From Stefan's report, his death wasn't an accident although we won't know more until Alana reports back."

"He was killed," Aggie said, spreading butter on one of the crackers on his plate. "Why? And what are we in for?"

"It has to do with the Paletti Notebook, for sure," Priest responded. "But why? And how?"

Priest replayed the mental tape of his conversation with Dr. Bordrick. Although Bordrick provided very little detail, it seemed obvious that the U.S. government had a stake in the Notebook. Priest didn't want to bring this up to Aggie just yet, but he had to consider if this search for the collection that Paletti started included more than they currently knew about.

"Good," Aggie said, mumbling through a bite of cracker.

"Good, what?" Priest asked.

"The butter!" he said with a smile. "Butter in Europe is always better than in the States."

Apparently, even murder and the imminent threat of more violence couldn't keep Aggie from enjoying food.

After about an hour, Priest's phone chirped. It was Alana.

"And?" he asked expectedly. There was a pause.

"I'm just at the office," she began, "and reviewing the record of the scene. I'll go there later this morning. Bao was found tied up and sitting in a chair. He looked like he had been beaten. There were bruises that are recent, within the last twenty-four hours. His throat was slit."

"Any evidence? Any hint of who was there?"

"Very little," she said, "except for that note they found pinned to Bao's shirt. The note Haber read to us over the phone."

"What does it say?" This came from Aggie, and it dawned on Priest that he hadn't shared that detail yet with his friend.

"*Ego sum ira Dei.*"

"Whoa!" whispered Aggie.

"What's whoa?" Priest asked turning toward him.

"It means, "*I am the wrath of God.*"

"Sounds ominous," Priest opined, then added, "but also a bit presumptuous. Whoever left that note thinks they're carrying out direct orders from God?"

By then, Aggie had pulled out his laptop, flipped it open and signed on to the Marriott weblink.

"What's your password?" he asked Priest.

"What?"

"I need your Marriott password. Come on. We don't have time to discuss this."

Priest gave Aggie the password that he had used at Marriott hotels around the world.

"Okay," Aggie said, sitting back and surveying the Google results. "I thought I remembered this."

Priest was familiar with Aggie's knowledge of biblical references and the arcane bits of information that clustered around religious subjects.

" '*Ego sum ira Dei*' is the motto of a cult that formed back in the early, maybe pre-, Reformation days. They called themselves *Arma Dei,* or Army of God, and considered their mission to protect the hierarchy of the Catholic Church, particularly the Pope himself, from all criticism and challenges. They have been known to resort to violence and there are recorded instances of them killing to accomplish their goals."

"Why would *Arma Dei* be in Vienna," asked Alana, "and why would they kill Bao?"

"There are no coincidences," Priest reminded her. "Bao supposedly had the Paletti Notebook, or proof of it, and the Notebook – from what we've found out already – may include a bunch of anti-Pope stuff in it."

"Not to mention a gospel that the Vatican considers heretical," chimed in Aggie.

"Yeah, not to mention."

"But how would *Arma Dei* know Bao had something like this,

and how did they get here so quickly?" asked Alana on the phone.

"Seems like that's what you're here to find out," Priest said. "Can you get a warrant to search Bao's apartment, then come by and pick us up to take a look at it with you?"

"Sure. I'll be there in about an hour."

CHINH'S APARTMENT, VIENNA

April 6, 2021

ALANA AND STEFAN HABER PICKED UP PRIEST AND AGGIE AT the hotel and together they rode to Bao Chinh's apartment. Using the search warrant that Alana had so quickly acquired, they prodded the desk clerk in the apartment building into hurrying along the hallway and getting into the flat that Chinh used.

Sliding the keycard past the door lock, a click was heard and they were admitted into the apartment. The clerk pushed the door open but stepped aside to let the three of them in.

The apartment had been sacked. Pictures askew, sofa cushions tossed onto the floor – some of them slashed open – drawers left half-open, curtains pulled aside. Priest went into the bedroom and saw a similar scene, although most of the art and wall ornaments had been pulled down and tossed aside. Aggie went into the kitchen and found the drawers open and cabinets emptied of their bowls and plates.

Alana looked through the closets and smaller spaces, sure that Chinh – if he had anything to hide – would deposit the treasure there. Haber remained at the door to keep the desk clerk at bay. While he was standing there, a man approached, coming down the corridor with what Haber interpreted as a bit of reluctance.

"You'll have to pass by," Haber told the stranger.

"But I can't. I am Franz Hesse. I worked with Bao at DFR Wien."

Alana quickly moved toward the door.

"What do you mean 'worked?' Don't you mean 'work with?'"

"No," Hesse replied, looking at his feet. "The news of Bao has already made it to the bank. We are aware that he was killed. Perhaps it had something to do with this."

Hesse held his hands out, cradling a large envelope that appeared to be stuffed to the point of bursting.

"He thought it wouldn't be safe to keep these himself," Hesse said. "I guess it wasn't safe to get rid of them either."

Alana took the envelope from him, peered quickly inside and signaled for Priest and Aggie to join her. Then she turned toward Stefan Haber and asked him to get the man's name, address, and any other information that he might have to help with the investigation.

"We need to look more closely at this," she said to her companions, pulling a couple of photographs out of the folder. The photos looked old themselves, likely decades old, and the ones that Alana held in her fingers depicted very old-looking sketches, drawings, and letters.

"Let's go back to the hotel," Priest said, and they slipped through the door just as Haber was completing his interview of Hesse.

"Stefan," she said to her colleague, "please take us back to the Marriott."

Priest, Alana, and Aggie retreated to the Marriott to look through the photographic record of the Paletti Notebook. They were astonished to see images of Renaissance art, sketches and drawings that depicted later-famous sculpture and paintings. Included among the photos were pictures of letters signed by Niccolò Machiavelli, heretical prophesies by Girolamo Savonarola, anti-Church screeds written by Cesare Borgia, plans by da Vinci to reroute the Arno River and isolate the people of Pisa, and first drafts of art with "Mich. B." in the corner, referring to Michelangelo Buonarotti.

But they needed something more; they needed clues from the pile of photographs that would help them find Chinh's killer and lead them to the Paletti Notebook.

Then they found it. The photographs were scattered across Priest's hotel bed and twelve pieces stood out. Although the printed paper of all the photos was the same, the lettering was different on these pages. They seemed to be part of a journal, a chronology of sorts, with European cities scattered throughout and a trail of clues that all were connected to the Paletti Notebook. Darwin pointed out the signature at the bottom of the final page, "Fra Nizza."

"Fra is the honorific title for friar," Alana said, examining the twelve sheets carefully. "From his narrative, it seems this Fra Nizza was a monk at the Abbey of Sant' Antimo near Montalcino in 1943. This could be a documented history of the Paletti Notebook as it traveled through the continent and passed from hand to hand among those who planned to use it for their own purposes."

"But we've only got a few pages," said Priest, "and judging from the discontinuous paragraphs, I think these pages are not connected." He looked up at Alana and wondered what the make of it.

The trio sat on the edge of the bed and passed the sheets back and forth as they read the pages that Fra Nizza had written. His notes pointed to the importance of the Notebook and the power that it conveyed to the person who controlled it.

"Hey," Aggie said, holding up one of the sheets of Nizza's journal. "Are you seeing what I'm seeing?"

"What?" Alana asked.

"People are dying all over the place for this thing." Then, referring to Nizza's notes, Aggie adds, "Armies have been destroyed, secret missions by several countries have come to terrible ends, people were crucified over it. Even the first guy, Pietro was murdered for it, and..."

"And Bao was killed," Priest added.

"Yeah," Aggie said, "exactly my point. Are you sure you want to go looking for this thing?"

Finding the Paletti Notebook had now become secondary to finding Bao Chinh's killer.

"Damn right," replied Priest.

FLORENCE -ROME 1553

FLORENCE - ROME

August 13-14, 1553

BERNARDO UTA WAS NOT A NOVICE, AND HE WAS NOT A MONK; he was a warrior. He had sworn an oath to Pope Julius III and the entire line of popes. Uta's oath as a member of *Arma Dei* was to protect the unquestioned dominance of the Papal throne, even if his life would be lost in the process. His army of "sainted soldiers" declared that they were imposing the wrath of God, and they had fought for the Church hierarchy for decades, ever since heretics like Martin Luther and Philip Melanchthon challenged Pope Leo X and the practices of Church in Rome. Members of *Arma Dei* swore an oath of allegiance to the Papacy, as did Uta when he joined the army of disciples in 1548.

His charge in this case was to find the thing called the Paletti Notebook, full of heresies from a scandalous gospel written long ago and letters and sketches by the men of Florence – artists, writers, even once-famous politicians – who dared to promote ideas contrary to Church teaching. Uta was instructed to find it and destroy everything in it by fire.

With the unwitting help of a winemaker at an inn near San Marco monastery, Uta had gained entrance to the monks' cells, identified the one where Pietro Paletti lived, and ended the novice's life in exchange for the apostasy of anti-Church writings he had hidden beneath the stones of his chamber.

Along the way, Uta had made slight changes in the plan that *Arma Dei* had given him. Rather than destroy the Notebook and all its contents, he decided that he would deliver them himself to Pope Julius III, in return for which he expected to reap more papal benefits than he could otherwise accumulate in his entire lifetime. The Pope would smile generously upon being presented with the thing called the Paletti Notebook, especially the sacrilegious Gospel of Matthias, and Uta could be a witness to the Pope putting this devil's concoction to the flames.

But first, he had to kill the monk called Pietro Paletti, an act he carried out with ruthless violence late one evening after the bells of *compline* had sounded in the monastery. Retrieving the collection called the Paletti Notebook, he ran from the cell and down the hallway, exiting the monastery grounds by leaping over a wall and down onto the ground outside it.

The following morning Uta spent some time examining the contents of the leather folio he now possessed. He saw a sketch of a naked woman, one that displayed much more than his imagination would have allowed, and a tiny "da Vinci" etched in the corner. He saw a letter that was an ongoing harangue against the Pope, with the abbreviation "C. Borgia" at the bottom. Uta saw a drawing of what he thought would be God, but the brain of the creature was scrambled.

Then he opened the rag that bundled the old text that he saw the night before.

Symbols that looked like crossed lines, arches, and circles filled the page. Uta could not make any sense of it, but he could tell from the yellowed parchment that what he held in his hands was very old. Leaders at *Arma Dei* had told him that such a thing would exist, and that it would appear just this way, so Uta didn't need to be able to translate from Coptic to Italian to know that this was the rumored lost Gospel of Matthias.

He closed everything up, pulled on his cloak, and headed for the stables. He had arranged to buy a horse that he could ride to Rome, and it was already saddled up when he arrived.

The days he spent traveling to Rome were uneventful. Uta stayed to himself and avoided busy roads because he didn't want to encounter someone who had evil intent. Being robbed or assaulted would be a problem but losing the Paletti Notebook would be a catastrophe. Not only did he want to please the leaders of *Arma Dei*, he also wanted to win the favor of the Pope for his bravery and cunning in bringing this particular heresy to destruction.

He reached the Apostolic Palace in mid-morning and approached the gate. He was stopped by the guards and ordered to turn around and leave. He knew no one at the Palace, nor how any of the important people looked, but he saw a man in an expensive robe with a long, jeweled chain hanging from his neck exiting through the gate.

"Sire," Uta said, bowing low and beseeching a moment. "I am from *Arma Dei,*" he began but was immediately shushed by the elegant man who grabbed Uta by the elbow and pulled him aside.

"Who are you?" the man asked. "And why are you here?" The urgency in his voice convinced Uta that the man recognized the name *Arma Dei,* but he also didn't seem pleased to hear it uttered in a public place.

"I am Bernardo Uta, a soldier in..." but the man put his fingers to his lips to make Uta quit speaking.

Looking around, the man then asked Uta, "Are you here on an important mission?"

"*Sì.*" Uta then, too, looked around before pulling from his bag the leather folder that he had brought from Florence.

"What is it?"

Uta needed to know more about the man he was addressing before revealing what he had.

"I am here to see Pope Julius," he began. "I have something for him that is very important."

"Well," the man rose taller when he spoke, "I am Antonio Trebiata, the Pope's assistant. He will not see you now but I will make sure he sees what you have there. And what, I pray, is it, sir?"

Uta gulped and peered closely at the man who introduced himself as the assistant to the Pope. He wanted to be the person who presented it to Julius, hoping in return to gain the papal favors he had wished for. Giving up the Gospel of Matthias to this man carried all sorts of dangers.

He whispered, "It is great art from Florence, and the Gospel of Matthias. The heretic."

Trebiata stumbled backward but then regained his composure. Concluding that this raggedly outfitted man couldn't possibly be in possession of something no one else had ever seen was inconceivable. But yet...

"Give it to me," Trebiata said with command.

"I cannot," Uta replied. "I am told to deliver it to the Pope himself."

"I told you, I am Pope Julius's personal assistant. If you give it to me, you give it to him. Otherwise, you must leave and never come back."

The guards who had sent Uta packing watched this exchange from a distance but they didn't like it when voices grew louder. They knew Trebiata and how the powers that he wielded at the Apostolic Palace could end a man's career, or life. So they thought it prudent to intercede on his behalf. The first guard approached and demanded to know what the issue was. Trebiata quickly told him that the beggar, pointing at Uta, had grabbed Trebiata's folio, pointing to the leather Notebook in Uta's hands.

"He grabbed it from me and now tells me that I have to pay to retrieve it from him."

Of course that was a lie and the guards knew it but, still, they were wary of Trebiata's power. They wrestled the Paletti Notebook away from Uta and dragged him away. Presenting the leather folio to Trebiata, the guard smiled at the man and held his gaze for a moment, hoping to get some recognition or thanks, but Trebiata turned his back on the guard and moved back toward the gate that he had just exited.

Trebiata retraced his steps and returned to the Apostolic Palace, keeping the Paletti Notebook tucked under his left arm with his right hand gripping the edge of it. Although he still had doubts about whether the beggar at the gate could actually have found this historic treasure, he wanted to be sure not to lose it before it could be examined.

Once inside his office in the Palace, Trebiata told a guard to call for Giorgio Vasari, a man well versed not only in art but in the history of art throughout the provinces of Italy. In fact, Vasari had recently published his book, *The Lives of the Most Excellent Painters, Sculptors, and Architects,* which told the stories of the great artists of the Renaissance. If the leather folio contained not only the legendary Gospel of Matthias but also the art of Leonardo da Vinci and others, Vasari would certainly recognize it.

When Vasari entered the room, Trebiata was standing over the Notebook, prepared to display its contents with a flourish well known as his custom. Vasari approached the table; Trebiata gave him a single glance, then he undid the leather belt and clasp, pushing the flap on the folio open. He reached inside and carefully withdrew some of the contents, mostly parchment and paper sketches, letters, and drawings.

Vasari's interest was first drawn to the art, engineering, and other sketches on the table.

There was an obscene sketch of a woman's vulva that disgusted Vasari, although he couldn't take his eyes off of it. There was no signature, but the art historian was familiar with Leonardo da Vinci's anatomical sketches and this seemed to be consistent with that work. There was another drawing of the image of God, but an overlay of lines gave a double impression, that of both God and the brain. Vasari knew the scandal that erupted when Michelangelo had painted the Sistine Chapel, and how one of the bishops saw an image of God that, when looked at slightly askance, appeared to be a brain. And he knew that Michelangelo had at times said that the real god is the human brain, in effect refuting the existence of divinity. Vasari looked at the sketch again and concluded that this was an early rendition of Michelangelo's thought process.

Then he picked up one of the letters. "This Pope has neither the blessing nor the approval of God..." he began, reading from it. Vasari skipped past most of the text to find the signature "C. Borgia" at the bottom. Another letter was signed by "N.M.," initials familiarly used by Niccolò Machiavelli, and contained passages doubting whether the world was created by God, and proclaiming that religion is the invention of man.

Trebiata stood patiently as Vasari reviewed the art and letters of the Paletti Notebook, smiling as he saw recognition dawn on the art historian's face.

"These are most definitely the work of the men in Florence some fifty years past. I have not seen such things before but I have been told that their views were much in line with this. Of course, publicizing these ideas would have had each of them excommunicated and possibly executed. But, yes, I do believe you have authentic products of these great men."

Then he turned toward Trebiata, and said, "But the Paletti Notebook is rumored to have something much older, much more heretical, much more..." and Vasari paused to choose his words carefully, "...much more interesting."

"You are referring to the Gospel of Matthias, yes?"

"Well, of course," Vasari replied, "but that doesn't really exist. It is a fantasy of the anti-Papists and the heretics."

Trebiata only smiled, then he reached into the leather pouch once again and withdrew a cloth-wrapped package tied with a string.

Vasari's breath caught in his throat. He watched intently as Trebiata untied the string and unfolded the cloth covering. Once open to view, Vasari could see the yellowed papyrus and the strange, indecipherable writing on the crisp pages stacked before him. He knew enough of the Coptic language to pick out portions of the writing and he was certain that this was in fact the heretical lost Gospel of Matthias.

The two men conferred in whispers now, wary of attracting anyone's attention from outside the room, but they became convinced that they had in their possession the long rumored Paletti Notebook, with all its sacrilegious contents, from Matthias in the first century to the Renaissance masters of just a few decades ago.

"His Excellency, Pope Julius must see this," said Trebiata. Vasari nodded but he instinctively knew that the Pope would want to destroy this blasphemous material. Many popes had searched for this treasure over the centuries, all swearing to put it to fire when it was found. Vasari had some sympathy for their concerns, since revelations contained in the Paletti Notebook could threaten the very foundation of Christianity. But he was also a man of art, an historian who dedicated his life to cataloguing and narrating the lives of the great artists, and he didn't want to lose this magnificent addition to his library.

Vasari recognized that Pope Julius was better known for his vanity and corruption than his sanctity. In the long line of popes who would be eager to burn the Paletti Notebook, Julius would be the one most easily distracted and allow the exhibits on the table in Trebiata's room to survive.

"We should tell His Excellency that we have come upon new information concerning the lost gospel but not tell him at this very moment that we have it," he said to Trebiata. He then convinced the man to let him have it for his own study.

"I am preparing a second edition of my *Lives* and would

greatly appreciate having time to spend with all of these things for my study."

"Even this blasphemous gospel?" asked Trebiata.

"Yes, I think we should keep them together."

They repackaged the materials and Vasari left the room cradling it under his arm.

VIENNA 2021

MARRIOTT HOTEL, VIENNA

April 6, 2021

"So, how are we going to manage this?" Aggie asked. "The photographs of the artwork are great, but they won't help us find the real things. We've got these other pages all in the same handwriting, one of them signed by Fra Nizza and dating from 1943. I can't translate the Italian..."

"I probably can," interjected Priest. "But the style of handwriting is different, so I'll have some trouble getting through it."

"Should we bring in an Italian language expert?" Alana asked.

"No," replied Priest, "I don't think so. We should probably keep this close to the vest for now."

He was thinking about the phone call from Bordrick, a conversation that he had still not revealed to Aggie or Alana. Despite those private concerns, it still seemed wise to limit access to these photographs to as few people as possible.

Alana stared at Priest for a moment, slightly confused by his reluctance to get help with the translation, but she didn't say anything.

"What have you been able to find out about Emil Gutman and Ira Hillyer?" he asked.

"Not much," she replied. "Both of their names were on the

register for that safe deposit box. Gutman was a local businessman, died in 1943 under suspicious circumstances."

"How's that?"

"He and Hillyer opened the safe deposit box. Then, just a couple days later, Gutman was found strangled, his body left in the alley as if the perpetrator didn't care if the body was found."

"What about Hillyer?" he asked.

"Can't get a read on him. Very little information in the files. No date or place of birth. No record of military service. Nothing really in his name except an apartment here in Vienna and the fact that he died in 1988."

"How did he die?" Priest asked.

"We're checking into that. I want to look for hospital records around that time to see if anything turns up. I'll let you know."

The three were sitting on the edge of the bed in Priest's room, with the photographic record of the Paletti Notebook scattered about the coverlet. Alana held up two of the photographs of Nizza's journal. "What do you see in the translation, Darren?" as she handed him a couple of the pages. He studied one of them for a moment, scrunched up his eyes and switched from one paper to the next.

"We need to arrange these pages first; and it would be nice if we could find what we are missing from in between." Thumbing through the pages, he added, "There are no page numbers, so I'll have to take a closer look at the bottom and top of each to see if I can get a read on what might have followed each narrative."

"If you do that, can you just skip to the end?" Aggie asked.

"Possibly, although look at this." Priest read slowly from one of the photographed pages.

Never speak of this to anyone.

"And this."

The soldiers were successful in recovering the Notebook; however, when they arrived in Florence, they were persuaded to disobey the orders from Pope Leo, considering the faithfulness of the city's managers to be in question. Instead, they decided to take the Notebook elsewhere.

"Where?" Alana asked.

"Not sure," was Priest's reply staring at the page in his hand. "The next page is missing. But I do worry that if we follow a short segment that we have here, the false starts might lead us down the wrong path if we skip too much of the journal."

To make this point, he read on.

...the Austrian squad, they got to Rome and found nothing...

"This sounds like a jumble," sighed Aggie.

"Yeah," Alana said, "so, just like a puzzle, we have to sort all the pieces out and assemble them little by little. Darren, you should work on a more complete translation. Nizza does seem to have chronicled the passage of the Paletti Notebook through time and place."

"Yeah," he responded, "and you need to help me find the rest of it. Without the entire Nizza journal, we're going to wander from place to place without a defined path."

"Let's say he had the Paletti Notebook," Aggie offered. "We don't know that, but what if he did? And how did it get from Montalcino to Vienna?"

Each of them pulled from the pile of photographs. Alana looked over the images of art while Aggie smiled in amusement at the Coptic renderings that seemed to come from a distant past, judging from the edges of the papyrus that appeared on the photographic page. Darren worked his way through one particular piece of the translation. He had noticed the name Vasari buried in the text written by Nizza. Knowing that name from literature, he decided to pursue the translation from that point.

"Listen up," he implored.

Vasari's text was very formal and lent me no special knowledge, but the drawers in the library that supported Vasari's work included additional documents. In these I found...

"What drawers?" Aggie asked.

"Not sure, but I got stuck there. Let me try again," as he returned to try the translation. "Here's more, but there are some pages missing in between."

From there, I went to Rome. I had no reason to suspect that would be on the itinerary that the Paletti Notebook took, but I was certain that the collection – and the Gospel of Matthias – would sooner or later have turned up there.

... I was led to an ancient...book by Giorgio Vasari, an historian who wrote about the artists from the Renaissance. This was the second edition of his seminal work, Lives of the Most Excellent Painters, Sculptors, and Architects, *which was published in 1568 just a few years before his death. I had hoped that his research, although now nearly five hundred years old, would enlighten me about the works of the artists that I had in the Paletti Notebook. Perhaps Vasari's notes would tell me something about what they did and how their draft works might have ended up in a restaurant owner's private collection.*

Vasari's text was...then...lent me no special knowledge, but the drawers in the library that supported...

"Here I'm a little lost. Something about letters to his wife, Niccolosa Bacci..."

"Whose wife?" Alana asked. "Not Nizza."

"No. Vasari. Something about references to a collection that he had recently come to possess. Here Nizza refers to Vasari."

"Never speak of this with anyone," was said in one letter to his wife. "Especially never to speak to Antonio Trebiata in Rome." Among his

papers I found various references to draft art and letters, then I stumbled onto a passage with the name "Paletti" written at the top and these words: "Signor Paletti has compiled a rich collection of art from our great period, one that I have named Rinascimento, *a period of our history when the art and genius of the men of Florence will stand against any in the long story of mankind."*

"*Rinascimento*," Aggie exclaimed. "That's the Italian word for Renaissance."

Then Priest continued.

I read through that letter then found others that contained references to Paletti. Then a short note, less than a letter, appeared.

"Cara mia," *it began. It was in Vasari's handwriting and I hoped that it was a note to his wife. I had to smile, though, since I knew that Vasari kept a mistress – ironically, his wife's sister – and so the reference to* cara mia, *could easily lead me astray.*

"Cara mia, *remember that your sister, my wife, has the Paletti Notebook. You must promise me that you will not let her divulge its contents to anyone." Apparently, he trusted his mistress more than he did his wife, her sister.*

"Okay, then," muttered Aggie. "So we know this guy Vasari had the Notebook, that he left it with his wife when he died... what else do we know?"

"More yet to find out, but this was hundreds of years ago. Besides, 'this guy' as you describe him was the greatest art historian of the Renaissance period."

"Well, excuse me," Aggie laughed, "and apparently he was sleeping with sisters."

Alana's eyebrows arched and Priest laughed. Then she smacked him on the thigh.

"I don't have a sister," was her retort.

Priest just grinned and returned to the translation.

"Steady as she goes, one page at a time," he commented, "although I do think we should stick to our earlier plan, and that is to follow Nizza's story like a tour guide while we try to find the other pages."

ROME – FLORENCE 1555

ROME – FLORENCE

May 30, 1555

"GOD'S REWARD," VASARI WHISPERED UNDER HIS BREATH. "OR God's justice."

The artist-historian was not a fan of Julius III so he had little pity for the suffering that his employer endured. When the pope's death came in March, he was suffering from a spell of gout and irritable nerves, and given to sudden spasms of anger. Probably all due to Julius's life of heavy drinking, expensive food, and pleasure, Vasari concluded.

Still, the sudden exit of his patron and the ascension of Pope Marcellus II introduced some uncertainty for Vasari and his future. Marcellus was not an impressive man, but he commanded attention from the court of the Vatican on the basis of his family connections and prior assignment in Jerusalem.

Happily or not for Vasari, Marcellus only lived for twenty-two days after being named Pope. The end came suddenly, Vasari recalled while sitting in his study with the contents of the Paletti Notebook spread out on the table before him. Marcellus showed no signs of ill health, but on the morning of May 1, 1555, an attendant noticed that the Pope's mouth was askew and dripping with spittle. The young aide called gently to Marcellus, touching his shoulder to get his attention. The Pope turned his head toward the man but his eyes seemed unfocused. The left eyelid drooped and the muscles on that side of his face sagged. With a low groan, Pope Marcellus II passed from this earth after serving as the Vicar of Christ for less than one month, and too little time to leave a mark of any kind on the Church that he was elected to lead.

Vasari barely had time to implement his plan to secure his arrangement in the Apostolic Palace under Marcellus when he was confronted with another pope, Paul IV, elected to the office on May 23. The new Bishop of Rome had no interest in art and literature; however he had developed a strong dislike for the Spanish people while serving as papal nuncio to Spain. When confronted with Spanish forces marching on Rome, Paul IV called upon friendly French armies to protect him and the city. But under the greater threat from the invading forces, only a compromise by the Pope would succeed in withdrawal of the Spanish threat, whereupon the Pope adopted a strictly neutral stance. The Spanish throne derided him as a fool while the French decried him as a weakling.

Paul IV remained interested in military affairs throughout his papacy, but he also established a strict code of adherence to Church doctrine. One of his proclamations including locking the Jewish population of Rome behind barriers in a neighborhood that emerged as the first *ghetto*. His unforgiving stance on doctrine and the orthodoxy of Catholic teaching worried Vasari. Such a dogmatic approach to Church teaching and the witch hunt for heretics might easily lead to the destruction of the great collection of art and letters that Vasari now possessed.

The artist-historian sat on a specially made, elevated stool that allowed him to perch above the work table and more clearly see the various papers spread out before him. His fingers touched some of the artwork and sketches made by the great men of Florence years before, then he tapped the ancient papyrus of the lost gospel that was included in the collection of the Paletti Notebook. He knew that the new Pope's rigid rules about heresy and supplication to the Church would inevitably produce a fiery end to the Notebook, including both the artwork and the Gospel of Matthias.

Vasari had only barely briefed his former employer, Julius III about the Notebook, little enough to be sure the Pope would not form an opinion about its contents. Marcellus II only lived for a few weeks and so the trail that led from Paletti to Vasari was broken. Unless he broached the subject with Paul IV, Vasari was confident that the new Pope would not know of the Paletti Notebook's existence, nor would his preoccupation with wars allow him time to form an opinion.

Which provided a perfect opportunity for Vasari. As a painter/sculptor of some note himself and born just outside of Florence, he had long harbored a bias for the artists at the dawn of the 16th century. It was to refer to this collection of genius – da Vinci, Michelangelo, Botticelli, Raphael, Verrocchio, and others – that Vasari had first used the term *Rinascimento*, or Renaissance. From that period and about these artists, he had published his great work, *Lives of the Most Excellent Painters, Sculptors, and Architects* in 1550, dedicated to Grand Duke Cosimo I de' Medici as the patron of Florentine art.

Now he found himself in possession of a unique collection of unknown art from these very men. If he protected it from papal wrath and helped the Paletti Notebook escape the various dangers posed in Rome, he could use the contents of the Notebook in his first revision to *Notes* that he was already planning.

Taking a sudden leave of absence – with an uncertain date of return – Vasari departed Rome in a carriage bound for Florence. Paul IV would probably not even notice his absence; besides, his patron Cosimo I had offered Vasari a contract to paint Cosimo's apartment in the Palazzo Vecchio in Florence. With the decline in papal interest in art and his long-held desire to return to the city of his youth, Vasari considered the confluence of events to be the perfect opportunity to relocate for his final years.

During his time in Rome and in the service of the popes,

Vasari had too often left his wife Niccolosa Bacci behind, and so this return to Florence would also reunite them for what they both believed would be the remainder of their lives. As an accomplished architect, he had designed a spacious house in Arezzo for them and he would spend his time revising his *magnum opus* and publish a second edition of *Lives* for posterity.

To do that, he knew that he would have to smuggle the Paletti Notebook out of Rome. The carriage that he hired for the journey to Florence was reserved solely for him and allowed enough room for him to bring several trunks of personal belongings. In a chest filled with some of his clothing and art, he hid the Notebook from view.

Antonio Trebiata, who had survived the three recent papacies, was still working as assistant to Paul IV, but he had long since lost interest in this collection of art that he had received from Bernardo Uta, the soldier from *Arma Dei.* Having given it to Vasari, Trebiata assumed he would not see it again, so Vasari wasn't concerned about that connection to the Apostolic Palace either.

The journey from Rome to Florence took three days, passing through open countryside on rough roads that connected little villages along the way. Vasari had enough respect for the possible danger from bandits that he also hired two men to accompany him, clearing the way ahead and watching for imminent threats from the roadside as the horses pulled the wagon north to Arezzo. When night fell each day, Vasari would choose an inn for rest and nourishment, commanding the driver and one of the men to take a certain chest up to his room. The guard pondered why Vasari would always order that one to be kept in his presence, even while leaving the other two chests on the wagon. But he was being paid handsomely already and decided that whatever was in that trunk, stealing it might cost more than the pay he was receiving. One guard was posted with Vasari in the inn while the other one remained outside with the wagon and horses, and so they proceeded until they reached Arezzo, not far from Vasari's beloved city of Florence.

Once there, Vasari was greeted by his wife while the driver and two guards unloaded his possessions and carried them into the house.

After a day of rest, and in the privacy of his home, the artist-historian finally got around to unpacking. He went first to the trunk in which he had hidden the Paletti Notebook and found it there among the folds of his clothing, intact and undamaged by the trip. He lifted it out of the pile and carried the leather folio to his studio, laying it gently on the large oak table that he used for his artwork. Pulling a high chair from the corner of the room – a chair much like the custom form that he had made for his studio in Rome – he pulled himself up onto it and undid the leather strap and buckle from the Notebook.

As he was unfolding the flap and withdrawing some of the contents, Niccolosa entered the room, stepping forward and laying a hand gently on his shoulder.

"What is this, sire?" she asked.

"This," Vasari said, proudly holding up a crinkled sketch of a machine, "is a drawing performed by Leonardo da Vinci."

Niccolosa stared at it, drawing herself closer to see the details, and touched the paper with her finger.

"This," she began, pointing at a spiral on the sheet but looking at her husband, "this is the work of Leonardo?"

"Yes. I believe it is a drawing that he completed for Cesare Borgia, a sketch of a plan to move the water of the Arno River."

"But the water in the Arno already moves," she replied with a chuckle. "Why does he have to do that?"

"I have read about this," Vasari continued. "Borgia had a plan to move the river away from Pisa, and so Leonardo had to find a way to move the water once a new trough had been cut."

"But why would they expend so much time and work to do that?" Niccolosa still spoke with the voice of a young girl, despite being in her later years, and her questions of surprise had a pleasing lilt to the sound.

"Well, you know," he responded, "Pisa has always held Florence in its power. The river runs from our city to Pisa, but it is only through Pisa that our ships can reach the sea. As long as the Pisans control that waterway, we are subservient to them."

"Yes, my husband, I have heard that from many sources, and I know that there have been many wars fought over it."

"So, Borgia's idea was to reroute the river, taking it around Pisa and leaving them with a dry riverbed, so that the people of Florence would be the masters of their own destiny."

Niccolosa laughed.

"I know that too, but I also know that the project failed."

"Masterfully!" he replied, and now it was his turn to laugh. "A great storm fell on the city in 1504, flooding all our streets and causing the dams that were erected to control the rerouted Arno to collapse. Many people died," he continued, though now without laughter, "and the project was suspended."

Then Vasari turned his attention back to the paper in his hands.

"This is the work of Leonardo. And this," he said, picking up another slip of paper, "is a drawing by Michelangelo that seems to be a beginning of a sculpture. If you look carefully at the curve of the head of that woman, the body in her lap, and the line that traces downward from the body, this seems to be a clear reference to the *Pietà,* the sculptor's greatest ever creation that stands in the Basilica of Saint Peter in Rome.

"And this?" he added, holding up something that held no drawings but only words. "This is a portion of a manuscript that I recognize as part of Niccolò Machiavelli's *The Prince.* It wasn't published until 1532, after his death, but we have read from the manuscript that he wrote years before that. In fact, this slip of paper may be one of the first drafts of that book in existence."

"Where did all this come from?"

"Two years ago, a beggar showed up at the Apostolic Palace

with this folder. He said it was collected by someone named Paletti in Florence..."

"There is a Paletti restaurant, isn't there?" Niccolosa asked.

"Yes, on the Piazza del Gran Duca, although it is now abandoned. I recall when it was run by a man named Sandro Paletti, but he died about ten years ago. Since then it was owned by his son and grandson, Pietro, who two years ago was murdered in the Abbey of San Marco."

"So, this Paletti collection," she asked tentatively, "you think that the Paletti family collected all this?"

"More precisely, Sandro Paletti. He owned the restaurant around the time that these artists were being brought to the city by the Medici family. He probably knew them and, somehow, he came into possession of all these sketches, letters, and so on."

"And then Pietro got the collection?" she asked.

"Seems that way. And then Pietro was murdered. The man who brought this to the Pope's palace said he was a soldier in *Arma Dei,* a secret sect who are sworn to protect the traditions and hierarchy of the papacy and the Catholic Church. He didn't admit to murdering Pietro Paletti, but he did admit to coming by this Notebook by unseemly terms. He also urged that it be delivered to Pope Julius III so that the contents of the collection could be destroyed as heretical."

"Then what are you doing with it?" she asked, showing a bit of alarm that her husband would have in their house objects that would be considered blasphemous by the Church.

"I do not care much for all the talk of heresy and blasphemy. I am an artist and I have spent my life chronicling the lives of the greatest artists of all time. I hope that this Paletti Notebook will be of service to me while revising my book."

"And what is this?" Niccolosa asked, pulling a tied bundle of cloth from the leather folio.

"That," said Vasari proudly, "may be even more interesting. It seems to be a gospel, possibly the lost Gospel of Matthias."

"How was it lost?"

"That's a long story, but the short version is that this man, Matthias, was a follower of Jesus Christ and he wrote this gospel about the Savior's life. It is the only such gospel in existence, one composed by a man who actually knew Jesus."

"And other than that, how is it different from what we have learned from reading the words of saints Matthew, Mark, Luke, and John?"

"Well," and Vasari couldn't suppress a sly smile, "it's very different. Matthias says that Jesus was not a god, that he was married, and that he had children."

Niccolosa stepped back suddenly as if she had been struck. She withdrew her hand from the bundled papyrus as if was on fire. Her eyes went wide and her lips parted in a silent scream.

"We cannot have this here," she said in awe and fear.

Vasari looked at his wife for a moment and then rose to comfort her.

"It is alright. This Notebook was delivered to me in my role as art historian for the Pope. I have a right to have it and I have a need to review its contents for the sake of the Church."

His explanation sounded complete if not a bit practiced, but it didn't allay Niccolosa's fears. She left the room and left her husband to ponder the possible evil things revealed in the Paletti Notebook.

FLORENCE 1574

FLORENCE

September 12, 1574

NICCOLOSA BACCI, NOW IN HER MID-SIXTIES, KNELT BESIDE the bed of her husband, Giorgio Vasari. They had shared many years together and, although she was not schooled in art or history, she absorbed some of her spouse's knowledge through his works. It had been a long and loving relationship, though regretfully it produced no children. Niccolosa suspected that her husband had become entangled with another woman prior to their marriage, a housemaid, and that this union might have produced offspring. But she chose to ignore the facts; suffering at times, perhaps, for not producing a child from her own womb.

The Vasari house was already prepared for his death, with black drapes being prepared for hanging from the stone portals of the palazzo they built in Arezzo outside of his beloved Florence. Though the artist historian had not yet passed away, the end was near and the servants mourned his imminent passing.

There was no laughter in the house, no joy; even the meals served to his wife were but meager victuals, shallow plates of boiled vegetables and meat with no seasoning to highlight the flavors that Vasari – in life – praised as the best of the region of Tuscany.

Niccolosa remained at his side as Vasari's breath labored from one moment to the next. He didn't seem to be in distress, and this fact was noticed by her. She couldn't tell whether it signified an absence of pain or simply heralded a slow decline and the piteous end that was near.

It had been a hot day in June, the twenty-seventh to be exact, which Niccolosa noted as the anniversary of their first parting, the day when Vasari had been called to Rome the first time to serve the pope so many years before. He had accepted many such commissions over the years of their marriage, and Niccolosa had missed him on each occasion, but the memory of that twenty-seventh so long ago recalled a little pain as she considered how her husband's fame had cost her their time together.

As the afternoon wore on, Vasari's breath became shallow. His eyes remained closed throughout and Niccolosa wished to see the fading blue color of his pupils just one more time. But it was not to be. Just as a servant entered the room to light a candle in the dying light of day, Vasari's chest heaved, a slight exhalation escaped his lips, and he passed away.

Niccolosa knew it as it happened. She let her hand brush his cheek as she kissed his lips just as she accepted the inevitable as the will of God. She gave the servant a slight nod, then rose to leave the room. There was one more very important task that she had to manage before nightfall.

Years earlier, her husband had been at work on the second edition of his book, *Lives of the Most Excellent Painters, Sculptors, and Architects,* a volume that was later published in 1568. He had used many sources for his information, mostly from the Medici library in Florence, but also from an obscure folder of writings and sketches that he refused to show to anyone – except Niccolosa. Something he referred to as the Paletti Notebook.

"Keep this here, with you, and never show it to anyone," he warned her. When he first brought it to their home in Arezzo in 1555, he said that it had come to him in his role as the art historian for the pope. But Niccolosa also knew that it contained heretical material that she didn't want to have in her possession.

After her husband's death, Niccolosa calculated that this folder – still in her house – would now be considered in her possession. She thought it blasphemous and dangerous, so she didn't want to expose it or let anyone know of its existence, but she also knew that she couldn't destroy it.

"Never let it go, but never show it," she remembered Vasari telling her. It was a difficult command, but one she intended to obey. Not to let it go, but also not to reveal it.

Niccolosa left her husband's room and retreated to his study. Behind a line of books, hidden behind a wooden wall, and in the crevice between wood and plaster, she removed the old leather satchel, placing it gently on the table. She looked over her shoulder to make sure that no servants were present. Confident that she was alone, she studied the strap and buckle holding the folder together, with only the tips of her fingers touching the surface of it as if she was afraid to make too much contact. Then she reached with her other hand and undid the strap and pulled open the flap of the folder.

While engaged in this simple task, Niccolosa recalled Vasari's second edition of his book, knowing full well that it contained no mention of anti-religious writings or art. For a moment, she took comfort knowing that her husband had omitted such material. Admitting some of the blasphemous writings that he told her were contained in the Notebook would in itself pose terrible dangers for her. Including such things in his revised book would be enduring evidence of his apostasy. And hers, by association.

"Maybe there is nothing against the Church in here," she murmured aloud, uttering a gentle prayer that she hoped would protect her from God's wrath if she was wrong.

Reaching inside the folder she withdrew a stack of papers. It was easy to tell that some were from Leonardo da Vinci and Michelangelo, some from the city's historian Niccolò Machiavelli, and some from Cesare Borgia. Glancing at the pages,

Niccolosa's expression changed and the blood drained from her cheeks. Yes, in fact, there were anti-Pope and anti-Church writings, even some direct criticisms of Florence's leaders, the *Signoria*.

She reached in again and withdrew a cloth-wrapped package, tied with a string. Untying it and unfolding the white cloth, she spread the first few pages on the table. Niccolosa couldn't read the pictographs and symbolic writing on the papyrus, but she remembered Vasari telling her that this was the lost Gospel of Matthias, and that the man who wrote it knew Jesus personally. She also remembered her husband telling her that Matthias wrote of Jesus as a rabbi, not a god, and that he had a wife and children.

While these thoughts came to her, she dropped the papyrus sheets as if touching them might be enough to damn her to hell. Quickly, Niccolosa bound the sheets up together once more, tied the cloth with the string, and placed it back in the folder, then returned all the other materials in likewise fashion and belted the strap in place again.

Now, today, September 12, her servants were readying her departure for Florence. After Vasari's death, she felt the house in Arezzo was too cold and lonely and, without his companionship, she needed the life of society in Florence.

But Niccolosa needed to bring the Paletti Notebook with her. She couldn't leave it in the house in Arezzo to be discovered by who knows whom; she couldn't risk her future safety on some villain or conniver bringing the heretical works into the open and blaming her for them.

She murmured her husband's words: "Never let it go, but never show it."

Niccolosa packed the Notebook among her personal things, refusing even to let her chambermaid touch the undergarments among which the folder was hidden. Once in Florence, she planned to find a suitable hiding place for Paletti's collection; until then, no one could know that she had it in her possession.

VIENNA 2021

MARRIOTT PARKRING, VIENNA

April 6, 2021

ALANA WAS FOCUSED ON CHINH'S MURDER BUT COULDN'T shake the fascination she had with the collection of photos of the Paletti Notebook. Priest reminded her not to assume too much but she too was well absorbed in the collection and couldn't stop pouring through the various images and trying to piece them together.

"Look here," Aggie said. "These pictures clearly mark the designs of Leonardo da Vinci's water wheel. And these," he held a document up proudly, "can be none other than his anatomical sketches of females."

Priest stared at the photo and realized that it was a very detailed and very intimate drawing of the female vulva. Certainly within the realm of da Vinci's curiosity, but Priest reminded himself that the great artist had a similar fascination with the genitals of men.

"Let's stick to the Nizza journal, if you don't mind," he reminded Aggie.

"No question," Aggie replied.

"Nizza appears..." Priest began, scanning the photos in his hands, "Nizza appears to have discovered – or should I say 'recovered' – the movement of the Notebook, but like any historian, he might have some gaps in the tale. Besides, Nizza's journal ends in 1943 so it leaves out decades between the end of World War II and modern times.

"And we have two challenges: We want to certify the authenticity..." he continued.

"You mean, *possible* authenticity," Aggie intervened.

"Yeah, possible authenticity," Priest said. "We want to certify the authenticity of the contents of the photos..."

"You said Bao referred to a guy name Leitner?" Aggie asked.

"Yeah, the art professor. But he also indicated another name, a Tobias Moser, an historian who might have something to say about this. I put a call in to Leitner; he's here in Vienna, but I don't know when I'll hear back."

"If you don't hear soon," Alana interjected, "I can help out. The city files can track him down."

They continued scanning the photos and looking for clues for how to connect the dots. The photos of ancient art and letters were fascinating, but they yielded few pointers. With his knowledge of Italian, Priest decided to take a bit more time and read the parts of Fra Nizza's journal that he had.

Aggie was intrigued by the collection depicted in the photographs, but he still had his doubts. To scratch that itch, he searched the art and letters for details that would confirm the origin of the materials, either by an artist's style of drawing, a writer's preferred wording, or other obscure clues that might be hidden on the paper. Pulling a photo of a letter written in Italian, he decided that he wouldn't be much help there.

"I recall that da Vinci used mirror-writing often," Aggie said aloud. "It was a primitive coding technique to keep people from stealing his ideas."

"Yeah, he was left-handed," Priest commented. "Might have been easier under the circumstances."

"How about this?" Alana chimed in, holding up a photo with a tiny sketch of some kind of machine with what looked like scribbled words in the upper right corner. Aggie took it from her, examined it briefly, then stood from the bed and went into the bathroom. Holding it up to the mirror, he called out to Priest in the other room.

"Darren, what is *imbracatura?*" he asked, sounding out the word.

"Well, it could be something like arm, or sling."

"And *gomito?*"

"That's elbow."

"This is difficult because the words are backward and in Italian," Aggie said. "And the handwriting isn't what we're used to nowadays."

"You're telling me," exclaimed Priest.

"I'm guessing that *articolazione* means articulated, or articulation," Aggie continued.

"What is the whole phrase?" Alana asked.

Aggie paused as if trying to get a running start on the backward Italian phrase.

"*Imbracatura per l'articolazione del gomito,*" he said. "Sounds like an articulated elbow of an arm. This is fascinating! Articulated elbow! Think of it."

"Think of what?" Priest asked.

"Well, we know that among the war machines that da Vinci designed for Cesare Borgia and the popes," Aggie continued, walking back into the bedroom area, "was an articulated trebuchet, a sorta catapult with an elbow that bends and adds speed to the object being thrown. This must be a tiny detail of that design."

"From what we know of da Vinci, he was very secretive and wouldn't share something like that with other artists and engineers. Why would that be in the Paletti collection?" asked Alana.

"Actually, I would look at it from another angle," Priest suggested. "Da Vinci probably made the drawing, but he didn't bring it to Paletti's to be swept up in the Notebook."

"Then what?" Aggie asked.

"Maybe Borgia had it. You see, if da Vinci drew it and

presented the idea to Borgia, Borgia might have had it in his possession, possibly while discussing it with the artist at Paletti's table. So it could be that this drawing ended up in the Notebook thanks to Borgia, not da Vinci."

"This actually might lend credence to the whole notion of a Paletti Notebook," Alana said.

"How, and why?" asked Aggie.

"Well, finding things that would have been kept hidden," she said, "and that would only surface due to someone else's carelessness – say Borgia, in this case – lends a little serendipity to the collection. It's a step in the art counterfeiting sequence that the perpetrator wouldn't be expected to think of.

"Hey," Alana said, switching her attention to a text that had just appeared on her phone. "I think I've got something. I can't top Aggie's background knowledge of *Arma Dei*, but they have appeared in recent times. Well, distant recent..."

"What the heck is 'distant recent?'" Priest asked.

Alana laughed.

"Okay, well, I guess I mean this century."

"Twentieth or Twenty-First."

"Yeah, both," she replied. "As we already heard, they are a pro-pope, pro-Church group who call themselves 'sainted soldiers.' They are focused on protecting the Church against all comers. And they have been known to take drastic measures when such appeared necessary."

"Like what?" Aggie chimed in.

"Like murder. It seems that *Arma Dei* has been the suspect in several kidnappings and killings involving bishops and priests who were accused of making unorthodox comments."

"Define unorthodox," asked Priest.

"Well, let's just say that the pedophilia complaints about American priests would not even make a headline compared to their behavior."

"Wow!" said Aggie.

"What else?" asked Priest, trying to get the commentary back on less salacious grounds.

Alana returned to her phone to read from the text.

"*Arma Dei* was formed in early Sixteenth Century, just prior to the Protestant Reformation breaking out. They anticipated the schism and decided to appoint themselves guardians of the Church. The pope at the time, Julius II, didn't mind their efforts; in fact, he encouraged them, although he didn't outwardly support them. *Arma Dei* wasn't deterred by the pope's 'silent partner' routine and a few surviving letters from members of the group indicate that they expected the pope to keep his distance. It was good, in their mind, since it allowed them to carry out justice as they saw fit."

"Including murder and mayhem, right?" asked Aggie.

"Yep. And they have done so for, now, hundreds of years," she added. "Which brings me to the present."

"Thankfully," Priest muttered.

"They keep themselves concealed," Alana continued, "in part by avoiding modern tools. They don't correspond by email or text, or not that we can find, but they pass messages using a very old technique."

"Letters?" Aggie ventured.

"No," she responded. "Horseback. My sources in Interpol tell me that they have made use of an elaborate network of horse farms, horse shows, and other equestrian events as cover to transmit their messages."

"Sounds laborious and not very tidy," Priest said.

"Yes, on both counts. But effective," Alana expounded. "Interest in horses is worldwide, allowing *Arma Dei* to infiltrate basically any country and communicate through signals and symbols without leaving much of a record."

"Right out of the horse's mouth," muttered Aggie.

"Yeah, but," Alana continued after laughing, "in some cases a note or written order was required. Still passed from hand to hand at equestrian events, and apparently some survived and have helped us to determine the cult's means of communication."

"So," Priest began, "where do we go from here?"

"Let me switch gears slightly," she added. "We now have high certainty that it was *Arma Dei* who killed Bao."

"I was accepting that as given all along," Aggie said.

"Well, no," said by both Priest and Alana simultaneously. "Too soon to draw such conclusions," Priest added.

"Well, not soon now," Alana said, tapping the screen of her phone. "Remember the sign that we found pinned to Bao's shirt?"

"Yeah," Priest recalled. "'*Ego sum ira Dei?*'"

"Exactly. Well it seems that the lettering style is important," she added. "The sign on Bao capitalized 'Ego' and 'Dei.'"

"That would be correct," interjected Aggie. "That's the correct manner."

"Yes," Alana continued, "but there have been copycats. We found about a dozen such taunts in other crimes in recent years, and all but two of these capitalized every word."

"You mean they also capitalized 'sum' and 'ira?' That seems a bit scant on information if you ask me," commented Priest.

"Yes, but no," she replied. "Capitalizing interior words in a phrase demonstrates a careless, possibly copycat, mode of operating. The true 'sainted soldiers' would not make that mistake."

"So," Aggie broke in, "what are the two instances where the proper capitalization was used?"

"Bao, of course. The other one was in 1943, here in Vienna."

"What happened?" Priest inquired.

"In his sermon, a priest presiding over mass at St. Peter's Catholic Church raised the apostasy of Savonarola."

"The heretic?" Aggie interrupted.

"Yeah, him. The guy they excommunicated and then executed in 1498."

"Why was that a problem for the priest?"

"He wasn't defending Savonarola, but he commented on the

guy's excommunication, and he said that the ancient friar's teaching was consistent with Protestant teaching and was focused on the sin of selling graces through the auspices of the Church."

"Still don't get it," Priest added. "That is still considered one of the gravest errors by Church hierarchy."

"I agree, but there's another way to look at it," Alana continued. "His sermon was thought to be supportive of the ban on selling graces, a clear reference to Martin Luther's complaint about the Catholic Church in Rome, and in defiance of Church practice at the time. Remember, the old guard at *Arma Dei* was willing to fight to protect anything and everything the Pope preached, which extended to his bishops and ordained representatives. *Arma Dei* wouldn't look kindly on some priest calling such a practice into question."

"What happened?" Aggie asked.

"The priest was dragged from the sacristy late at night and hung from the arches in the interior of the church. A sign saying '*Ego sum ira Dei*' with upper and lower case letters, was pinned to his cassock."

Alana left the hotel and returned to her office at *Bundespolizei* headquarters to follow up on the Chinh murder.

Priest got a call from Leitner and reached an agreement on meeting that afternoon. He and Aggie left the hotel, catching a cab to a small restaurant in the old part of the city chosen by Leitner. The professor was willing to meet with them and discuss the Paletti Notebook but he wanted the meeting to be discreet. News of the recent murder in the warehouse had filtered through the city, including the name of the victim, and Leitner was nervous considering he had just met with Chinh. He even worried that he might be implicated in the murder because of his meeting with the bank manager.

"And don't bring those photographs," he warned Priest on the phone, "or whatever it is you have."

When they arrived at the establishment, Priest and Aggie entered through the door and looked for a man who described himself to them on the phone. It was a small dining room with a bar on the left side. All dark wood and sconce lights at each booth, so the lighting wasn't great. They were looking for a man sitting alone and probably facing the door, as if he was waiting for someone. At first, they didn't see anyone who might be Leitner.

"When he said 'don't bring the photos,'" Aggie said, "I felt there was something fishy. He's probably not going to show."

"I don't read it that way. He met with Bao and didn't seem too concerned at that time. Sure, recent events might make him skittish, but why would he agree to meet with us when I called?"

"Possibly because the last guy he met with is now dead? Could it be that?" Aggie asked derisively.

"Yeah, well, there is that."

Just then, a man sitting with another man waved and signaled them to come over. Introducing himself as Andres Leitner, he then introduced Tobias Moser, the other expert that Chinh had mentioned. Priest and Aggie took the two seats across from them and settled in.

"What's that?" Leitner asked, pointing to Priest's rucksack.

Priest didn't reply right away, and Leitner showed his displeasure.

"Did you bring the photographs?" Moser asked.

"I told them not to," said Leitner with his fist pressed to the table to stress the point.

"Actually," Priest responded, "I did bring them, but it's mostly because I didn't want them left behind in a hotel room."

"Can I see them?" asked Moser. "Looking at photos doesn't bother me."

"Maybe having your throat cut will," said Leitner testily.

"First, let me thank you for meeting with us," Priest said,

holding the palms of his hands out in supplication. "I know that you spoke to Bao and he relayed your opinions to me. What's happened to Bao is terrible; he was my friend. And what happened to him is almost certainly related to the Paletti Notebook, or should I say to some people who either want it or want to destroy it."

"And they'll do whatever they have to do to carry out their mission," Leitner added, in a slightly calmer tone.

"Well, we don't know that yet either, but killing for it doesn't seem to be outside their tool kit," said Aggie.

"I want us to find the Paletti Notebook in part to avenge Bao's death," Priest suggested patiently, "and, not incidentally, to reduce the threat the Notebook's existence poses to other people. So, with that, can we discuss what you saw when you reviewed the photographic contents of the safety deposit box at DFR Wien?

"From where I'm sitting," Priest added, "the photographs lean in the direction of proof that the Paletti Notebook exists."

"And why do you think that?" asked Leitner.

"Well, it's hard to take photographs of something that doesn't exist."

"Fakes of art masterpieces are easy to make. Photographs of fakes are even easier," Leitner replied.

"Let me see these a bit more closely," said Moser, holding his hand out to get Priest to produce the materials from his rucksack. He examined them carefully, then pulled his glasses up above his eyebrows to study them again, replacing his glasses before handing them back to Priest.

"They certainly appear to be authentic, but as Andres here says, the process of photographing something introduces even more variables and leaves open more avenues to alter the subject being considered."

"What do you think, though?" Aggie asked, addressing Moser since he was the first to ask for the photos.

"The images represented in these photographs are very

intriguing, no question," Moser explained, "but fakes are easy and without the source material itself, it's hard for me to make a determination."

A waiter appeared and Moser pulled his napkin across the few photos that he had on the table.

"Can I get you something to drink or eat?" the man asked.

"Yes, please," Aggie responded, more to distract the waiter's attention from Moser than to place an order. "I'd like a Negroni," he continued, then turned to the others at the table.

"I'll have a glass of Blaufränkisch wine," said Priest.

"No, nothing," said Leitner.

"For me," Moser interjected, thoughtfully considering his options, "I'll have an Aperol Spritzer."

When the waiter departed, Leitner spoke up.

"There have been rumors for centuries about something called the 'Paletti Notebook,' a fantastical collection of scribblings of artists and letters from powerful people in Florence, the time between the periods of rule by the Medici."

He spoke of the Medici, the birth of the Renaissance, and so on.

"The rumors of a Paletti Notebook centered on the notion that some guy named Paletti kept a journal of these artists' activities, even scraps of their work. The notebook is said to contain his own remembrances of the artists and politicians, even including sketches the artists made and letters written by the politicians and intelligentsia of the time. The rumors also suggested that a lost gospel, possibly from Matthias, ended up in Paletti's collection.

"But it's just a myth. Probably started by Giuliano de' Medici on his return to power in Florence to use this Paletti fellow as proof of his family's continuing contribution to the art and history of the city. Nothing's ever been found. It's like the Gospel of Mathias. A fiction."

Priest sat quietly for a moment and tried to assess the information he was getting, including the doubts cast by Leitner on the search.

"You know about *Salvator Mundi*, right?" asked Leitner. "It's a famous painting attributed to Leonardo da Vinci and rediscovered in 2011. Well, it's a fake. Probably painted by da Vinci's students, perhaps by his paramour, Salai, the "little devil" that he kept by his side for many years. Look at the sphere in the painting, the folds of the robes, the full-on face, the shape of the mouth...all wrong for da Vinci. And yet, it still knocked down $450 million dollars at auction in 2017.

"One last comment," Leitner added, leaning in. "The Paletti Notebook? If it exists? The Paletti Notebook would be worth ten times that much."

"Wow!" was all Aggie could say as he slumped back in his chair.

"Well," Priest responded, "That's why we're here in Vienna. The photos found at DFR Wien suggest that a great collection of arts and letters exists. Let's go back one point," he said, sitting forward at the table. "Let's assume, for the moment, that these photographs accurately capture documents, drawings, whatever, that are real. Look at the photos again," he entreated, and Leitner and Moser both leaned in and focused on the materials on the table. "Would you be inclined to credit the men mentioned in the journal..."

"Wait, what journal?" asked Leitner.

"Well," Priest began but he realized that he may have offered too much detail. Oh, well, no going back now.

"There are two journals that are included among the contents of the Paletti Notebook."

Aggie smiled, picking up on the fact that Priest was now talking of the Notebook as if it existed.

"There are two journals," Priest repeated, "one by Sandro Paletti himself describing the materials that he had gathered and the men from whom he collected them."

This produced nods from Aggie, stoic silence from Leitner and Moser.

"And another journal apparently written in the 1940s by a monk, Fra Nizza."

"Maybe a third journal," commented Aggie, but he didn't go further.

"Who is this Fra Nizza, and what does he have to do with the Paletti story?" asked Moser.

"We haven't decided yet whether Fra Nizza ever had the Paletti Notebook," began Priest, "or when he had it if he did, but the parts of his journal that we have contain a lot of historical information about it, who had it, where it was kept, how it changed hands, and so on. Unfortunately, we only have a few pages of it."

"You said around 1940," interjected Leitner. "That's more than four centuries after this Notebook was first collected."

Aggie smiled once again, hearing Leitner buying into the story of the Paletti Notebook and talking about it as real.

"Yes," Priest replied. "Around then. We're still looking into it but we think that Nizza had the Notebook, or was aware of its existence around the time he wrote his journal – in the 1940s – that he feared for its survival, considering the Nazis' preoccupation with ancient art in Italy during the war, and that he might have – emphasis on 'might have' – had it in his possession in the closing phases of World War II."

"This sounds like a great mystery novel," Leitner said, leaning back in his chair, "but we need more proof."

Moser reached over and tapped his colleague on the arm.

"Let's leave proof to the experts," nodding in the direction of Priest and Aggie. "I think what they want from us is an assessment of whether these materials could have been produced by the 'great men' of Florence."

"For me," Priest interjected, "I think the bottom line – at least at this point – is can the documents, sketches, whatever –

in this pile," he said tapping the photos on the table, "possibly be the real thing?"

"Yes," said Moser, "and possibly no."

"That's not what he's asking," replied Aggie. "Can they be real?"

"Yes, definitely," said Leitner, surprisingly coming out of his 'doubting Thomas' routine. "It is possible that a guy named Sandro Paletti lived in Florence around 1500 and collected a bunch of simple drawings and letters from the great men who lived in the city during that period."

"We know of the fortunate set of circumstances that brought them together," Moser explained, but was interrupted by Leitner.

"Actually, it was fortunate, but not accidental. The Medici family invested heavily in the arts, and people like Botticelli, Raphael, da Vinci, and Michelangelo ended up in Florence thanks to the Medicis' deep pockets."

"Okay, yes, true," Moser said, replying to his colleague's history lesson, "but there was still some luck here. First, these great men were all alive at the same time..."

"Some aging men and some young protégés," commented Leitner.

"Yes, some young, some old, but all in Florence at the same time. But there was more. For example, Niccolò Machiavelli lived his entire life in Florence..."

"And at the same time as these artists were there," added Aggie.

"Precisely. Machiavelli was a government man, a stateman, and very well educated. His seminal book, *The Prince,* was the result of his time in Florence. And most literary scholars have concluded that the book's main character was modeled on Cesare Borgia..."

"Who was also in the city at that time," inserted Leitner.

"Yes, although he moved around quite a lot, including to

Rome and elsewhere. But he spent a good bit of time in Florence among these other men."

"All agreed," Priest said. "But can we go back to the point about the things depicted in these photographs? Can we go from possible to probable?" Priest asked.

Leitner stared back at him for two beats, then picked up the photographs once more to study them. Leaning in, just inches from Priest's face, he responded.

"I think it's not only possible, but probable!" Leitner responded.

This brought a broad smile and a "whoa" from his colleague, and Priest and Aggie sat back with victorious smiles on their faces.

"But," Leitner continued, "you have nothing if you don't have the source material. Get it."

BAR ONYX, VIENNA

April 6, 2021

Priest's phone buzzed and the screen read "Restricted." That's not the kind of call he would normally accept, but these were strange times. Given the number of threats and attacks in recent days, he thought it wise to accept any contacts.

"Priest," a male voice said. "We should meet."

"Why?" That seemed like a prudent response on his part, especially since Priest had no idea who he was talking to.

"Because I said so. And because your government would be very upset if we didn't."

Still, not a lot of information. Priest's government, as the caller said, could be upset either way.

"Again, why?" he asked. After a pause, he retreated. "Okay, where and when?"

"Bar Onyx. Topside of the DO & CO Hotel on Stephansplatz."

"I know where it is."

"Nine o'clock," he said.

"So, we can't do it any earlier? I have a date and..." Priest said with as much levity as he could muster.

But the phone line had gone dead.

Priest didn't think it was a good idea to include Alana and

Aggie in this information yet, or even let them know he was meeting someone. Partly to protect them. This informant could be dangerous or deranged. Or both. Or even useless. But he had to explain to Alana why he would be busy at nine o'clock without raising suspicions. He still hadn't told her much about working for the U.S. government, so he couldn't use that as a cover. He also knew that he would have to pay up for a lie later on.

So he told her he was meeting with a Russian agent. She laughed, then looked at him sideways and shrugged her shoulders. There were some things she knew she would never know about him and she decided not to pry too much. In his earlier life as Armando Listrani, he had met and dealt with Russian agents, even older ones who were veterans of the Russian KGB, but Alana wouldn't have had access to the Armando Listrani file, nor would she have been able to connect it to him if she did have access.

"So, is this Russian agent a pretty girl?" she teased, although Priest detected a bit of concern in her voice.

"Not unless she has a gravelly voice," he quipped. Sensing that he was giving too much up, he changed the subject.

"You'll be home with Kia, right?"

"Uh-huh."

"Can I call you afterward?"

"Sure," she said. That would give her an opportunity to judge how long Priest would spend with this anonymous, possibly "pretty" Russian agent.

Stephansplatz was the heart of Vienna, not just "at" the heart but actually "the heart." It was not far from Priest's hotel at Marriott Parkring and the proximity made it convenient for him on each of his visits. He and Alana had developed a romantic relationship but he couldn't stay at her house and risk difficult questions from her daughter, so he booked a room at the Marriott on each trip. He walked to Stephansplatz most mornings and returned many evenings to enjoy the social setting, the sidewalk bars and restaurants, and the general feeling of international amity that was the hallmark of the city.

At nine o'clock Priest stepped through the door of the DO & CO Hotel lobby and took the elevator to the second floor where Bar Onyx was. The rounded glass front of the hotel rose from the paving stones of the plaza below, up to the level of the bar on this floor and above, offering a sweeping view of Stephansplatz below. He was glad that his bartender friend, Piotr, was not there. Piotr had his own personal collection of acquaintances developed from the jet set crowd that visited his bar, and once he became friends with Priest, he liked to regale his American guest with the stories of actors and politicians, with occasional risqué stories of the peccadilloes of diplomats. Priest was fine not to run into Piotr on that evening; he didn't want to be recognized at the moment and be catalogued in the company of whoever this was he was about to meet.

He chose a chair facing the glass wall looking down on the plaza below, a seating that put his back facing the barroom. No waiter arrived right away, so Priest looked out at the teeming crowds of tourists that filled Stephansplatz every afternoon for sightseeing and every evening for the nightlife.

After a few minutes, a man in a charcoal gray jacket and black jeans approached. He sat down next to Priest without invitation and stared straight ahead. His gray-specked beard and full head of hair suggested someone of middle age, but his skin was smooth and taut and gave the impression of someone intent on physical health and exercise. The two men sat for a moment without speaking until the waiter arrived.

"I'll have a gin and tonic," Priest said.

"Vodka. Neat," the stranger added.

They sat quietly after the waiter departed and, still longer, until the waiter returned to deliver the drinks and left.

"You might find the following information disturbing," the visitor began.

"You mean more disturbing than meeting with a stranger

who won't identify himself, who won't look me in the eye, who drinks vodka straight, and makes curious and threatening statements about the United States?"

The visitor looked at him finally and smiled.

"Yes, all that," he replied.

As a wartime interrogator who clocked many months in the Iraq and Afghanistan conflicts, Priest had heard many things that were probably more disturbing than anything this man could tell him. He turned his head slightly to see the visitor better. Priest thought of Deep Throat, the historic informant during the Watergate investigation. Mark Felt came forward much later to reveal that he was the guy who gave Woodward and Bernstein their greatest leads and blew open an investigation that ended a presidency. The visitor looked something like that and, yet, at the same time he looked like a generic kind of middle-aged guy. Fair appearance and somewhat innocuous looking, but not one to attract attention. Priest decided that the same "everyman" look was probably what allowed Felt to fly under the radar for so many years.

"You are looking for the Paletti Notebook," the visitor said. "I've been instructed to tell you more about the thing that you are searching for."

Priest sipped from his gin and tonic and watched as the visitor tipped his tumbler of vodka to his lips.

"What do you know about it?" the visitor asked.

"Come on," Priest replied, showing a little irritation. "I'm not going to accept an anonymous invitation from a guy who won't introduce himself and then begin the conversation by telling what I know. What do you know?" he pressed.

The visitor took another sip and then stared out the window.

"You know that the Notebook has a lost gospel in it," the man began, "and letters from some of the historic writers of the Renaissance. And some art."

Another sip of vodka.

"But what you don't know is how these items in the Notebook – and some others that are not so old – matter to the cultural and political influence of America."

Nothing in Priest's research extended beyond the Gospel of Matthias and the art and letters of the Renaissance.

"What else?" Priest asked. He knew that anything affecting U.S. influence, political or otherwise, always involved other nations. Russia? China?

"The most recent addition to the Notebook is a journal left by a Fra Nizza from 1943," Priest added. "He left a chronology of the Notebook up until that time..."

"No, more than that," said the visitor. "Later."

Priest waited for an explanation but the visitor remained silent.

"What?" he asked finally.

"The Notebook received some information sometime after Fra Nizza had it, in 1943, when it was in the possession of a German officer..."

"Let me guess," Priest cut in. "Hillyer."

For the first time, his visitor looked at Priest and smiled.

"Yes. Hillyer. But his name isn't important at this time. Some materials from the U.S. government were put into the Paletti Notebook that the Americans would like to have back."

"Which Americans?" Priest knew that this wording would either lead to stickier evidence or a dead end.

"That isn't important at this time."

"It is to me," Priest protested. He recalled the conversation with Dr. Matthew Bordrick before his flight to Vienna and began to ponder who in the States wanted the Notebook more. And what it meant to each of them.

"Which Americans?" Priest repeated.

The stranger sipped the tumbler of vodka and considered how to answer the question.

"The historians mostly, but probably the high ranks of Congress."

This didn't satisfy Priest, but it did whet his appetite for the Notebook.

"If I find this Paletti Notebook," Priest began slowly, weighing his words, "to whom should I give it?"

"You've already been told to whom to deliver it."

"I was told to give it to..." but Priest paused, suddenly anxious about revealing Bordrick's identity. He didn't trust the shrink, but he knew that giving up a name might have an unintended consequence. And his visitor almost succeeded in using an old technique from Priest's past in military intelligence. Pretend to know the answer so the interviewee would think there's no risk in divulging what he knows.

"I was told to give it to someone working for the President."

"Good," the visitor said, draining his vodka. "Then you should do it."

"And, because this information is so important to the U.S...." Priest began.

"I'm not at liberty to talk about that. But, yes, it is important to the person who gave you the order to find it."

Priest wanted to pretend that President Pendleton had given the order, but he was beginning to think that it originated with Bordrick.

The visitor lifted the empty glass to salute Priest, then rose and headed toward the elevator. Priest swirled his gin and tonic, the ice cubes clinking against the glass. After a minute or two, he drained it and moved toward the elevator. He knew that continued contact with the visitor would be useless, and possibly dangerous. So he wanted to leave enough time and space between them so that they could descend to the public space of Stephansplatz separately.

MARRIOTT PARKRING

April 7, 2021

Sleep didn't come easily to Darren. The hotel bed was comfortable and, yes, he missed Alana but it was more than that. He couldn't stop thinking about the Paletti Notebook, the warnings and cautions offered by Leitner and Moser about its authenticity, and numerous places and times logged into Fra Nizza's journal. Of course, he also imagined the threats that they were facing and regretted Bao Chinh's murder as if he, Priest, was somehow responsible.

Aggie joined him in the hotel restaurant for breakfast and they decided that their effort on this day should be to piece together Nizza's journal, translate all or most of it while farming out the passages that Priest wasn't comfortable translating, and arrange the journal almost like a travelogue.

"We can find someone here who speaks Italian," Aggie commented. "Shouldn't be hard." He seemed to know that Priest was on edge letting anyone else in on their search, though.

"I'm more interested in the German," Priest said.

"Alana can handle that."

"No. I mean the pages that are in German and encrypted in code."

"Yeah, sure," said Aggie.

They were finishing their coffee when Priest's phone rang.

"Hey," said Alana on the other end. "How're you doing?"

"I'm good," he replied. Alana knew from his recounting of the discussion at Bar Onyx from the night before that there may be some loose ends that he was worried about. He didn't tell her that much, but she was a skilled interrogator and knew when bits of knowledge were being left out.

She was mindful that Priest carried the burden of all of his assignments. She also suspected that there was something else, something that he wasn't telling them. For his part, some of Priest's anxiety stemmed from the call from Dr. Bordrick and the meeting at Bar Onyx.

"Okay," Alana continued, "I want to make sure that you and Aggie are alert for any dangers. Bao didn't die by accident, and he didn't die peacefully. There's a threat out there, I guess this group of crazies called *Arma Dei,* and I want you to be looking over your shoulder at every turn.

"Yeah, we're good," Priest replied. Hearing her concern he switched roles and suppressed his fears in order to convince Alana that he was aware, alert, and ready to engage.

Well, maybe not engage.

"Do you need a license to carry?" Alana asked Priest.

"No, I don't."

She remembered their first time together, two years earlier, when he was under nearly constant threat. Despite his excellence on the firing range, Priest never carried a weapon. She carried a sidearm, a Beretta, even though her role in investigation might not have required it, and she had saved his life on one occasion, and maybe reduced threats to him on others. So when she heard him say "we're good" and "no" he didn't want a weapon, she wanted to remind him of what she said that time a couple years before.

"Maybe you should carry a sidearm."

"Nope. I'm good."

Aggie listened in on this conversation and knew – even from

the one-sided nature of his eavesdropping – that Alana was right. Priest was skilled with a handgun and should probably carry one. And Alana could get him the permit here in Austria. He didn't say anything but decided to raise the issue later with Priest.

What Alana and Aggie didn't know was that Priest's change of identity would actually make getting a license in a foreign country extremely unlikely. The U.S. government had arranged for his new identity, complete with Social Security card and fictitious past, but there was no easy way to include a marksman qualification without raising some alarm bells. So they hid his military background completely, including his certification from the range.

Aggie and Priest finished with breakfast and were ready to go back up to the room. Priest had the photos from the Paletti Notebook in his rucksack hanging from the back of his chair. He didn't trust the room safes and wasn't about to leave the photos of the Notebook unattended in the room. When they were ready to leave, he signed the breakfast check and they went back to his room to study the contents once again, with a focus on Fra Nizza's journal.

"I'll have mine neat," Aggie said as they entered the room.

"Neat?"

"Yeah. You know. Without ice or other additions."

"You know we're making coffee here," Priest said with a chuckle as he pulled the Nespresso maker toward him on the counter.

"Sure, I knew that. So I don't want any of that maple syrup or honey added to my coffee."

"Yeah, sure. I knew that," Priest replied with a smile.

While he made a round of coffee, Aggie helped himself to the photographs of the Paletti Notebook in Priest's rucksack.

"You know, I'm thinking," Aggie began, "while you're translating those parts of the Nizza journal, why not just go to the end and find out where the Paletti Notebook was last?"

"I considered that, but there are gaps in the pages. And so far in my quick translation and reading, I've found several mentions of places like Paris, Perugia, Venice, even Athens, where the Notebook was thought to be, but it wasn't. Seems like many people, from popes to kings and their armies were looking for this thing and many times their quest turned up empty.

"So if we just go to the end, we may miss the real clues as to its current condition and location."

"Okay," Aggie replied. "Gotcha."

Priest handed Aggie his coffee and sat down on the bed with his coffee cup on the nightstand.

"Let's take what Alana gave us, including the twelve pages of Nizza's journal and start to piece together the itinerary of the Notebook," Priest said.

"What about the pages of German writing?"

"I think those may matter later, but not yet. Besides, some of them appear to be in some kind of code, as well as in German. From what I recall of cryptography, and the style that the code is in, it must have been rendered in more recent times. For now, we need to follow Nizza from 1500 to around 1940 and see what we can find out."

"Besides," Aggie said with a grin, "you don't speak German."

"Yeah. That. Let me read some from this page of Nizza's journal."

Several years ago, I was asked to take charge of a collection that I had not previously known anything about. It was in 1938, just at the beginning of the Nazi scourge that was creeping across Europe. I was told that the collection involved great art of significant age, and great writings of the leading men of Europe, from Spain, Italy, and elsewhere. I was surprised by the assignment but surprised even more when I was told to keep the existence of the collection in strictest confidence.

With whom can I discuss this? I asked but was told "no one."

"No one?" I repeated. "Then to whom am I responsible? To whom do I answer?" And I was told that I was answerable only to God.

Priest occasionally paused to focus on the translation, making sure not to get words or phrases wrong, then continued.

Then I was given some more unsettling information. "The collection is known as the Paletti Notebook," my mentor said. "It contains not only great art but a gospel of uncertain origin."

"What is uncertain about its origin?" I asked.

It is said to be the Gospel of Matthias. To be more specific, the lost *Gospel of Matthias.*

My heart suddenly began to beat fast. I had heard of the mythical gospel, but it didn't seem to me that anyone had actually ever seen it. Or so we had been told. But this assignment assumed that the Paletti Notebook contained a copy of it – perhaps the only copy – and that this discovery would make the Gospel of Matthias with all its heresy a reality.

"I don't know if I can possess such a thing," I responded. "You have no choice," came the reply. "You are a servant of God and Jesus Christ."

"But neither God nor Jesus Christ would want this thing to exist," I said, and I received only a knowing nod in reply.

"Why didn't he just destroy it?" Aggie asked. "It sounds like he was a bit in fear of it and didn't want to possess it. As if the Notebook had some spell on it that could prove dangerous." Priest shrugged his shoulders but then returned to the text.

Since that time, I have been the unwilling caretaker for a collection of art and letters attributed to some of the greatest men who ever lived. Brilliant scholars like Niccolò Machiavelli, geniuses like Leonardo da Vinci, warriors like Cesare Borgia, artists and sculptors like Michelangelo and Raphael...even heretics like Girolamo Savonarola, all men excommunicated or threatened with excommunication for their apostasy – their works appeared in this collection. I have sorted through the contents of the Paletti Notebook and have come to understand and appreciate that it represents the single greatest assembly of genius in, perhaps, the history of the world.

"Wait," said Aggie, holding his hand up. "So Nizza did have the Notebook, and all its contents."

"It seems so. Let me continue."

And as my breath settled on this undertaking, I had to come to terms with the Coptic writing attributed to Matthias, a contemporary of Our Lord Jesus Christ, His disciple and one of His fondest friends. My training in this ancient language was lacking, so I pursued a refresher with more vigor, studying old texts and a codex that I was able to borrow from a friend in London. As I studied the language, words appeared on the pages that I was reading as if a magic wand had been drawn across the lines and revealed their meaning to me.

Matthias, if he ever really existed, was a dear friend of Our Lord and followed His every move. He knew Jesus for many years, especially from his early adulthood and into His service to God, but Matthias wasn't admitted to the inner circle of disciples until after Judas had betrayed our Savior and hung himself in shame and dishonor.

It was then that Matthias entered the inner circle of Jesus's life, though it happened after Our Lord's crucifixion at the hands of the Romans. Although they comprise the heart of the New Testament, we have long known that the gospels of Matthew, Mark, Luke, and John were written in the late-First Century, nearly one hundred years after Jesus's life and, therefore, composed by men who did not know Our Lord. Matthias stands out as a singular rendition of the chronicle and teachings of Jesus, written by a man who followed His sermons and acts, and who was present at His death and resurrection.

"Wow," Aggie exclaimed. "This is serious stuff. I spent a lot of my childhood in Catholic schools, Sunday school, and whatnot, and I don't think any of the nuns or priests would be happy hearing this."

"Yeah, I was exposed to the same teaching and I agree. It's not hard to imagine why the Church considered this stuff by Matthias to be heresy." Then he returned to reading.

If the Gospel of Matthias contained in this Paletti Notebook is authentic, it could become the greatest discovery in history – and the most heretical writing the Church would have to face. If, as some reports posed about Matthias's writing, the gospel contains passages describing Jesus as a man – not a god – and a man who entered into a marriage contract with a woman and produced children, the contents of the Paletti Notebook could shake thousands of years of Church teaching.

Once I had developed a level of comfort with the translation of the Coptic text, I moved on to the next, obvious, step: Tracing the provenance of the Paletti Notebook to confirm its origins and, perhaps, to confirm its authenticity. I began with Matthias, although I had few sources that originated with the gospel itself. So I had to rely on more recent narratives.

"Here's where it gets good," Priest began, "but I'm having a little more trouble reading through his handwriting. I'll try."

Sandro Paletti himself had maintained a journal and included references in it not only to the men whose work he had collected but also the history behind them. Most of the work of da Vinci, Machiavelli, and others required no deep history; Paletti was their contemporary and simply collected the works as they were produced and discarded.

But his journal included a lengthy description of the Gospel of Matthias and how he had come into possession of it. He reported that Leonardo da Vinci brought to Paletti's restaurant a single page of the papyrus that made up the gospel, proudly showing off his new find to the others gathered there. His journal described the manner in which he, Paletti, stole the gospel from Leonardo by paying the artist's male companion, Salai, a paltry sum for the theft. And the journal described how the gospel was then in his possession, although his own level of education prevented him from understanding the meaning of the Coptic symbols written on the pages.

There was a brief entry in the journal in handwriting that was almost indecipherable. I concluded that it was written either by someone without training or education, or by someone suffering from a physical ailment that resulted in tortured writing. It said that the entire collection would be passed to Sandro Paletti's grandson, Pietro, when he died.

That is where Sandro Paletti's journal ends. But the story goes on from there.

"Okay, the story," Aggie said, rubbing his hands together in anticipation. "Let's get to it."

Just as Sandro had commanded, his collection was passed on to Pietro on the event of Sandro's death in 1546.

As an historian, I was given freedoms not accorded other monks in my circle. I asked for and was granted permission to go to Florence and Rome as part of research that I was conducting.

"What kind of research?" the abbot asked me.

"In service of God," I responded. Fortunately for me, the abbot was a man of little culture and less learning, and he cared not much about historical research. He let me go with a wave of his hand and I proceeded to pursue my understanding of the Paletti Notebook.

I thought it prudent to omit telling him that I might also be going farther afield, including Paris.

Here the pages ended, and left Priest at a loss for words.

"I need some time to work through this," he said, choosing some other photographs of pages from the pile and turning toward the desk to get more focused.

Aggie's phone rang and when he looked at it, he held the screen up to Priest and triumphantly declared, "See! I get calls from Alana too!"

"Yeah, Alana. What you got?"

"A search warrant."

"Really?" Aggie replied. "What did I do?"

"No, Aggie, not for you! The bank! Or more precisely, the safe deposit boxes at the bank. I figured after Bao's apartment yielded very little, perhaps he left something back there."

"We already have the photos," Priest shouted from the distance of the desk.

"Yes, we do," she replied, "but there's no harm in poking around the bank. I think the bank manager's murder is sufficient reason to think there may be clues in his place of business."

Aggie hung up the call and said he'd meet Alana for the search at the bank, while Priest busied himself with the translation.

"Sounds good. You know where I'll be."

DFR WIEN

April 7, 2021

Alana and Aggie met at the door to the bank. It was not far from Café Central and Alana knew to collect two coffees for them and meet Aggie with a gift.

DFR Wien had occupied a prominent spot on this street for many years, just a few steps up from the roadway and perched on granite risers to emphasize its girth and height. The façade sported tall columns that themselves supported a triangular pediment above the massive bronze doors. Soaring windows with polished brass frames allowed pedestrians to peer inside the lobby of the bank, windows that begin at waist level and rose nearly the full thirty-foot height of the bank's first floor ceiling.

Despite their heavy appearance, the doors opened readily at the push of my hand, as if a mechanical assist had been engineered into the design so that each visitor to the establishment would begin with a pleasant feeling of being welcome.

A serious calm presided over the lobby. There were eight teller windows on the left wall and three formal-looking desks positioned opposite them along the right wall. A handful of hightop counters occupied the middle of the long rectangular room, around which stood patrons scribbling notes on small slips of paper. It was like a throwback to the 1950s. Instead of the sound of computers clacking and the invisible movement of capital along micro circuits, here were real people, real tellers, and real forms and papers to fill out to initiate transactions.

Alana and Aggie stepped in through the doorway and took in the serenity of an old-fashioned bank building. They were greeted by Franz Hesse, Chinh's employee who supplied the photos to them the day before.

"*Guten tag*," he said, reaching out to shake their hands. "What can I help you with?"

"We have a search warrant to review Bao Chinh's personal computer and to explore the safe deposit boxes in the vault," said Alana.

"All the boxes?" asked Hesse, a little taken aback.

"That shouldn't be necessary," she replied. "After we look through Mr. Chinh's files and check the one box in question, that should be it. Unless something that we discover leads to other questions."

"Okay," Hesse responded. "Let's go," and he led them up the few steps into the manager's office, formerly occupied by Bao Chinh. Alana explained that the search warrant gave her permission to access Chinh's computer, so she asked Hesse for the password. He had to return to his own office to retrieve it, but soon came back to give it to her.

A search of files dating backward from the present time showed no unusual activity. Alana even checked Chinh's own bank accounts to be able to discount the theory that he was killed over money. Aggie looked through the file cabinets and among the books and registers on the shelves. Nothing turned up.

After finding nothing of direct importance there, they descended the steps and entered the vault. Hesse had brought along his master keys and opened the safe box where the Paletti Notebook photos had been found.

It was empty. Not even a staple remained.

"There is nothing here," Alana said with some disappointment. Just then her phone chirped.

"Yes?" she asked. "Okay. I understand. I'll be right there."

Then she turned toward Aggie and explained that she would have to leave right away, on business unrelated to the current investigation.

"You're here," she said to him and, turning to Hesse, continued, "I hope you will honor this search warrant in my absence, for Mr. Darwin, so that he can continue to look around. He might find something in the files to help us."

"Certainly," responded Hesse.

Alana turned to go, proceeded up the few steps out of the vault and walked across the expanse of the bank lobby. On her way out, she brushed by three men she thought were acting suspiciously. The bulge in the jacket of two of the men was familiar to her; it represented a concealed weapon.

"They're not coming to make a deposit," she said under her breath. "At least not money."

Alana turned around and followed the men as they made a direct line toward the entrance into the vault area. Just as one of the men reached inside his jacket, Aggie appeared in the doorway of the vault and began coming up the steps. The other man with a weapon reached into his jacket too as the third one stepped aside, scanning the room for any interference.

Alana had her Beretta on her hip and drew the weapon to balance the attack, quickly shouting to Aggie to take cover. Drone pilots like Aggie aren't trained in close-order combat, but he knew enough to get out of the line of fire. The sound of both the men's weapons discharging simultaneously drove bank clerks down below the counters and drove customers scattering for cover. Aggie had obeyed the warning and was now pulling the heavy vault door closed, protecting him from gunfire while depriving the gunmen of access to the sensitive area.

Hesse was not as quick as Aggie. He took a round to the upper arm and fell back down the steps.

"Get down!" Alana shouted to the room, as she closed on the armed men and cut the distance to Hesse.

The attackers were less interested in Hesse than they were in getting into the vault, so he escaped further danger. Aggie didn't take any fire since he was then behind the door. The two armed men saw their plan falling apart so they turned to run from the bank.

By then, Alana who had trailed them back into the building, stood between them and the door. She took aim at the one in front, hitting him in the chest, then spun to her left as the other shooter approached. She couldn't handle all three men so she paused to consider her options. The third one, the observer, ran at her and rammed into her, knocking Alana to the floor as he and the second shooter escaped out of the bank lobby, leaving their fallen comrade behind.

Alana was on her radio right away calling for back-up while running toward the vault. She quickly examined Hesse who seemed to have suffered only a flesh wound, and she called out to Aggie, telling him the coast was clear. He emerged from the vault and looked around as clerks and customers began to rise up from their hiding places.

"What the fuck!" Aggie said, looking down at the slain gunman. "Bao, and now this?" he exclaimed.

Alana stood next to him as street policemen filled the lobby and clerks tried to calm the customers.

"Well, there are some extreme Christian sects all over, but hard to know if this is one of *Arma Dei*," she replied.

"Yeah, maybe, but check out the tattoo."

As Aggie pointed out the tatt on the man's forearm, a man appeared from the startled crowd of onlookers. He peered into the circle, saw the tattoo, and quickly backed away.

"What's that about?" Aggie asked, seeking to get the man to re-enter the group and tell what he knows.

"That cruciform tattoo on his wrist," the man told them,

pointing to the man Alana had shot dead. Before Alana or Aggie could ask for more information, he ran away.

Examining the tattoo, Alana took a photo of it with her phone which she immediately transmitted to Haber at the precinct.

"We'll get something on this pretty soon," she told Aggie, "but I'd like to clean up this mess first."

MARRIOTT PARKRING

April 7, 2021

"OKAY, WHAT THE HELL," AGGIE SAID AS THEY ENTERED THE hotel room with Priest. "Why is *Arma Dei* out to get us?"

"That should be easy to figure out, Aggie," said Priest. "At least as long as they think we have a bead on the Paletti Notebook that they're trying to get."

Alana had already called Priest with a report on the day's activities, taking him away from the translation of Nizza's journal. Instead Priest turned his attention to the group in question to have a report as soon as possible.

"I'm going on what you said earlier," Priest said, consulting his phone for information. *Arma Dei* has a long record of violent tactics. Seems like they've zeroed in on the Paletti Notebook and they're trailing us to find it, then probably planning to eliminate us from the equation."

"Wonderful," said Aggie ruefully. "Eliminate us."

Alana only looked on with concern.

"Yeah. Us," Priest added. There was a bit of hesitation in his voice that Alana detected, a hesitation borne of the fact that he had not yet told them about his assignment from the U.S. government. Alana wondered if there was something Priest wasn't telling them, and when it would come out.

"By the way, Alana," Aggie said, "I don't think I thanked you for saving my life."

"No sweat," she responded. Looking at Priest, she added with a smile. "I'm used to saving guy's lives."

"We need to solve Bao's murder and get the Paletti Notebook...sooner rather than later so we can get out of this mess we're in," said Aggie.

"Let's get back to Nizza's journal," Priest said. "I've only been able to translate the opening page or two, but nothing yet about where he found the Notebook, or where he chased it to."

He proceeded with another portion of the translation and read Fra Nizza's words aloud:

It seemed to me that the logical first place to look would be Florence. That is where the great men lived and it is where the story apparently begins. But it was a nearly useless trip. I visited the city, spoke to priests, artists, museum curators, and even strangers on the street. I could find no one who had ever heard of a man named Paletti or anything about a collection of art from his time.

Except Alberto Falfani. He was a new monk when I met him in 1944, a young man who entered the service of God when he was still only sixteen. The great world war was on and he didn't want to fight, so he thought that a life in service of the Lord was preferable. As he told the story, though, he was soon captured by the Nazis, taken prisoner, and tortured. They told him they were looking for the great Paletti Notebook and assumed that the monks of San Marco would know where it was hidden. This was something Falfani knew nothing about, but they tortured him on the premise that, as a monk and as a resident in the abbey, he would have stories to tell. Well, he didn't and he suffered for it.

Falfani was so struck by the hatred of the Germans that he wondered how God could create such creatures. In the end, he abandoned his novitiate and foreswore the vows he had taken.

He told me he knew the name Paletti and said that he remembered tales of a restaurant that existed on the part of the Piazza della Signoria that was formerly known as the Piazza del Gran Duca. But he knew nothing more.

"You should check with the abbot," he said. "There's long been a legend about a monk named Paletti who was murdered in the abbey."

I followed his suggestion. Records of such events would be closely guarded, but some of the friars at the abbey were eager to trade on the folklore they had heard of the legend. It seemed that a young man named Pietro Paletti entered the monastery after killing a man on the streets of Florence. He sought refuge in the abbey, which was granted, but he was soon murdered in his cell one night after evening prayers.

I put together what I knew and concluded that Sandro Paletti's notebook had been passed to his grandson, who was subsequently killed. But if Pietro was in possession of the collection when he was murdered, it could have either remained in its hiding place in the abbey or been taken somewhere by his killer.

I visited San Marco and asked to speak with the abbot. "Yes," he said, he remembered Alberto Falfani, but was reluctant to discuss the long-held rumors told about a monk named Pietro Paletti. His explanation didn't seem plausible, and his words seem to evade my questions. After long questioning, and me reminding him that rumors of a monk being murdered could only be put to rest with the truth, he relented.

"If every rumor about mysterious things happening behind the walls of the abbey were believed," he said, "you could fill a book!" Slowly, with some apparent hesitation, the abbot did concede that there is a legend that dates back to about 1550 concerning a young man who joined the abbey to avoid punishment for killing another man in the streets of Florence.

"Paletti?" he asked questioningly. "Possibly."

Does the legend also speak of a great collection of art? I asked him.

The abbot shrugged off the question but acknowledged that he had heard this also.

At this point, Priest paused, struggling a bit with the translation and deciphering the handwriting.

"Some of the telling refers to an army of God, men who take up arms to protect the Pope and the teachings of the Church," he said. The abbot seemed to be warming up to my questioning, as if he now felt he had permission to reveal all the tawdry details of the story, so he told me that this army of God were said to have killed Fra Pietro for his Notebook. "I don't know what was in the notebook or why these men would kill for it, but that's how the story goes."

After that the abbot excused himself, looking like he had second thoughts about telling such stories. He crossed himself before turning away, retreating to the cloister of the abbey.

"There's a lot to consider there," Alana noted. "Sounds like the person known as Pietro Paletti might have existed..."

"At least in the legendary sense," Aggie said.

"Yeah, I guess. Is there any more, Darren?"

"Here's where I got turned around. Sounds like Nizza got enough from the abbot but...wait...here's something. The handwriting is pretty bad. In addition to being in the usual penmanship of European style, it looks like it was scrawled in a hurry."

As I prepared to leave, a monk stooped from age approached me. He said he knew the story of the murder of Fra Pietro Paletti, and he provided many details, including that the young monk's father owned a restaurant during the "Great Time" as he called it, his words for the Renaissance.

"Fra Pietro was murdered for a bundle of drawings!" the old monk said, a smile of amazement in his voice. "Can you imagine? For drawings!"

"But there's more," he told me. The old guy took a step closer to me and raised his chin so that he could whisper directly into my ear. "You didn't hear about the note, did you?" he asked. I shook my head.

"Ego sum ira Dei, *he said quietly. The utterance made me draw back. It was a Latin phrase for "I am the wrath of God." I didn't know what the old man intended, or whether he could carry out some divine justice right there in the courtyard, but I wanted to be on guard.*

His smile revealed missing teeth and wrinkled lips, but he assured me he meant no harm. "It is what was written for Pietro."

"How do you mean?" I asked. He told me that a note had been left on Pietro's murdered body, saying just that.

"Were the drawings ever found?" I asked him.

"No, I don't think so," he replied. "But I have heard that the killer took them to Rome to present to the Pope."

I asked him why the Pope would be interested and the old monk smiled again.

"Oh, you don't know, do you?" he said gleefully. "There was something more in Pietro's satchel, something much more valuable than the drawings of the artists."

"What?" I asked.

"A gospel. A very old Gospel."

I already knew of the legend of the lost Gospel, one written by a man named Matthias.

Priest wrapped up his translation with that passage, promising to work on more later.

"Seems like the Paletti Notebook might have followed Pietro to the abbey and possibly was taken to Rome," said Aggie.

"That's where we should follow it. In the meantime," Priest added, "let's talk about who we're up against."

Alana sat on the edge of the bed, Aggie took a seat at the desk, and Priest paced the floor.

"*Arma Dei* seems are pretty serious about getting the Paletti Notebook," he began. "And maybe others."

Alana quietly considered why Priest mentioned "others."

"These guys went after me..." Aggie said.

"Well, not exactly," Alana interjected. "Yeah, they were ready to shoot you, if necessary, but they were after the Notebook. Not you."

"That doesn't make me feel any better," Aggie responded.

"From what we know," continued Priest, "*Arma Dei* wants to

destroy the Notebook and all its contents, considering them blasphemous or heretical."

"And seem ready to kill to reach their goal," said Aggie. "It seems like we have a choice to make. We can abandon this quest and, in the process, maybe survive, or we can continue with it and just fight our way along."

Priest demurred, looking down at the floor, but not ready to respond directly to Aggie's question.

"What is it, friend?" Aggie asked. "You know I'm not afraid to face down these thugs, but if you have something to say, I need to know why we're doing this."

Alana looked at Priest to try to guess what he was thinking. Priest remained impassive for a few moments, then looked up and spoke.

"Okay, this is hard to admit, but I have some information that I've been keeping from you."

Alana showed a little surprise, but her pursed lips and the expression on her face indicated that she expected such a revelation all along. Aggie just stared at his buddy, having been through other situations that presented them with risk, but not willing to give in. They waited for Priest to speak.

"I asked you to join in the search for one reason – a good one, I might add – involving the lost art of the Renaissance and possibly, just possibly, a gospel that could alter the world's understanding of Jesus and the early Church."

"Right," Aggie nodded. "Got that."

"And, in the process, Bao was killed and we turned our attention to finding his killers, too. But there is another reason," Priest continued. "I was contacted by some individuals in the U.S. government who warned me that we have to get to the Paletti Notebook first."

"Did these individuals say why?" Alana asked.

"Yes, and no."

"Can I guess? The 'individuals' that you mention," Aggie

persisted. "Would they happen to get their mail delivered to the White House?"

Priest smiled. Aggie knew that he reported to the White House but, in this case, the command came from one rung lower on the ladder of power.

"Yeah, sorta, but no. I was assigned to find the Notebook by a screener for the President, not the President himself."

"A screener," Alana deadpanned. "What's a 'screener?'"

"It's the guy who creates separation between the primary target," Aggie opined, " – probably in this case the President – and the person interviewed. Hence, 'screener.' Darren, you mind telling us who the screener is?"

"Wouldn't be a good idea. At least, not right now."

"So, what," Aggie continued, "you don't trust us?"

"Come on, man, you know that's not fair. I trust you more than anyone. Both of you. But I need to give you some distance here." He paused then reconsidered his comment. "Until a little later."

"Until you need us again," Aggie grumbled. It was the first time in their relationship that Aggie and Priest seemed to be at odds. Priest just stared at his friend, hoping that his near silence on this mission wouldn't end their relationship.

"Alright," Aggie said, "sorry. I didn't mean that. But I almost got shot today and who knows what else is waiting for me out there?"

That last was said with a chuckle, as if he knew the danger, accepted it, and was willing to stay by Priest's side no matter what.

"Sorry, friend," Priest said, but Aggie only shrugged. "So, we have to get on with this, and I think we should follow Nizza's prompt to visit Rome and see what we can find there. That's assuming the story the old monk told Fra Nizza back in the 1940s was right."

"I need to get something to eat," Alana suggested. "I'll go down to Champions and pick up some burgers and fries..."

"And a couple of beers," Aggie added.

"Yeah, well, of course."

"We've got all this stuff here on the bed and desk," Priest said indicating the spread pile of photographs. He looked at Alana and decided he needed to give her some space. "I'll stay and watch it and you two can go down to Champions. Bring me something special."

"No," Aggie said. "I'll stay. I've been watching you two and you need some alone time together."

"Alone time?" Alana laughed, then shot an angry glance at Priest. "You sure you want to risk leaving Darren alone with me?"

"Yeah, sure," Aggie replied. "Or not. Anyway, I'll stay. You go get the food. Don't worry. I won't run away."

Priest and Alana left the room, carefully checking the door lock to ensure that it engaged. They walked down the hallway and entered the elevator. Pressing the "down" button, Priest looked at Alana with a pleading expression.

"I'm sorry, honey. Really, I am. I wasn't sure whether telling you about this connection to the White House would be good. And whether I should tell you early or late."

"Solved that!" she replied with a note of anger in her voice. They rode the rest of the elevator descent in a chilly silence.

As they exited the elevator, they saw four men loitering in the hotel lobby. It was past check-in time so the crowd had thinned, but there was something not quite right about their look.

"Did you see that?" asked Alana, as they walked by. It was a mostly useless question since she knew that Priest would be attentive to those around them.

"Yeah, but it might not mean anything."

"Good," Alana muttered, "because the handgun grips I saw in their jackets would normally have worried me."

She smiled wanly at Priest, but knew that they would have to deal with this.

As Priest and Alana moved toward the glass door to Champions at the end of the Marriott lobby, the men moved toward the elevator. A man standing there as the doors opened on the next carriage was pushed away by one of the men, preventing him from joining them on the upward ride.

"That's enough," said Priest, convinced that these men were up to no good. "I'll take the stairs and you catch the next elevator."

Priest grabbed the bellhop and shoved him toward Alana, telling him to commandeer the next elevator and take her to their floor. Priest grabbed another bellhop and dragged him to the stairway entrance, screaming at him to unlock the door so that he could ascend the steps.

Out of breath but still able to engage, Priest exited the stairwell on their floor. The four men they had spied in the lobby were already walking down the corridor and, soon, another elevator door opened and Alana came running toward him. The men saw Priest and Alana and picked up their pace. They reached the door to Priest's room where Aggie was waiting, and Alana pulled her Beretta from the holster.

"Halt!" she screamed, pointing her handgun at them while running in their direction.

The men turned around but continued to walk backwards towards Priest's room. One of them held a keycard – probably a master, Priest surmised – and one of them drew his weapon. It was clear these weren't just hotel guests and they were going straight for Priest's room.

"Halt!" Alana screamed again, a loud order that probably was also heard by Aggie.

Shots were fired in both directions. One of the men took a round to his right leg, another one was shot in the temple and dropped quickly to the carpeted floor. Priest commandeered a maid's cart to use as protection and Alana squeezed in next to him.

More shots were fired while one of the intruders swiped the

keycard past the lock on the door. The action brought the men to pause in firing their weapons, but as one of them pulled on the door handle, Alana squeezed off two more rounds to slow their entry to the room. He pushed the door open a crack but then met resistance. Apparently, Aggie caught on to the action in the hallway and pushed back against the door to deny them entry.

The struggle to get the door open, coupled with Alana raining shots down the hallway were enough to convince the men to give up the attempt. The three surviving men turned and ran down the hallway toward the stairwell, leaving their dead companion on the carpet.

Alana followed the escaping men to the staircase but reasoned that she couldn't catch up with them. She stopped and called her precinct to report the incident and told the desk cop to immediately contact the hotel. Then she clicked off and picked up a service telephone in the hallway and dialed "0" hoping that would miraculously reach the front desk. The intermittent, repetitive buzzing sound convinced that it wouldn't, so she slammed the phone down. By the time she was able to place a call to the front desk, she was told that three men, one of them limping, had just rushed through the lobby and out the side entrance onto Weihberggasse street.

When all seemed to have ended, Aggie pulled the door open and exclaimed, "Shit. This isn't fun anymore!"

Priest was checking the fallen man, blood oozing from his head wound, and quickly determined that he was dead. Rifling through the man's pockets, Priest found no forms of personal identification, although there was a short notice, in bulletin style, written in Italian. He knew he'd have to spend more time on the translation but could already see two instances of the phrase *Ego sum ira Dei* in the text.

"Looks like he has a connection to *Arma Dei,* he said to Aggie standing in the doorway.

"Look, every time you guys leave me, gunmen come

running," Aggie said, following with a strained laugh. "I think I should stick with you from now on."

Alana had returned to the man sprawled on the carpet as hotel staff came running from the elevator.

"We have this under control," she said. "Police from my office will be here soon. Please notify your front desk to expedite their entrance and passage to this floor." On that command, a woman from the hotel stepped away to phone the desk.

The police arrived and the hotel staff began knocking on doors to explain the incident to the other guests. No one had been able to enter Priest's room so the photographs remained undisturbed, but Alana kept the police out of the room during interrogation. She knew that the evidence spread out on the furniture would raise uneasy questions.

When the medical staff had taken the body away, Alana excused herself to return to the office and help process this event. Aggie and Priest went back into the room.

"Whew," Aggie began. "This is getting interesting!"

"Is that what you call it?"

"I have other choice words," he responded, but glaring at Priest, added, "but I'm saving them for you."

"It's getting late," Priest said. "I'll wait up for Alana but you should get some shut-eye."

"Actually, I think I'll have to keep one eye open the whole time," came the reply, and Aggie left the room.

ROME 2021

VATICAN LIBRARY

April 8, 2021

Alana called Priest later that night but said she would have to go home to check on Kia. Priest thought her voice had softened but he remembered the edge she had when she found out he had kept from her the involvement of the White House. He hoped that her return home – rather than to the hotel to see him – didn't reflect a lingering tension between them.

In the morning, Priest called Alana while he was sitting with Aggie in the hotel breakfast room. She seemed to have recovered and the edge was gone from her voice.

"How's Kia?" he asked.

"She's fine. Sorry to have missed out on seeing Washington, and tired from all the traveling. But she'll be okay."

"How are you?" he continued, but Alana didn't answer.

Once they moved beyond the awkward pause, he asked about the investigation, and for more information on Gutman and Hillyer.

"Not much there," she replied in a flat voice. "I'll keep looking."

Priest glanced over at Aggie who was staring away and absently stirring his scrambled eggs.

"Say, do you mind if Aggie and I go to Rome? We'd like to follow up on the bit in Fra Nizza's journal about the Paletti Notebook going to Rome."

"Sure," Alana responded, but Priest was once again concerned about the note of detachment in her voice.

"Are you okay?" he asked her.

"Yeah, sure. We have a lot to talk about, Darren. We've been together for a while, although admittedly having to commute long distances to see each other has not been the best. And I'm not...well, let me begin again. I'm uncomfortable knowing that I don't know much about you."

Priest listened without commenting. A lump formed in his throat.

"And I need to know more. And when you piped up about working for the White House, well, I mean, I suspected something like that, but if you trust me – and if you want me to trust you – we have to, well, I mean...Shit, Darren. We need to talk."

By then he was holding the phone closer to his ear so Aggie couldn't hear Alana's voice. And yet Aggie could tell by the look on his friend's face that this was a troubling conversation.

"I know. I understand," Priest replied. "And I do trust you, with everything. With me. With my heart. Okay, I agree, we need to talk. We'll get back from Rome by tomorrow morning. Can I call you then?"

"Yeah, sure." After a pause to reset her tone, Alana asked, "What can I do while you're gone? On the investigation, I mean?"

"Could you get in touch with your friend Rafaela Indolfo on the Rome police force? I'd like to get her help getting into a library."

"Okay, sure, but why that? Can't you just visit a library without her help?"

"Not in this case. I mean the Vatican Library."

"Yeah, of course you do," and it was the first time Priest

could detect a little humor in her voice. "I'll call her as soon as we're off."

"*Buon giorno*," said the voice when Priest answered his phone. He and Aggie had just arrived in Rome when the call came in. It was Rafaela. "What can I do for you?"

"We're conducting an investigation and would like to review some materials in the Vatican Library."

"Yes, Darren," Rafaela began, "but you know that the Vatican is a sovereign nation. We, the Rome police, have no jurisdiction there."

"Of course, yes, I know that. But I believe that a professional of your caliber would have contacts in many different police departments..."

"*Sì*," she responded.

"Even in the Vatican."

"*Sì*."

"So..."

"Okay. I'll see what I can do. But one thing, Darren."

"What's that?"

"If you break my friend's heart, I'll break your head."

A long sigh on Priest's end of the line.

That left little room for doubt. He knew that Alana and Rafaela went way back and had maintained a close relationship for years. So, obviously, Alana had confided her concerns to her Roman friend, or Rafaela had deduced it from Alana's voice. Priest knew that he would have a lot of repair work to do when he got back to Vienna.

They stepped to the curb at the airport and took the next cab in the taxi line.

"*Città del Vaticano*," Priest told the driver as he pulled away from the curb.

The cab ride took about thirty minutes winding its way

around the vast monuments of the Eternal City. Rome was established thousands of years before Vatican City became an independent state in 1929 and, although it remained sovereign in its own right, the architecture of the buildings in this seat of the Holy See blended into the landscape of the city in such a way as to become enfolded within it.

Priest had been in Rome many times and Aggie was currently living there, if a six-month stay in any city counts as "living there." Yet, passing by the Colosseum, the massive monument to Vittorio Emanuele, the Palatine Hill overshadowing the sunken Circus Maximus, and Forum still brought out the child in each of them. It was hard not to be amazed in this city, not only for its age, architectural beauty, and vast reach, but also to recollect the role played by ancient Rome in the annals of Western history.

The taxi crossed the Tiber River on the Ponte Vittorio Emanuele II, with the hulking Castel Sant'Angelo on the right and roads leading up to the grand entrance to St. Peter's Basilica on the left. The driver took them down the Via della Conciliazione, a broad avenue with the basilica looming in the distance, then dropped Priest and Aggie off on the edge of the elliptical plaza in front of St. Peter's. Although the basilica resides in the midst of Vatican City, to get to the museum and apostolic offices they had to go around the church.

Aggie kept looking up at the rows of statues of saints that top the façade of St. Peter's – still in awe of the grandeur of this structure – and Priest had to frequently grab his friend's arm to steer him blindly around the building toward the entrance where they would meet Rafaela.

Rafaela was waiting for them at the appointed spot, shook hands with both men, but assumed a more professional manner for this mission. She spoke to the guard at the gate, presented her credentials and a piece of paper from her shoulder bag, and they were allowed to enter.

The Vatican Apostolic Library holds historic texts from

various religions that are greater and older than anything else in the world. Certainly, on all subjects relating to the Catholic Church. And like other rooms and studios in the Vatican, it was covered with magnificent art on walls and ceilings, and sculpture from the greatest artists over two millennia. Originally conceived in the early 1400s, the library was formally introduced in 1475 to bring together under one roof the Church's literature and teachings and, not incidentally, the writings of Popes and other Church dignitaries.

Priest had already determined from his reading of Nizza's journal that he was interested in anything written or kept by Pope Julius III. The pope was born Giovanni Maria Ciocchi del Monte and was elected to the papacy in 1550, just before the time that Pietro Paletti was murdered so any involvement by the papacy in the theft of the Paletti Notebook would have involved him. If the old monk described in Nizza's journal was right, and the Paletti Notebook was taken to Rome, it would have no better destination than Pope Julius III's office.

Priest also knew that *Arma Dei*'s goal of destroying the Notebook would not have been realized since the collection appeared to still be meandering through Europe for centuries – possibly ending up somewhere near Vienna. So he hoped to find some record of it in the files attributed to Pope Julius.

Rafaela remained with her charges until they had gained access to the complex of rooms that make up the library. A young woman who introduced herself as the assistant curator, received Rafaela's credentials, and then bade goodbye to the Roman cop as the curator led Priest and Aggie to a series of rooms that might contain the things they sought. She pushed open a heavy wooden door that was ornately carved in relief – Aggie couldn't resist touching the intricately carved panels on the door – and into a room that took their breath away. The vaulted ceiling was covered with an intricate painting of the books of the Old Testament; on the walls hung framed paintings that clearly dated from early to late Renaissance.

"Look at that!" Aggie exclaimed. "A Tintoretto!"

Running in a straight line down the middle of the long room were observation tables that Priest remembered seeing in other ancient libraries. The design of the tables would fit long flat drawers underneath for storage of materials, while the surfaces were covered with sheets of glass. Gooseneck lamps were positioned every few feet, each with its own on/off switch and each sporting a dimmer dial. In between each lamp was a small computer screen, and two of them were lit up.

The assistant curator had been instructed by her superiors to cooperate with Rafaela Indolfo's request, so she showed Priest and Aggie to some cabinets by the side. Prior arrangements made by Rafaela ensured that the books and materials they cared most about would already be available, saving them precious time to source them.

The men were allowed to view ancient texts and notes written by the closest advisors to Pope Julius. Fortunately, the Vatican had begun digitizing all the ancient records back in 2014 so access was easier and didn't require opening creaky old books.

"Hey, check this out," Priest said to Aggie, but his friend just stared at the ancient papers in confusion.

"Darren, I don't speak Italian. What's there for me to check out?"

"Okay, right. Anyway, there's a guy named Antonio Trebiata, assistant to Pope Julius, who writes..." he began, tracing the lines on the screen with his finger. "Who writes about a collection of art brought to the Pope in 1555. It was a collection from Florence and included many of the great masters of the day."

Then Priest paused and considered the next passage carefully.

"And look at this," he said. He straightened up from the screen as if height or distance would make it clearer to him, then leaned in again. "He also writes about an ancient gospel, one not known to any man..."

"Bingo!" exclaimed Aggie.

"But, no, wait. He writes that the collection of art and the gospel were taken from the Vatican."

"By whom?"

"By Giorgio Vasari." responded Priest.

"Vasari," mused Aggie. Priest had already described Vasari but Aggie wanted more, so he checked his phone for information. "Right here, I thought so."

"Trebiata says here that Vasari was preparing a second edition of his book and he convinced him, Trebiata, that is, to let him take the Paletti materials with him for study."

"Okay, sounds benign."

"Yeah, but..." Priest added, "he writes in this note that Vasari never returned the Paletti Notebook. Vasari died in 1574..."

"And Trebiata lived until 1585," Aggie interjected.

"How do you know that?" asked Priest, impressed with his friend's sudden facility with Italian.

"It says it right here, on the frontispiece of what you're reading. "Antonio Trebiata, 1514 – 1585."

Priest laughed but followed Aggie's comment.

"So Trebiata outlived Vasari, probably stayed in the Vatican all that time, and would have known whether the Paletti Notebook was ever returned."

"And I suppose," Aggie continued, "that Trebiata was just covering his ass here, writing that Vasari had the Notebook last in case anyone came looking for it."

They were attended throughout their research by the assistant curator who had been sitting quietly at a side table. At this moment, she spoke up, offering another complication.

"*Sì*," she said, "it is as you say. But if Vasari took the Notebook when he left Rome in 1555. If he died in 1574, where is it now?"

For a moment, Priest realized that her presence in the room might compromise their work, but they were past worrying about that and had to press on.

"Antonio Vasari went to Florence in 1555?" Priest asked.

"Actually, he moved to Arezzo," she said, "to the house that he had built there for him and his wife."

"His wife," Aggie began, "did she outlive him?"

"*Sì*," she replied. "Unusual for those times, when many women died young. But Niccolosa Bacci, his wife, did live on."

Priest had already gleaned as much from his translation of the Nizza journal, but he wanted confirmation.

"Do we know what happened to her after his death?" Priest asked.

"I recall that she moved back to Florence, considering the big house in Arezzo to be too empty, too lonely."

"You know a lot about Vasari," Aggie said. "How is that?"

"I wrote my thesis on his life, and his book," she responded.

"Fantastic," Priest cut in. "So we know his wife, Niccolosa, right?"

The woman nodded.

"We know she moved back to Florence. If he had the Paletti Notebook, there's no way she would have left it in an empty house in the countryside."

"*D'accordo,*" she responded. "Agreed."

Turning to Priest, Aggie said, "Looks like we're going to Florence." Then turning toward the assistant speaking to them, "Can you tell us anything about where she lived in Florence?"

"*Sì*," and she wrote some notes on a slip of paper and handed it to them. "But you probably won't find what you're looking for there."

"Why?" Priest asked.

"Vasari was an artist, as you know. He had apprentices, including a man named Luca Mandori. Times were tough back then, and when the widow Niccolosa Bacci died, Mandori decided to sell everything the master owned. He was short of finances, or so the records show, but he could have survived selling only a small collection. Instead, he sold everything that Vasari had produced."

"Not sure how that affects our search," Aggie said.

She turned to the other computer screen, tapped a few keys, and brought up a digital image of an old letter.

"We don't know the origins of this, but it refers to Mandori. I'll read it to you."

I was able to discover that Niccolosa Bacci, Vasari's wife, left their home in Arezzo after his death in 1574 and returned to Florence. Given his entreaties, I could not but assume that she brought the Paletti Notebook with her to that city. However, the signora followed her spouse in death not long after that. Before she died, she passed on knowledge of the Notebook to an apprentice of her husband, Luca Mandori, who kept the Paletti Notebook. As his sponsor had died and even, then, his wife, Signor Mandori found himself in need of finances. To correct his plight, he smuggled the Paletti Notebook out of Florence to sell it to Alfredo Ferrante in Pisa. Ferrante decided that instead of paying for the collection, he would rather acquire it by simple torture. So he had Mandori taken prisoner, subjected him to torture on the strapado, *until he relented.*

The woman paused to explain. "The *strapado* is a terrible device. A man's arms are tied behind his back. Then he is hoisted up by his hands and dropped several times toward the ground, wrenching his arms upward behind him, dislocating his shoulders."

Then she resumed reading from the screen.

By this method Ferrante retrieved the Notebook and Mandori was later hung in his prison cell.

At this point, it seemed that the Notebook was kept in Pisa. That is, until 1605.

Judging from the chronological ordering of the narrative, not to mention the handwriting that Priest was able to see, he was now certain that what the assistant had in her hands was an excerpt from Nizza's journal. She said she didn't know its provenance; Priest smiled thinking how much she would like to see the pages of Nizza's journal that he had.

The curator continued.

Given the continuing conflict between Florence and Pisa, the originators of the Notebook – the people in Florence who considered it their own – mounted a campaign to retrieve it. Appeals were made to Pope Leo XI – a Medici – to retrieve the Paletti Notebook from Pisa. He agreed to dispatch soldiers to Pisa and force the return of the Notebook to Florence. He gave specific instructions to house it in the monastery at San Marco which his Medici ancestors had reconstructed in the 1440s.

The soldiers were successful in recovering the Notebook; however, when they arrived in Florence, they were persuaded to disobey the orders from Pope Leo, considering the faithfulness of the city's managers to be in question. Instead, they decided to take the Notebook elsewhere.

"There is also a list of the things to be sold," she added. "Mandori was careful to itemize everything that he was offering for purchase. Among the list of Vasari paintings and sketches, he included references to great art from other artists of an earlier time – minor drafts, sketches, even letters from some of them. Among the items on the list was a reference to an ancient manuscript, one written in a foreign tongue, and captured on papyrus."

"I'm amazed that you know all this," Priest said, still holding back his own information about Nizza's journal. Aggie looked at his friend, understood his plan, and remained silent.

"Remember, I wrote my thesis on Vasari. But even I couldn't understand all of the entries on Mandori's list until I met you and heard you talking about the Paletti Notebook. Mandori's list fits the Notebook's collection perfectly, right down to the gospel you speak of, from the man known as Matthias."

"Who was Alfredo Ferrante?" asked Aggie.

"A very rich man, but otherwise, not an important one. Ferrante wanted the entire collection, but hearing the price he was offering, Mandori had second thoughts and tried to keep the Paletti Notebook out of the sale. Turns out that this was precisely what Ferrante wanted most. You know the Florentines and Pisans were always fighting back in those days..."

"And Ferrante, the guy from Pisa, ends up with Florence's greatest ever collection," said Priest.

"*Sì*," she replied, "for a while."

"And..." said Aggie, prompting her for more information.

"That's where the popes and the Vatican come back into play."

PISA 1605

PISA

April 2, 1605

Alessandro Ottaviano de' Medici had been denied a life in the priesthood by his mother, Francesca Salviati. She didn't want him to follow a life in the Church; instead, she hoped that he would marry and produce children, continuing their branch of the Medici line. He enjoyed the rewards of living a life in civil society, including the many titles and positions of honor granted him by his mother's influence, but he never gave up on his hope to enter the priesthood.

Upon his mother's death in 1566, he returned to his religious studies and was ordained not long afterward.

In the early 1600s, having risen through the hierarchy of the Church over the years, through assignments as Archbishop of Florence and Prefect of the Congregation of Bishops, later as Cardinal Alessandro de' Medici, he found himself just a short reach from the papacy itself.

Clement VIII died on March 14, 1605, bringing about a conclave of cardinals to choose his successor to the Chair of St. Peter. They deliberated for two weeks before selecting Alessandro, the scion of the Medici family, a man committed to the legacy of the family though one without children to carry on its name.

Alessandro chose Leo XI to be his name as pope, referring reverently to his great-uncle, Pope Leo X. If he couldn't carry on the Medici name by bearing children, he would extend it by adding to the lineage of Medici popes. He was installed on April 1, 1605, but he had some family business to attend to and he wasted no time in addressing it.

The day after his installation, Leo XI called his advisors together, including military experts, to discuss the rumors that the Medici rivals in Pisa, the Ferrante family, possessed a great collection of art first assembled by a fellow Florentine by the name of Sandro Paletti. The pope was told the story of the Paletti Notebook, how it had caused the death of a young monk in their native city, been taken to Rome, then smuggled out of Rome and to Arezzo, then returned to its rightful place in Florence. He was also told that it had resided in the household of Giorgio Vasari, a man who had died many years before, then brought by Vasari's wife back to Florence.

It might have been safe there, they said, but upon Niccolosa Bacci's death, an apprentice in Vasari's studio sold it to Alfredo Ferrante in Pisa. From their account, and from all they knew at the time, the collection now being called the Paletti Notebook, complete with its art and the mysterious Gospel of Matthias was still in Pisa.

"We will have it returned to us," pronounced Leo XI, spoken as the leader of the Roman Catholic Church but also as a Medici and a Florentine. Given his access to military forces, no one doubted his intention of regaining the great treasure.

And so, on April 2, he dispatched an army of men to Pisa to find and recover the Notebook with all its contents intact. Although he was now in Rome, he ordered the commander of these forces to bring the Notebook back to Florence and gave specific instructions to house it in the monastery at San Marco. The abbey held special significance to him and his family due to connections it had with the Medici.

The commander, Vittorio Sensa, had no plans to lay siege to Pisa. That would take too long and would not be the right strategy if the goal was only to collect the Paletti Notebook. Instead, his men infiltrated the city, spending days getting to know the Pisan people, and establishing contacts and comfort that they could use to get intelligence on where the treasure might be.

There was a castle on the outskirts of Pisa named after the Ferrante family and Sensa knew the collection would have to be there. But instead of a full assault on the structure, which might prove unsuccessful considering its stalwart design, Sensa decided that he would devise a plan to enter it surreptitiously, using the information that his men could glean by plying the local men with wine and fattened meat.

The opportunity came after two weeks spent in Pisa. One of his soldiers, Filippo, had met a young woman at an inn, and the young lady's father approached him. The proprietor was himself drunk and seemed ready to sell his daughter, until Filippo changed the topic to the Ferrante *castello*.

"You don't want my daughter?" the father said, shaking his head in an inebriated way, surprised that the young man at the table would turn down such an offer. The girl was standing by the side and slapped her father in the head.

"*Sei un maiale,*" she shouted. "You are a pig," then told the young man to not even think of such a thing.

The drunken proprietor, Drago, turned his attention back to his visitor and smiled through rosy cheeks.

"So, my friend, what do you want if not my beautiful daughter?"

Filippo told him that he had heard about the magnificent *castello* where the Ferrante lived. "Is it truly as beautiful as they say?"

"Well, yes, of course," nodded the old sot. "Of course," he repeated.

"But you wouldn't know, would you?" asked Filippo.

Drago stood up as straight as the wine would allow and said, "I have knowledge of these things, my friend."

"How do you know?"

"I bring him his wine, once a week."

"And where do you deliver it?" Filippo asked.

"To the kitchen, of course," the man guffawed. "Where else?"

"But you know the way in, how to get inside the castle, to reach the kitchen, no?"

"*Sì*, I do," he replied, swaying slightly.

Filippo pried Drago for more information and offered to help with the next delivery. Then he reported to Sensa what he had learned, and how he would be able to enter the Ferrante castle soon on a pretense that would not raise any suspicions.

Two days later, Filippo was at the inn again, this time early in the morning. Drago was sitting at one of the tables, his head down on the wood, seeming to be asleep. As Filippo approached and tapped the man on the shoulder, Drago raised his head and bared his blood-shot eyes.

"Still drunk," muttered Filippo. "Maybe that's better for me," and he altered his plan. He would accompany Drago to the castle with the wine, but in his drunken state, Drago would have to let Filippo take more control of the delivery. Which would give him more time to enter the castle and look around.

That plan worked and Filippo was able to sketch the layout of the castle and a route from the entrance to the kitchen. Wandering the halls carefully so that he would not be discovered, Filippo was also able to determine where the living quarters were.

Two days later, Filippo returned to the inn to find Drago again.

"It's too early for another delivery," the owner told him.

"No, it isn't. We haven't brought Ferrante any wine for a

week," he lied. But he knew Drago was too drunk to remember anything, so the old man conceded.

This time, when Filippo entered the castle, he knew where and how to open an outside gate and then an inside door to let in the other soldiers under Sensa's command. They flooded the castle, overwhelmed the guards protecting the place, and swarmed toward the most private quarters, including Count Ferrante's chamber. When the count himself appeared, they cut him down in a single swipe of the blade, then turned on the man's young mistress still lying naked in the bed.

"Now, tell me where the great treasures are kept in this castle," Sensa said, holding the tip of his knife close to the woman's bare breast. She rose tentatively, pointing with her finger, but avoiding any sudden movement that might end up with her breast being ripped from her body. Slowly, she turned her feet toward the door. Sensa admired her nakedness and had trouble dispelling his more immediate thoughts, but he decided that anything he wanted to do with her could wait until he had secured the Paletti Notebook.

For her part, the woman knew that displaying her nakedness might help her survive.

Sensa and the woman walked down the hallway from the bedroom, past soldiers staring lasciviously at her body, and stopped at a heavy wooden door, supported by iron hinges and held locked by a heavy iron padlock. She turned around, as if looking for someone in particular, and saw him being held by the arm by one of Sensa's men. Signaling to the man, she told the soldier to release him, and he approached her.

"Produce the key," she commanded, demonstrating a remarkably strong sense of herself despite being naked and encircled by heavily armed men. "Produce the key," she repeated, and the man obeyed.

He reached into a pocket of his leather pants and withdrew a heavy key that fit the lock on the door. Swinging it open, he allowed Sensa and his army to follow him into the room.

Sensa asked about the collection of art and letters known as the Paletti Notebook, without mentioning the rumored Gospel of Matthias. He didn't want his men to hear too much.

The keyman guided him toward a chest at the back of the room, opened it, and produced a large leather folder buckled with a strap. Sensa carefully opened the folder, pulling enough of its contents out to conclude that it was the collection of art that he expected. Then he unfolded a clothbound stack of brittle papers. Untying the string, he glanced at the papyrus, shrugging his shoulders when he saw that they were filled with circles, square-shaped symbols, and swirls that he didn't recognize. But it was enough from his briefing to conclude that this was the Coptic Gospel of Matthias.

Sensa put the materials back into the satchel and tied it up again. Then, tucking it under his arm, he told his men that they could help themselves to the other jewels and precious items that remained in the room. With his solitary treasure in his possession, Sensa turned to leave the room, but not before gripping the elbow of the same woman who still stood naked before him. He led her out of the room as he departed, leaving his men to ransack the Ferrante treasure.

"Sire, I have terrible news," said the messenger, addressing Sensa. "His Excellency the Pope, sainted Leo XI, has died," the man said, bowing low before Sensa. It was sometimes dangerous to be a messenger bringing bad tidings, so it was common for such a man to bow in supplication, hoping that his head would still be attached when he tried to straighten up again.

"How did this happen?" asked Sensa.

"In his sleep. Suddenly. It is God's work," replied the messenger, who then bowed again and backed out of Sensa's room.

Pope Leo XI only survived twenty-six days in office, long enough to launch this attack on Pisa and secure the Paletti

Notebook, but not long enough to see it returned to its proper place in Florence, to the possession of the Medici family.

Vittorio Sensa had some decisions to make. Yes, he had the Notebook now, but it was something of greatest value to the Medici pope. Still, he had been commanded to secure it and return it to Florence, which he decided he would do.

He knew that Ferdinando I de' Medici, Grand Duke of Tuscany, was the patriarch of the family in Florence. To attain his title and marry the woman he had fallen in love with, Ferdinando had to renounce his role as cardinal. He then married Christina of Lorraine in 1589, and fathered many children, ensuring the continued reign of the Medici in Florence.

Sensa knew that Ferdinando had a keen interest in art, and this knowledge factored into Sensa's thinking of the proper place for the Paletti Notebook. For the moment, however, he assumed that the Paletti collection would be safe in his hands.

According to papal instructions prior to his untimely death, Pope Leo XI had ordered Sensa to retrieve the Paletti Notebook and place it in the abbey of San Marco, the original sanctuary for the treasure when Pietro Paletti fled to the safety of the abbey in 1553. But Sensa now felt that the Medici, whose hold on San Marco was by then more tenuous, would be the proper custodians of this great collection as the family that had done so much for the city of Florence. He didn't know the abbot at San Marco, so following the death of the pope who issued the original command, he felt he had the freedom to alter the commission.

Upon his arrival in Florence, Sensa was greeted with great fanfare by Ferdinando I and his wife, Christina. They were aware that he was on a mission begun by their Medici cousin and that the mission was carried out in memory of the late Pope, and they rewarded Sensa handsomely when he delivered the Paletti Notebook to them.

"Sire, honorable Duke," Sensa said, bowing to the royal couple, "it is with great pleasure that I commit to your custody an historic treasure, one that deserves the eternal gratitude of the Medici family for its collection, and that rewards the people of Florence for their eternal contributions to the world of art and letters."

He stepped forward to the dais on which sat Ferdinando and Christina, kneeling on the brocaded cushion one step below their mount, and bowed his head. In his extended hands rested a leather satchel secured with a leather strap and buckle. An attendant relieved him of the treasure and, rising the final step to Ferdinando's throne, handed it to the duke.

"Thank you, Sensa. You have done well, and you have acquitted yourself of the assignment from my cousin, Pope Leo XI. Your reward will be bestowed on you as you enter the gates of heaven."

Sensa was not surprised by the delayed payoff, expecting that his life as an officer of the Medici court would not always yield worldly incentives. He bowed his head, spread his arms in supplication, then rose to exit the room.

ROME 2021

VATICAN LIBRARY

April 8, 2021

Priest and Aggie stood in rapt attention at the assistant curator's retelling of the history of the collection of art that they knew of as the Paletti Notebook. They had access to some of Fra Nizza's journal, possibly more than she had, but the extent of her knowledge of the legend and its possible whereabouts was impressive.

"That's where the popes and the Vatican come back into play," she said.

"May I ask, what is your name, signorina?" Priest inquired.

"I am Benedetta Incisa. I am a direct descendant of Lucretia Borgia."

Priest quickly summed up the lineage and replied, "So, that makes you a direct descendant of Pope Alexander VI."

"Yes, that is correct," she replied with a knowing smile.

"Now I know why you are so connected to papal history!" said Aggie, although he immediately regretted saying so.

Benedetta only smiled. She was not ashamed of her heritage and she had long since grown accustomed to people being amused by it.

"So, let's go back a little bit," Priest suggested. "You said that's where the popes and the Vatican come back into play."

"Yes. Pope Leo XI, also a Medici, issued an order soon after he was elevated to the papacy. The order was to retrieve the great collection of art that was becoming known at that time, around 1605, as the Paletti Notebook. He was especially concerned about the rumors of an ancient gospel appearing amongst the collection. So he sent an army under the command of Vittorio Sensa to Pisa to get it back."

"Did they?"

"Yes, they did. And they brought the collection back to Florence. The pope had told Sensa to deliver it to the abbey at San Marco and he thought, as a Medici, he should be able to have control of it. But he died only a few weeks after becoming pope and was succeeded by Paul V, from the Borghese house of Siena..."

"Siena, huh," said Aggie. "Not exactly a friend of Florence either."

Benedetta chuckled.

"No, not a friend. Anyway, Sensa decided on his own that Pope Paul V – not being a Medici – should not get the collection, so he brought it directly to Florence and handed it over to Ferdinando I, the Grand Duke of Tuscany – and definitely a Medici."

"But you said this is where the popes came back in," Priest said. "What did you mean?"

"In 1628, Ferdinand II..."

"Related to Ferdinando I?" asked Aggie.

"No," she replied. "Most definitely not. Ferdinand II was from the Hapsburg family in Austria. Anyway, he was the Holy Roman Emperor from..." she paused, "I think from 1619 to somewhere near 1637. He felt that as HRE, he should be able to control all things of value in the empire. Including works of art. He had heard rumors about the Paletti Notebook and how it ended up in Medici hands – a family that he especially despised – and he decided to take it from them and bring it to Austria."

"Did he?" asked Priest.

"He tried. In 1628 he sent his legions to Florence. Maybe I should tell you about his Counter-Reformation efforts. When he was told of the existence of the heretical Paletti Notebook, he sent an army to Florence to bring it to him. By that time, Ferdinando II, grandson of Ferdinando I, was the Grand Duke of Tuscany. Again, a Medici. He wasn't about to let the emperor take the Paletti Notebook from him. Battles were fought, some conspiracies arose, but none were successful in prying the Notebook from the Medici."

"So it remained in Florence."

She nodded.

"Still, I don't know how the popes were involved," queried Priest.

"Urban VIII was the pope at that time. He was a great patron of the arts – hence his interest in the Paletti Notebook – but he was also a great critic of the sciences. Pope Urban opposed Copernican theory and the teachings of Galileo. Meanwhile, he lavished money and time on artists, both past and present. He was born in Florence so maybe he was predestined to favor the arts.

"Remember Paul V?" she asked. "He was so impressed with Maffeo Barbarini that he made him a cardinal around 1606. Barbarini – who later became Urban VIII – was pope at the time that Ferdinand II decided to attack Florence to find the Paletti Notebook. Although not a Medici himself, he – Barbarini – knew that the Medici family had supported his election as Pope, so he sided with their claim to the collection of art."

"And, in the process, Urban's troops defeated the Holy Roman Emperor's quest..." Priest said.

"And the Paletti Notebook remained in Florence," said Benedetta.

"And the gospel?" Aggie asked.

"Any discussions of that have been lost to history. But it doesn't seem like the collection was broken up. At least there's no record of that."

"So, my guess is that the collection stayed in Florence," Aggie said.

"For a time," Benedetta said with a smile.

"Okay, I'll bite," said Aggie. "For how long? And where did it go from there?"

Benedetta filled them in on a little more information, but most of her research failed to identify the collection as the famed Paletti Notebook. Her notes indicated similar contents – not the gospel though – and so she assumed in her conversation with Priest and Aggie that they were on the same subject.

"I know it was in Florence as of 1628, protected by the Medici family," she said. "Let me look into it a bit more and follow up with you on what I find."

"Yes, thanks," Priest replied. He gave her his phone number and thanked her again. "Please let me know anything you find out. It would be a great help."

"Is this really that important?" she asked.

Priest just nodded.

VIENNA 2021

CAFÉ CENTRAL, VIENNA

April 9, 2021

As soon as Priest returned to Vienna, he called Alana.

"Benedetta Incisa," began Priest, "she helped us with the research in the Vatican Apostolic Library."

"Is she young?" asked Alana.

"Yes, and very pretty," he said, fighting taunt with taunt. They had not had time to talk about Alana's concerns, but Priest didn't want it to hang like a cloud over them. He thought that humor might be a defense; then again, it might not.

"She's a direct descendant of Lucretia Borgia and a pope," he said for effect.

Alana was silent, probably still absorbing the "very pretty" comment.

"What did you find out?" she asked. Her voice was a bit flat but at least they were communicating.

"Lots of popes involved. Lots of killing and skullduggery," he said. "How are you?"

He offered that as a plea for calm, but also because he would normally ask that question when they had been apart.

"I'm fine," she replied. "Look, Darren, I said we need to talk, but I don't know if this is the right time."

"We're in the middle of some pretty heavy stuff," he said, "but I still think we need to clear things up."

"Maybe later."

"No, maybe now. It's still mid-morning. Can I take you for coffee?"

Alana remained silent for a period longer than Priest wanted, then agreed.

"You're at home, right?"

"No," she said, "I'm at the office."

"Can I meet you at Café Central in about twenty minutes?"

"Yes. Sure."

"See you then."

They met outside the café and entered together. There was no touching, something that Priest took as a bad sign, and there was also a certain nervousness. He was well adapted to interrogation and could read people's intentions from their movements and demeanor. He concluded that Alana was still mad and might need some time to work through their present situation.

They chose a table near the window and sat somewhat close together. They didn't speak to each other, addressing only the waiter when he took their order. When he departed the table, they resumed their silence at first.

"So, can we talk?" Priest said finally.

Alana didn't reply or look at him right away, but he could see she was weighing how to respond.

"About us?" she asked, "or about the job?"

"Us," he said quickly, turning toward her.

Again, silence from Alana. About then the waiter returned with their coffee so they kept their mum attitude until he had left. Priest noticed the glassy look in Alana's eyes, not on the verge of tears but not revealing any emotion either.

"Okay, I'll break the ice," he said. "You know that I love you, Alana."

She looked at him suddenly. She had thought that, although

he had never said so that directly. Then tears began to gather at the corners of her eyes. She looked away to hide them.

"You have to trust me, Darren. I can't live with a man I don't know."

"I do trust you, but you know what classified work is like. I can't share all of it."

"Okay, I get that. But do you think you could have at least told me that we weren't just solving Bao's murder? That you were working with the White House on some Top Secret mission?"

The force of her voice made him look down at the table and hold his tongue. It sounded like she was ready to let him have it and he decided the best strategy was to let her go on.

"Really, Darren. I know that you are on secret missions that I can't know about. So am I. I even know Darren Priest is not your real name."

That drew a worried look from Priest.

"But when I'm putting myself on the front lines," Alana continued, "possibly risking my life, can you at least let me know what I'm in for?"

Again, repentant silence from Priest. He didn't look at her but remained focused on his hands folded on the table next to his coffee. She was reaming him and he needed to let her get it out of her system. He only hoped that this would provide an emotional release that could usher in some accord.

"Bao was killed," she continued. "Aggie was shot at. We were attacked both at the bank and in your hotel. If we can't make the attacks stop, if we have to accept them as the price for doing this job, I at least expect you to tell me everything I'm risking my life for.

"I have a daughter, you know!" Alana nearly shouted.

Priest took this last reminder with a pained look. He knew that, and he loved Kia too, but he couldn't dispute Alana's complaint. She had much at risk, and he needed to find a way to manage that better.

"Okay," he said. "Let me tell you what I know."

He proceeded to fill her in on the details that he got from Dr. Matthew Bordrick at the White House, from the unnamed visitor at Bar Onyx, and how these facts fit into the slow accumulation of information they were getting about the Paletti Notebook.

"Why does the White House care about a bunch of art, even a gospel that we're not even sure is authentic?" she pleaded.

"I was only told that the Notebook has great importance to the U.S. and I need to find it before others do. I guess by 'others' they meant *Arma Dei.* I think there may be some things hidden in the encrypted text that we don't know yet. And I need you to know that I wasn't aware of *Arma Dei* either until we arrived in Vienna."

Dark thoughts passed his mind, thoughts about Bordrick and how he'd like to strangle him right now.

"So there are two competitors for this prize," she continued, her voice slowly softening. "*Arma Dei* and your government."

Priest nodded, and they dropped into silence for a moment, sipping tentatively at their coffee.

Alana turned only slightly toward him, laid her hand on his thigh, and exhaled in a sigh that made Priest feel that things may be getting a bit better between them.

"Well, you damn sure better survive this mission," she said to him, unapologetically turning her tear-filled eyes toward him. "Because I love you too and if you die here, I'm going to kill you."

They ordered another round of coffee, served sheepishly by the waiter who couldn't help observing some of the quarrel. Darren continued to describe the meeting he and Aggie had with Benedetta, and what they learned through her coaching.

"From what she told us, I'm not certain I know where the Paletti Notebook is," he said, "but I have a pretty good idea."

"Where?"

"The last we got from the timeline around 1628, the Notebook was in Florence, probably in the custody of the Medici family."

"That's four hundred years ago," Alana clarified.

"Yeah, so probably not still there," Priest chuckled.

Just then Aggie appeared at their table.

"Where did you come from?" Priest asked.

"Outside the window. Right next to you. I had to wait until Alana was finished dressing you down for all your errant behavior.

"Wait, Alana," Aggie stammered, turning toward her. "Dressing someone down is American slang for criticizing them. I didn't mean undressing, which is, of course, completely different. I mean, I thought..."

She laughed and replied, "Well, actually either would have been fine with me."

For all his self-confidence, Aggie blushed.

"Well this is a family café, you know, so none of that," he replied, "even thinking of it, I mean undressing...not the dressing down...oh, forget it."

The three of them were able to laugh at that, so Aggie sat down and ordered a coffee. Which gave Priest an opportunity to brief him too on the involvement of the White House.

"Thought you'd get around to telling me," Aggie responded. "I would have hoped sooner rather than later, though."

"We were just talking about what might have happened to the Paletti Notebook in the last four hundred years," Alana said to Aggie.

"You mean between 1628 when the emperor tried to wrestle it away from Grand Duke Ferdinand II? Yeah. Lots of years since then."

"Benedetta," Aggie began, quickly realizing that he may be stepping on sensitive ground, "uhh, yeah, Benedetta."

"You mean the 'very pretty' one?" Alana smirked.

"Uh, no," Aggie tried to retrench. "I mean, yeah, she was pretty. Darren, you didn't really tell Alana that Benedetta was pretty, did you?"

"Yeah, sorta, but you had to be there."

"Okay, sure," Aggie replied. "Whatever. Actually, she is pretty. Anyway..." he retreated, now he was stretching for words. "Maybe I should look her up after this is over..."

Alana laughed quietly, not at Aggie's expense but at the humor that he could always bring to their meetings.

"It still begs the question," Priest said, "or many questions. By the way, Alana, what did you find out about Ira Hillyer?"

"Still not much. Just that he died here in Vienna. The hospital records say it was gunshot wounds."

"When, and was there a record of who was attending him?" Priest asked.

"It was in 1988. I cross-checked it with police records and there is a hint that maybe he was shot by Nazi hunters, but the case was never solved."

"So, should we assume he was a Nazi?" queried Aggie.

"Pretty much, if you trust the police records. Instead, I checked with the Israeli defense establishment and various groups of Nazi hunters," she continued, "and they confirmed that there had been several suspected Nazis tracked down in Vienna, including one in 1988. I don't think they have very many false positives, you know, identifying someone as a Nazi when in fact they weren't. So if we take that on its face, the Nazi hunters..."

"Where are they from?" Priest asked, "and can we get in touch with them?"

"Yeah, but let me finish," she said with her hand held up for pause. "The Nazi hunters tracked him down and shot him, back in 1988 as I said. But the investigation at the time didn't say anything about who they were, individually I mean, although we know their organization. It's based in Berlin. They tracked Hillyer down and chased him, literally a running gun battle through the streets of Vienna. He was hit, mortally wounded, but the ruckus attracted the attention of the police. Before our guys could close in on the incident, the Nazi hunters had disappeared, leaving Hillyer bleeding on the sidewalk."

"Then what?" Priest asked.

"He was taken to the local hospital where he died of his wounds."

"Did anyone check the premise that he was a Nazi?" Aggie inquired.

"Yes, but it was hard to confirm," Alana noted. "Like I said, there's very little information about him in the record."

"Let's see, Hillyer co-signed for the safe deposit box with Emil Gutman in 1943," Priest tried to sum up the facts, "soon after which Gutman died under suspicious circumstances."

"Sounds like there has to be a connection between the safe deposit box and Gutman's death," suggested Aggie.

"Yeah," Alana added, "leaving only Hillyer in control of the materials stored there. And now we think that Hillyer was a Nazi."

"We know that we have some German writing among the photographs from the Paletti Notebook," Priest said. "Both Hillyer and Gutman sound German. It could be that one of them inserted those notes."

"Some of the German is straightforward," Alana commented. "I can translate that and help out."

"And the rest of it is encrypted in some kind of code that I don't recognize," said Priest. "That'll take a bit longer but we should probably get on it."

"Let's go back to the hospital for a moment. Did you find anything else about Hillyer's passing there? He died from gunshot wounds, but did you find anything else?"

"Only the names of his doctors. Oh, yeah, one more thing. He was visited by a priest in his last hours. A Father..." here Alana consulted her notes, "Father Andrew Noonan."

"Is he still alive?" asked Aggie.

"Yeah. Still living here in Vienna."

"So, we can talk to him?" Priest asked.

"I think so. I'll check with the precinct and find out where he is."

Leaving the café, Priest's phone chirped. He didn't recognize the number but figured out that it was Rome by the extension.

"*Buon giorno*," came a female voice. "It is Benedetta, Signor Priest."

He smiled, then suggested that she call him Darren. Even that degree of minor intimacy made him think of Alana, and he wondered if she would be put off by it.

"*Sì,* Darren. I have something for you. We traced the path of the Paletti Notebook to 1628 but that was all I had for you. At the time, anyway. Do you remember that I mentioned that popes continued to maintain an interest in the collection?"

"Yes, I do."

"Well, do you remember Clement XI?"

"Not specifically, although I just read some notes about him," he replied, referring mentally to the entries from the journal but not wanting to state this in the conversation with Benedetta.

"It turns out that Clement XI tried to bring the Notebook back to Rome."

"Did he succeed?"

"It doesn't look like it. I went through the inventory of Vatican treasures during that time – around 1701 – and although I'm not sure, there are no references to something that fits the description of the Paletti Notebook."

"How did he plan to do it?" asked Aggie, once Priest had turned the speaker on his phone. "Oh, sorry," he added, "this is Aggie, Aggie Darwin. We met yesterday and..."

"*Sì, signore,*" she replied, a smile coming through the telephone connection. "I remember."

Aggie continued, "Was it an overt attack, or a covert mission?"

Benedetta could be heard giggling on the other end of the line.

"*Signori*, I am but a simple museum curator, not an – what do you say, *espioneour*? – I don't know about these things. What I did was check the inventory under Clement – he was the pope from 1700 to 1721 – from just before the mission to Florence in 1701. There are changes, many changes – I have to tell you that it was not easy to walk through all these records."

"Yes, Benedetta," Priest cut in. "I know that, and I know that you have volunteered your valuable time to help us."

"Okay," she said, "okay. I looked at the Vatican inventories. It seems like something as important as the Paletti Notebook would stand out. Unless it was hidden, or unless it didn't really exist."

"So," Aggie inquired, "you didn't find it?"

"No, I didn't," Benedetta replied. "But I went a step further. If it remained in Florence in that year, 1701, it would have been an important part of someone's collection."

"Someone?" asked Priest.

"Yes, someone like a Medici."

"Were they still in charge of Florence at the time?" asked Aggie.

"Very definitely," she replied. "Cosimo III de' Medici, the next to last Grand Duke of Tuscany from the Medici line. I figured if I couldn't find evidence of this collection in the Vatican inventories, perhaps something would show up in Florence, in the Medici Library.

"He married Margherite Louise d'Orleans, a granddaughter of King Henry IV of France. The marriage was arranged and the ceremony was conducted in proxy, so neither Cosimo nor Margherite knew what they were getting into. It turns out that Margherite had expensive tastes and she demanded jewels from the Medici fortune and insisted that Cosimo treat her as visiting royalty rather than as his wife."

"Sounds like a wonderful start," said Aggie.

"Yes, well, it didn't go well. They had several separations, although in their brief times together they managed to produce three children."

"I'm sorry, what does this have to do with us?" Alana asked. She was curious but seemed to Priest as if she was also a bit put off by the long narrative prepared by the "very pretty woman."

"Okay, so here's where it gets interesting," Benedetta continued. "If the Paletti Notebook was in Florence, it would almost undoubtedly be in the possession of the Medici family. In this case, Cosimo III. And if Cosimo had a wife jealous of the family's treasures, he might have felt the need to hide if from her."

"Lots of 'ifs'," Priest chimed in, still showing his impatience.

"Yeah, sure, but here's where it is. Cosimo knew of his wife's extravagant ways and her eagerness to get at the Medici fortune, so he hid some things from her. His counselor suggested a secret room in the Medici palace, and he kept a secret inventory of all the things held there."

"Like what?" Priest asked.

"Lots of things, including jewelry, gold coins, contracts with other nations that would bring money into the coffers of the Medici bank – which was sorely needed in this time – and other things."

"And?" prodded Aggie.

"There is an entry in that book concerning a collection of ancient art. The entry claims credit for the Medici family for bringing these great artists to the city, but it also lists some of the things with specifics. Like 'sketch by Leonardo da Vinci of moving water,' 'head of the great sculpture David,' 'letters from the great and grand Niccolò Machiavelli'... and so on."

"And?" repeated Aggie.

"This secret list, of items kept in a secret vault in the Medici palace, includes this: 'A collection of early art by our masters, and a very early gospel not yet translated.'"

"Is there a date on this inventory?"

"Each entry has its own, and this one about the gospel is from 1705."

"So, despite Clement XI's attempts to take the Paletti Notebook back to Rome, he failed."

"Spectacularly," replied Benedetta.

"What's so spectacular about that?"

"Besides the subject of the inventory at the Medici palace, do you know what was happening in Florence in 1701?" she asked him.

"No," responded Priest.

"Most people think of that period in Florence as relatively calm," Benedetta continued. "A period when art and music prevailed. It turns out that it was also a time of great political upheaval in Italy – Tuscany, and Florence specifically."

"How does this matter to us, right now?" asked Aggie.

"Clement XI had launched a series of military campaigns across the peninsula, sometimes siding with the Spanish crown, sometimes with Austria. He also believed in destiny, and that as the Vicar of Christ he was destined to resolve conflicts far and wide.

"Well, he also determined that the Paletti Notebook would bestow authority and divine power on him. Which is pretty funny, in hindsight, since the Paletti Notebook was filled with heresy and blasphemy. In any case, Clement XI decided not just to invade Florence and take the Notebook, but to destroy the city if he wanted afterward, as a sign of his omnipotence."

"Did he?" asked Aggie.

"Yes, he laid siege, but no, he didn't destroy the city. In the end, the Medici family was too smart for him and managed to keep the Paletti Notebook far from view until after the Papal forces gave up on the mission."

"So, the Notebook was in Florence as of 1701," concluded

Aggie. "Now, all we have to do is find out where it went in the succeeding three hundred years."

"I think we need to go to Florence and look around," said Priest. Turning to Alana, he asked, "Alana, could you get Rafaela to help us with a private tour of the Medici library?"

"Sure."

FLORENCE 2021

MEDICI LIBRARY

April 9, 2021

"ALANA," PRIEST SAID, "BASED ON WHAT WE HEARD FROM Benedetta, it's possible that the Paletti Notebook is still in the Medici collection."

"In Florence?" she asked.

"Yeah. Don't know for sure, but she said that her records indicate that attempts to dislodge it from the Medici in 1701 were unsuccessful. That's why we need Rafaela's help."

"But don't we have evidence of Fra Nizza having it, or at least seeing it much later?"

"Yeah, and I'm tempted to pull that string, but we're still trying to find out how he got it, if in fact he actually had it. Tracing the path of the Notebook might help with that and might also confirm whether the collection stayed intact. There's a quick flight from here to Florence this afternoon. We'll be back tomorrow."

"Does Aggie have to go too?" she asked, and Priest laughed.

"He says he doesn't want to be left alone anymore."

"Sounds like a real tough guy. Okay, call me when you get there. I'll signal to Rafaela that you'll need her help."

"Tell her we'll arrive this evening but not go to the Medici library until tomorrow morning."

"Oh, so you've lowered your standards. It's not the Vatican Library; just the Medici collection."

"Ha, ha," he replied derisively.

"Any pretty girls there?" she asked, teasing him.

"I don't know yet," he said, picking up the theme, "but if your friend Rafaela is there, I'll be careful. She said she'd break my head if I broke your heart."

"Sounds good to me," Alana commented. Priest couldn't tell if she was joking.

In the cab from their hotel in Florence the next morning, Aggie and Priest tried to sum up.

"Okay," Aggie said, "we have to follow the trail left by Fra Nizza. Have you translated any more of his journal?"

"Yeah, I have. I did it while you were sleeping on the way back from Rome. Let me read the next passages to you."

"The last we heard," Aggie chimed in, "the Paletti Notebook was in Florence, in the possession of the Medici family, right?"

"Yep," said Priest. "Here you go."

I have traced the Paletti Notebook to Florence and, without truly knowing where it was – since this was not revealed in the records – I assumed it was safe, or at least concealed.

I discovered from my research that in 1701, Pope Clement XI sent forces to Florence to recover the collection. I don't know who he sent and if they were capable of such a mission, but the logs and records I've read indicate that the Notebook was kept from Clement's army and it remained in Florence under the watchful eye of the Medici family.

"I know that part," Aggie said. "We've already covered that."

They arrived at the Medici palazzo just as Priest's phone chirped.

"*Buon giorno*," Rafaela said. "You are in Florence, no?"

"Yes. We're pulling up to the Laurentian Medici Library on the Piazza San Lorenzo."

"*Perfetto*. Now, I want you to go inside and ask to speak with Signor Proprio Mostello. He's the curator there. I've spoken with him and he is aware of what you are looking for."

"How do you know what we're looking for, Rafaela?" asked Priest.

"Come on, my friend," she responded in a friendly, teasing voice. "You do not know that I know everything that goes on in my country?"

Priest was certain that she could not actually know everything. In this case, he assumed that Alana had briefed Rafaela and, given their close relationship, he began to worry that Alana had told her Italian friend too much.

"*Grazie*," he replied as they exited the taxi.

The palazzo, now serving as a museum, was built in the grand style of the Renaissance. The original designs came from Michelangelo but, following his departure from Florence in 1534, construction was carried out under the supervision of Vasari and other architects. Since that time, the palazzo has dominated the streets and surrounding neighborhood of that sector of the city.

Priest and Aggie walked up the few steps into the main entrance and were greeted by a uniformed but unarmed guard. Asking for Signor Mostello, they were directed to an inner office, where they were once again greeted at the doorway, this time by a young woman.

"Signor Mostello is waiting for you," she said in a pleasant but professional voice. "I will take you to him."

They were led down another hallway and up one flight of stone steps, well-worn from centuries of visitors. Passing through the door indicated by their escort, they saw a grey-haired man with reading glasses perched on the tip of his nose.

"Sir, excuse us," Priest began. "You are Signor Mostello?"

"Yes, I am. And you? Signor Priest?"

"Yes, and my colleague, Signor Aggie...no, actually, Arnold Darwin."

"Ah, yes," Mostello said with glee. "A descendant of the great scientist?"

"No," replied Aggie, sheepishly. "I wish."

"Signor Mostello," Priest intervened, "we are looking for evidence that a thing called the Paletti Notebook was – or perhaps still is – in the Medici collection. Here, in this museum."

"*Sì*," he said, nodding his head and pulling the reading glasses down from his nose to hang by the strap around his neck. "I know of this thing, but it is not real. Is it?"

"Well, we think it is, but we're also trying to find that out," Aggie answered.

Mostello thought for a moment, tapping the side arm of his glasses on his teeth.

"I know of it. I know the legend. And I believe that the story has it that the Medici owned it for a time. Long ago."

"Do you have records, inventories, or registers of the Medici library's contents?" asked Priest. "Possibly from around 1701?"

Mostello smiled broadly, proud of the collection entrusted to him.

"Most certainly we do. We have careful lists of everything that is stored here. Let's see, you are looking for...when?"

"Records from 1701."

"That's very specific," Mostello commented. "And why did you decide on that year?"

"In the Vatican Library we found reference to Pope Clement XI trying to get it – the Paletti Notebook, that is – from the Medici in Florence in 1701."

"Yes, I know about Clement's raid on our city at that time."

"Yes, so," Priest continued, "we have records that talk about his raid, and that he was unsuccessful. So, if he was trying to get the Paletti Notebook in 1701, and he didn't, we thought the inventory that you have charge of might indicate its presence here, at that time."

"I see," Mostello commented, thoughtfully. "Let's look at this."

Unlike the digitized records in the Vatican Apostolic Library, the records in Signor Mostello's collection were mostly paper. Priest assumed that digitizing of records would proceed as usual, but here – today – not so much.

Mostello opened the glass and wood door to a deep display case. Inside, on several shelves were leatherbound books with page edges that spoke of many years of use. He reached into one shelf and withdrew a large book, about six inches thick, twenty inches tall, and twelve inches across the front. With some effort, he moved it to the table in the middle of the room.

Once Mostello had settled it on the table, he lifted his reading glasses, perched them on his nose, and swung the thick cover to the left. Inside, the yellowed pages were covered with small and intricate lettering, three columns in all. The left-most column had a few words for each entry, a description of sorts; the second column had a year – Aggie saw in amazement that the hand-written entries began about 1640 – and the third column was blank, at least for most of the lines. Some names were inscribed about every ten lines, and made Priest think of the old-fashioned library card format where the borrower's name would be written into the ledger.

Mostello, using a long, thin wooden stick to point to each line – preventing his fingers from touching the paper – scrolled down the pages, turning them as he sought the year in question. On the fifth page, "1701" appeared in the second column. Priest wasn't sure if the date and the name entered beside it represented the person providing the document or the person removing it from the collection, but he would let that question pass for the moment.

Mostello's pointer moved slowly down the left-hand column of the "1701" entries, muttering aloud as he read the words written to label or describe the entry. After turning two more pages and encountering the first entry of "1702," he stopped. Straightening up, he turned to Priest and Aggie.

"There's nothing here that would suggest a notebook of art and letters," he explained. "Nothing with the name Paletti attached to it."

"Perhaps we have the year wrong, or perhaps it was entered before or after 1701," offered Priest.

Mostello smiled but looked a bit peeved at the thought that he would have to search longer and harder. Taking on a resigned look, he lifted the pages back several years until he encountered the first "1700," gave Priest a look of disappointment, then pointed his wooden stick back at the page beginning "1700" to initiate a new search.

Drawing the pointer down the page and muttering words to himself, Mostello quickly skimmed the lines on all "1700" pages. He skipped over those with "1701" and resumed his tedious search from 1702 through 1705.

"*Nulla*," he said. "Nothing."

"*Permesso*," Priest asked for permission, and lifted the page to return to 1704. "What does this say?" he asked, pointing to a word in the left-hand column that looked a lot like Paletti.

"Politti," responded Mostello. "It is the name of one of our governors, someone who served on the *Signoria* in that year."

Priest nodded, looked at Aggie, and shrugged his shoulders.

"So, then, nothing," he said reluctantly.

Mostello didn't respond or gesture. He just looked at Priest as if he wished this tedious exercise would be over.

"You've heard of the Paletti Notebook," Priest said. "Isn't that true?"

"*Sì, signore*," was the reply. "But it is probably only a rumor. You thought that this Notebook would be in Florence in this year, this 1701, with the Medici. But we cannot find it."

"What of Paletti, the man?" Aggie asked.

"The man?" responded Mostello. "What good is that?"

"Well, we'd like to establish, perhaps, even that he existed."

"There are stories of a monk, someone from San Marco many, many years ago. He was killed in the abbey, a gruesome story. The legend says that his name was Paletti. Perhaps that is who you are thinking of."

"Yes, perhaps," said Priest. "Is there a way to know even that much?"

"There is an old man here, in Florence," Mostello said, but then laughed. "Not as old as the time you want. Not as old as 1701!" he chortled. "But he was a monk back in the war. World War II. He was at San Marco. Maybe he knows something about the stories you've heard."

"What is his name?" Aggie asked.

"Falfani. He is very old. Alberto Falfani, I think. He is a regular at Rivoire ristorante, on the Piazza della Signoria. I would ask there."

Priest and Aggie thanked Mostello for his hospitality, excused themselves from the room, then descended the steps and exited the palazzo.

"That wasn't very helpful," Aggie noted.

"Yeah, sorta," said Priest. "But considering the thing we're looking for, and the secrecy that has always surrounded its existence..."

"You mean the myth of the Paletti Notebook?" asked Aggie, returning to doubting the entire enterprise.

"No, not a myth. I think it existed; in fact, I am more certain now than ever, considering everything we've found. It just wasn't in the Medici collection. Or, maybe, just not listed in the Medici collection."

They were heading toward the piazza in front of the Duomo, the common name for Florence's *grande dame*, the cathedral of Santa Maria del Fiore. After covering about two blocks, Priest tapped Aggie on the forearm, but didn't look at him.

"What?" whispered Aggie.

"I think we've got company."

"Where?" Aggie asked, scanning the vista in front of them.

"Not in front. In back. Don't look."

"How can I see what's in back of us, then? And how can you see?"

"It's an old habit. Wherever I walk, my eyes turn toward glass windows and doors. Any that are ajar allow me to pick up reflections of actions going on around me. I saw three guys walking about fifty feet behind us, not looking like tourists. And when we turned that corner back there, so did they."

"It must be painful to be a spook," said Aggie, and he had to fight the urge to look around. "What now?"

"Let's turn another corner and see if they follow."

They did so, but once they had turned ninety degrees, Aggie lost his will power and twisted his head around. Just as Priest reported, there were three guys intently staring at them, wearing loose clothing and sporting a bulge in their armpits.

And just as Aggie took that in, he was hit on the head with a powerful blow, one that came not from the threat he perceived behind them, but in front. Priest had resisted the urge to look around so he saw the frontal attack coming. Although one of the men was able to club Aggie, Priest executed a swinging motion with his leg that tripped up the attacker, buckling his knee and dropping the man to the ground. Another one shoved Aggie to the wall while a third man pushed a gun up into Priest's gut.

"Now," he muttered into Priest's ear, "this way," as he shoved Priest toward the street. In seconds, the men they spotted following them had caught up to the action and entered the fray. A gun flashed and one man collapsed on the sidewalk. Another club came out but Priest used the confusion to escape his captor then block the club with his forearm before it crashed into Aggie's skull. In the melee, the two groups of men fought each other, a skirmish that allowed Priest to drag Aggie out of harm's way. As he looked back over his shoulder, he saw the men from each side engaged in close-order combat. Another shot rang out, another man dropped to the ground, and Priest pushed Aggie through a doorway into a souvenir shop on the streetside.

"You alright?" he asked.

Aggie shook his head and looked like he had his bell rung, but recovered quickly.

"Yeah, I think so. Who was that? What was that?"

"I'm not sure of the three in front of us, but I saw some signs from our followers that convinced me that they're CIA."

"You mean they're on our side?" Aggie asked.

"I wouldn't be too sure of that. But they did save our asses. Come on. Let's get out of here."

Priest asked the proprietor if there was a back way out of the shop, and got a shaking, nervous finger pointing toward the back of the display case in response.

Although they had been diverted from their original path, Priest and Aggie made their way toward the Piazza della Signoria in hopes of finding Alberto Falfani. Once there, they had to ask for the Rivoire, but found it across the piazza from the Palazzo Vecchio. Having no idea who Alberto Falfani was, or what he looked like, they began asking the waiters.

"*Sì, signore. È lì,*" came the response as the waiter pointed toward a table under the awning. A very old man sat there with a very young woman. "That is Signor Falfani," said the waiter in heavily accented English.

Priest and Aggie walked toward the table, well out of the sun, and approached the man indicated. He was of average height, with short gray hair and a stubble of a beard. His clothes fit very loosely, as if they were old and had not kept up with the weight loss that comes with age. He was talking to the young woman by his side and looked up as Priest approached.

"*Mi scusi, signore. È Signor Alberto Falfani?*" Priest asked.

The old man looked at the woman seated next to him, and she patted him on the arm.

"*Sì,*" she responded for him. "He is Alberto Falfani. And who are you?"

"I am Darren Priest, and this is my colleague, Arnold Darwin."

"Why are you asking for my grandfather?" she replied.

"We visited Signor Proprio Mostello at the Medici library, and we had some questions that he said your grandfather might be able to answer."

She gave Priest a look of suspicion, but then replied.

"Before I let you ask him any questions," she said, "may I ask you one?"

"Yes, certainly."

"Why do you want to ask my grandfather questions?"

It seemed like a logical query, and Priest had to smile at her intuition. He explained that he and Aggie were searching for some lost art and were helping the Italian government to find it. That last was a bit of an exaggeration but Priest hoped that, if put to the test, Rafaela would back him.

"What kind of art?" she asked.

"Very old art," Aggie said.

"But our questions for Signor Falfani are tangential to that," Priest added.

"Tangential?" she said. "How?"

"The art we are looking for might have been at the abbey San Marco. And your grandfather here might know something about that."

The young woman translated Priest's comments for Falfani, and he raised his hand as if swatting away a fly.

"What did he say?" Aggie asked, but the woman only smiled.

"I don't think you want to know what he said. It was about San Marco, though."

Priest explained further what he was looking for, and whether the name Paletti meant anything to her grandfather. They were interested in a thing called the Paletti Notebook – even in English, this phrase brought a look of recognition to the old man's face – and anything he might know about the Paletti family.

She translated all this for Falfani and he looked directly at Priest when he answered. She translated his response.

"He says there have been stories of the Paletti family for a very long time. That, in fact, this very place, this Rivoire, sits on the property where once was the Paletti restaurant." She paused to let the old man continue his reply.

"He heard stories of the terrible things that happened in the abbey, including the murder of a monk centuries ago. Of the same name as Paletti."

"So, the Paletti family existed?" Aggie interjected, but Priest remained focused on the woman and her grandfather.

"*È stato ucciso!*" the old guy whispered. "He was murdered," she translated.

"What else does he know about this?" asked Priest.

The woman took over the conversation for her grandfather, telling Priest and Aggie that Signor Falfani had been a novice monk at San Marco during the war. He was only sixteen years old and hoped to take the robes of a monk. But the Nazis came and demanded that the monks in the abbey cooperate with them. The Nazis insisted that the abbey held some great treasure, some art, some letters that they intended to take with them. The young Alberto wanted to cooperate, but he knew nothing of this and could not give the Germans what they wanted. So they beat him, and tortured him. When the soldiers were convinced that he could not give them the treasure or any information about it, they left.

"He was scarred, in both body and soul," she said, patting her grandfather's arm. "He couldn't understand how God could create such monsters. So he left the abbey, foreswore his vows, and never returned."

"This place," she continued, "this place is where the Paletti restaurant used to be."

"What?" said Aggie incredulously. "You mean, here? Where we're standing?" He wasn't prepared to be confronted with such solid evidence of something they had sought so long to find.

"Yes, here," she said, pointing to the ground they stood on.

"*Nonno*," she said softly to Falfani. "*C'era un ristorante Paletti, non è vero?*"

"She asked if there was really a restaurant Paletti," Priest translated for Aggie.

"*Sì,*" the old man replied, pointing to the establishment behind him, the restaurant that served these sidewalk tables where he sat. "*Giusto qui,*" – "right here" – he continued, pointing to a corner of the building behind him. "*Giusto qui,*" he repeated pointing to the wall of the restaurant.

Aggie followed the direction he was pointing and stooped down to see what looked like an etching on the stone at the lower corner of the building.

"Holy shit, Darren! Check this out! I mean, holy shit!"

Priest went to Aggie's side and looked down at the stone forming the lowest corner of the building. Etched into that stone he could barely read worn letters spelling "Paletti" and below it, "1488."

VIENNA 2021

SISTERS OF MERCY HOSPITAL, VIENNA

April 9, 2021

Priest and Aggie flew back to Vienna and tried to piece together what they had found so far. Not the Paletti Notebook, since it wasn't in Florence, and not any more information to help them in their search for it. But one thing they did find: Evidence of the existence of a Paletti restaurant right where they were told it would be.

By the time they landed in Vienna, Alana was already on the phone with Priest to join in the conversation.

"So, the guy really lived," Aggie said, somewhat triumphantly.

"Yeah. Seems so," Priest acknowledged.

"Now what?" Alana asked.

"Doesn't seem like it's in Florence," Priest replied. "So, we go back to the scraps of photographs that we have and try to draw more inferences from it. I was working on this translation on the flight down to Florence, so let me run it by you."

They stepped into a taxi at the airport and on the way to the Marriott Parkring, Priest returned to the translation to read aloud to Aggie.

In 1797 there was a threat to all Italian treasures from outside our country, raids conducted by outsiders anxious to take possession of Italy's great heritage. In that year, the French commander Napoleon Bonaparte sent Jacques-Pierre Tinet out to other countries in search of great art to fill the rooms of the recently opened Louvre Museum.

Here, Priest paused, peering closely at the photo of that page of Nizza's journal.

"I'm having a lot of trouble here. Nizza's manner of writing is like a cross between the penmanship common in Italy – and not common in the States – and something else."

"It looks 'monkish,'" Aggie offered, peering closely at the page.

"What's 'monkish?'" asked Priest.

"Young men entering the order as novitiates came from many backgrounds. There were certainly a few outcasts from wealthy families, those who had been driven to the life to atone for perceived sins, and there were many who were uneducated and poor. The peasant class. Reading and writing were considered a service to God so, to even the playing field, all novitiates were trained in an abbey-specific way regardless of their background. Nizza's writing seems to be like that. The penmanship in his order was highly stylistic which makes it harder for you to get into it."

Aggie looked out the window as the cityscape of Vienna came into view, dominated by the spire of Stephansdom, the cathedral at the center of the old city named for St. Stephen. Priest focused on Nizza's journal and suddenly lit up with a chuckle.

"Wish we had seen this before," he said. He called Alana for her to hear, then proceeded to read aloud.

Tinet spent most of his time in Italy, including Perugia, Rome, Venice, and Florence. When he arrived in that latter city, he found fabulous works of art that the French confiscated. He was also able to uncover the legendary Paletti Notebook and bring it back to Paris with him.

"Wait a minute," said Aggie. "So the Notebook was in Florence."

"At least in 1797."

"But the Medici records didn't reveal that."

"No," Priest concurred. "But Nizza is telling us that it was there, and that this guy Tinet pinched it for the Louvre Museum."

"That's the first record we have of the Paletti Notebook leaving Florence," Aggie said to summarize the status, "at least after it had been returned there by Vittorio Sensa on the pope's orders."

"Hold it," Alana said. She was still on the phone with them but switched to check an incoming message on her phone. "I have something on that Father Noonan, the guy who gave Hillyer last rites. He is still living here, in Vienna, although he suffers from late-stage cancer. He's being treated in the Sisters of Mercy Hospital here in the city."

"Aggie," Priest said turning to his friend, "how about you join me in visiting Father Noonan?"

"I don't know. Are there going to be any guys with clubs and guns?"

"Don't know," Priest chuckled. "Alana, could you pursue that lead on the 1797 thing with the Louvre. If the Paletti Notebook ended up in Paris, they may have records. That is, if they're willing to reveal them."

"Sure," she replied. "I'll check with Clarice Bonnet. She's an assistant curator at the museum. If I'm not mistaken, she specialized in the international art market, making waves when she wrote her dissertation about the confiscation of art from other countries by European powers."

"Great," Priest said. "Sir," he said, addressing the cab driver. "Change of plans. Please take us to the Sisters of Mercy Hospital."

Priest and Aggie arrived at the hospital on Stumpergasse and walked through the doors to the visiting area. They had no badges to display but Alana had called ahead and used her authority to get them easy access. They asked to see a patient named Andrew Noonan.

"He's a priest," Aggie added helpfully, although that didn't seem to impress the nurse at the check-in desk. She called to a colleague behind her and told the woman to escort the men to Father Noonan's room.

Up the elevator and down the hallway, then the escort stopped at a particular room. She pushed the door open a bit to admit them, then left them alone in the room.

Priest noticed that it was a private room, which would help in questioning him. He saw wires and tubes connected to the gray-haired patient who breathed through an oxygen mask. Approaching the bed, he spoke softly.

"Father Noonan," Priest said softly. There was no response.

"Father Noonan," he repeated with a little greater volume, and the patient opened his eyes.

"Father," Priest said, "we would like to ask you a few questions. Is that alright?"

The patient nodded.

"Did you know a man named Ira Hillyer?" Priest asked.

Noonan did not reply. He did not nod his head or give any sign of recognition. And his head rolled back away from Priest.

"Did you perform last rites for a man, back in 1988, by the name of Ira Hillyer? We understand that he had been chased down by Nazi hunters and was shot in the streets of Vienna."

Still no reaction from Noonan, although he did turn his head back to look at his visitors.

"We understand that you heard this man's confession and gave him last rites. We have reason to believe that not only was he a Nazi officer, but that he possessed a collection of letters that are extremely important. Documents that we must find to avoid further injustice, injury to innocent people, and tragedy. So, let me repeat, did you hear Ira Hillyer's confession?"

No response from Noonan.

"If you did," Priest continued, "and if you can tell us something about the man, many lives may be saved."

Noonan just looked on impassively. It was clear that he was listening to Priest and he seemed to understand what was being said, but he offered no reply.

Priest and Aggie tried some other lines of questioning but got nowhere with Noonan. At a certain point, they decided that pursuing this interview would yield nothing, so they said goodbye to the man, promised to come again and check on his health, and then left the room.

———

After Priest and Aggie were gone, Father Noonan stared at the ceiling. His eyes were wide open, he was fully conscious, and he was recalling the moments he had spent with Ira Hillyer so many years ago. He had heard many confessions and dealt with the sinful thoughts and acts of so many of his congregation, but what Hillyer told him stood out plainly. Noonan would never forget.

Hillyer, on his deathbed, confessed to being an officer in the German army during World War II. His real name was Karl Hilgendorf and, although he had not participated in the atrocities involving the gas chambers and deaths of millions of Jews, he had stolen many things from countries that the Germans conquered. He confessed to mistreating many women while using the powers of an occupying army, and he confessed to taking many secret collections of art and letters from the Italian people.

What struck Father Noonan the most was the description that Hillyer/Hilgendorf gave of a particular collection. He said it included sketches, drawings, and engineering designs from the men in Florence around 1500, men like Leonardo da Vinci, Michelangelo, and Raphael. The collection also had letters from Cesare Borgia and Niccolò Machiavelli, prayer papers from the heretic Savonarola, and other things. If true, Noonan was quite certain, the treasure that Hilgendorf stole would be worth more than any collection ever found.

And that was not all. Hillyer, in his confession, admitted to keeping an ancient papyrus manuscript. It was on brittle paper and written in a foreign tongue with picture words and hieroglyphs. Hillyer was told by the man who gave it to him, someone named Gutman – a man that Hillyer also confessed to killing – that these words were in Coptic, an ancient Egyptian language and that the documents were probably the only surviving copy of the lost Gospel of Matthias.

"Where is it?" asked Noonan when he spoke to Hillyer back in 1988.

"I have it hidden," came the reply.

"If I am to absolve you of these sins, you must make reparations. And the first step in reparations is to undo the sin, return the stolen goods, and prostrate yourself before the Lord our God asking for forgiveness."

"I don't know how much of that I can accomplish," Hillyer said, seeming to doubt his own remorse, "but I can deliver the stolen goods to you to dispose of as you wish." His words came through coughing and whispered breath.

Noonan leaned in to hear Hillyer's words more clearly. The dying man revealed the location of the collection of art and the Gospel of Matthias, and he then fell instantly into a deep sleep, induced no doubt by a combination of drugs and the deterioration of his health.

The priest left him that way and walked out of the room, his head filled with thoughts of the terrible things that a German officer might have done during the war, but also with the wonder of things that might be found in the treasure that Hillyer had just divulged to him.

PARIS 1797

PARIS

1797

NAPOLEONE DI BUONAPARTE WAS BORN ON THE ISLAND OF Corsica to Italian parents, Carlo Buonaparte and Letizia Ramolino who themselves were descended from minor Italian nobility. Although of Italian extraction, his history lists him as French and it was in France that he made his mark on the world.

In 1797, Napoleon was in the middle of his ascent to power in France. At the young age of twenty-eight, he had already distinguished himself during the French Revolution, saved the ruling French Directory from royalist insurgents in 1795 and, in 1796, became a national hero for a string of resounding military victories against Austrian and Italian forces.

Assigned to lead the Italian campaign just days after his marriage to Désirée Clary, he had another boost in stature by subduing the armies of the Piedmont and bringing them under the control of the French government. And it was in Italy that he developed a fondness for the art of the country, commissioning various officers in his command to bring back treasures for his own collection or for the glory of France.

The Louvre Palace was originally built in the late 12th century as a defensive castle for Philip II but urban development reduced its role as a fortified structure. In 1546, it became the royal residence of French kings until 1682 when that distinction passed to the Palace of Versailles. When Louis XIV moved his household to Versailles, he left the royal collection of art at the Louvre. That collection continued to grow until, in 1793, it was declared a formal museum based in large part on confiscated art and sculpture that French leaders had brought to Paris from their conquests abroad.

Soon after the opening of the newly christened Louvre Museum, Napoleon decided to take advantage of his assignment in Italy to seek out great works of art to fill the museum's sprawling rooms left empty by the departure of the royal family. Although a large contingent of art experts intended to supervise confiscation of the art, Napoleon had ideas of his own and followed leads for art not included on the lists supplied by the experts.

Advisors had long told him of ancient treasures, among them the rumored Paletti Notebook. Napoleon was told that it was a collection of the greatest art from the masters of the Renaissance. Considering the great art already possessed by the French government, he doubted the "one-and-only" nature of the legend, but he was intrigued by the stories.

Jacques-Pierre Tinet was one of Napoleon's closest art advisors. He served not only in the capacity of art critic but also as an art historian, astute at identifying great works but also knowledgeable of the history and provenance of the works he studied.

"Are the stories of this Paletti fellow true?" Napoleon asked his art advisor.

"*Oui, monsieur*," Tinet responded, "or so I think. There is every reason to believe the legend, as there have been stories told of its existence and the struggle to possess it for nearly three hundred years."

"But," Napoleon pressed, "do you believe it exists?"

"*Oui*," Tinet said flatly, but he went on to remind Napoleon that the thing called the Paletti Notebook contained not finished work, but drafts. They were drafts of the most prized paintings and sculptures ever created but, still only drafts.

"And the Gospel? The one by the man called Matthias?"

"We should have to see, my lord. I would have to find it and bring it home to you. Then we will know."

"Yes," Napoleon mused, stroking his chin.

"Even having these first drafts would be miraculous," Tinet told him. "Great works that hang in your museum are fine, but sketches and drawings by the masters would be more instructive. And more precious."

Napoleon decided that he should send Tinet throughout Italy in search of art treasures but instructed him to focus on the places where he might find the Paletti Notebook.

That instruction sent Tinet to Florence.

At that time, the Medici family still resided in Florence but had fallen from power. Nevertheless, they were known to possess great art treasures and Tinet knew that the forebears of the Medici clan were responsible for bringing the great artists and thinkers to the city throughout the 15th and 16th centuries.

Tinet met with the Medici patriarch at the time and queried him about the art and historical collections that the family still held. The two enjoyed a long meal of exquisite food and wine while performing a delicate dance around the real subject.

Who would possess the great art of this Medieval family?

Tinet knew that his assignment from Napoleon would brook no failure, and he prodded his host to find out what they had and how he might come into possession of it.

"What would it take," Tinet asked, "for example, if I asked you to give me the Paletti Notebook?"

The four Medici family members who sat at the dinner table with the Frenchman were dumbstruck. The legend surrounding that collection was long-told, but its actual existence had been debated for centuries. That Tinet would think they held it was a stretch, but Tinet's bluff hit pay dirt. The Medici knew that the Paletti Notebook was in their collection and they also knew that the French were conquering forces with the power and wherewithal to confiscate it.

They recognized the weakness of their position and opened the discussion up to a bargain. In exchange for a small sum of money – something that the occupying army of France was not required to do – the Medici family released the Paletti Notebook to Tinet and agreed to not interfere with his taking it back to Paris.

Tinet brought the Paletti Notebook back to Paris, complete with the artwork and sketches of Leonardo da Vinci and his fellow artists, the political writings of Machiavelli and Borgia, and the rants of the excommunicated heretic Girolamo Savonarola. Included in the collection was an undecipherable text written in pictographs, swirls and lines that Tinet couldn't read. He kept it with the Notebook collection but, otherwise, ignored it.

The Paletti collection was introduced to the Louvre Museum but since it did not contain finished art, the curator at the time sent it to storage in the museum's work rooms, thinking that his attention was needed elsewhere.

"I'll look at this odd collection later, when I have time," he said.

The Paletti Notebook remained in the back rooms and storage of the Louvre for many years, untouched by curator's hands and unseen by visitors to the museum.

PARIS 1871

PARIS

April 4, 1871

GIUSEPPE GARIBALDI SEEMED TO HAVE A NOSE FOR TROUBLE. As a young man, he supported a form of Italian republicanism and joined his mentor Giuseppe Mazzini in calling for the unification of nation states across the historic borders of Italy. Some of his incentive to push for unification involved liberation from Austrian control, a resistance to outside influence that he preached throughout his life.

When he led a failed insurrection in the north, he was sentenced to death but fled to Marseille, and then on to South America. Not content with idling sitting out his exile, he joined the resistance in opposing Brazil's claim to power. His marriage to Ana Maria de Jesus Ribeiro da Silva seemed to have tamed Garibaldi's wanderlust, at least for a time, but he kept an eye on political struggles in his homeland from that vantage point.

After returning to Italy, he was once more chased abroad by the government of Piedmont and he landed in the United States. It was the Second War for Italian Independence in 1859 when he decided to follow his instincts for rebellion once again and return to Italy.

In 1860, Giuseppe Garibaldi led his Expedition of the Thousand into Sicily to conquer the ruling power there, the Kingdom of the Two Sicilies. They were successful, having marched across the massive island and the event set up the creation of the Kingdom of Italy in March 1861.

As monumental as this feat was, Garibaldi remained unsatisfied with the status of society in other countries that he had visited. He wanted to evangelize, to change the order of politics, and he wouldn't rest with just making changes in Italy. He had broader ambitions.

Garibaldi had long considered the collection of city states in Italy to be strongest if they formed a united front against the world. "Look at the Etruscans," he told people, "when they formed the Etruscan League. And the city states of Greece when they confronted the world beyond their islands." He pushed the regions of Italy to form a republic, a union of states that would stand against the world.

And Garibaldi took stock of the magnificent culture created by the Romans and Italians over the centuries to make his point of Italian exceptionalism – the political and governmental functions, the literature, and the art. Italy was the greatest of all the great, he believed, and he would not countenance discussion of another version of history.

So, it was with this confidence that he wanted to bring everything that was handsome and historic in Italian culture together. Garibaldi considered the Renaissance – started on Italian soil, of course, but centered in Florence – to be the greatest gift of art ever for mankind. And he knew of a way to prove it.

He had heard rumors of a thing called the Paletti Notebook, a collection of great art from the greatest men to have ever lived. The Notebook contained their designs, sketches, and some final renditions, all created in the early days of the Renaissance and born of the genius of Florence. With such a legendary collection to be had, he wanted it for Italy. According to the story, the Paletti Notebook had other pieces, both political and religious, but he didn't care about those. He was focused on the art that would be found in it, and he wanted it for the Italian people.

In 1871, Garibaldi was in Paris, a member of the Paris Commune, a revolutionary government that reflected his philosophy for a united world. He knew that the Notebook had been stolen from Florence in 1797 by the very nation that Garibaldi now supported, France. The French administrators had contrived to gain possession of the Paletti collection during Napoleon's attack on Italy, and the spoils of Napoleon's crusade had ended up in the Louvre Museum. Of that, he was fairly sure, having read the diary of a man named Jacques-Pierre Tinet from that period.

Garibalddi planned to use his influence in that position to find the Paletti Notebook and bring it to Rome where he intended to serve as one of united Italy's first leaders, so he sent a small squad of his supporters to the Louvre Museum to inquire as to the possibility that such a thing exists.

"Signor Alisotti," he said to his assistant. "Go and speak with our French friends at the Louvre. I want you to ask them about a collection of art that is known by the name Paletti Notebook. See if they have heard of it."

"Yes, of course," Alisotti replied, "but how would we know when we have found it?"

Garibaldi described the contents of the Paletti Notebook as he had heard of it and sent Alisotti off to bring it to Rome. While Garibaldi entertained his pro-French guests in the Paris Commune, Alisotti was meeting with the curators at the museum. At first, the French custodians of the art were reluctant to talk to him and avoided many of his questions. After three visits, however, Alisotti gained enough information to at least suspect that the Paletti Notebook was there, in the back rooms in the basement of the museum.

"Have you seen it?" queried Garibaldi.

"No, I have not, but the French were not smart enough to hide their pride behind their lies. When I asked if they had very much Italian art, they laughed. When I asked if some of it might be from Florence, they laughed again.

" 'How old is the art?' I asked them. And then they fell for my contrivance. They bragged that their Florentine art was over three hundred years old. 'From 1500,' one of them boasted."

"And they took you to see it?" asked Garibaldi, repeating his earlier question.

"No, as I have said," repeated Alisotti. "But I know where they keep this old art and I plan to return to get it from them. How can I do it, Generalissimo Garibaldi? Do we have some special authority, some special power?"

"Yes, we do," responded Garibaldi as he lifted a heavy pistol from the table and handed it to Alisotti. "This is our special authority, our special power. Now, go find the Paletti Notebook and bring it to me."

Alisotti did as he was instructed. The next day he revisited the Louvre and asked to see the same custodian of art. When he asked the man if he could see the rooms where they stored the old art, he was rebuffed. He produced the weapon from the pocket of his overcoat and pointed it at the head of the man, demanding obedience.

"That is," Alisotti clarified, "if you want to see your family tonight."

The storage room of the Louvre was crowded with paintings, sculpture, and other art. Alisotti assumed most of it was stolen, an assumption he repeated to himself several times to relieve his conscience of the next sin he planned to commit.

He went through the piles, pulling stretched canvas aside one by one, peering into large boxes of vases and porcelain, and moving crates filled with heads, arms, and bases of sculpture that had once enjoyed full bodies to attach to.

Alisotti found a fat leather folder at the bottom of a stack of paintings and brought it to the table in the center of the room. Just as Garibaldi had predicted, the contents of the folio revealed themselves to be the lost art of the early Renaissance. Sketches by the great men, letters by heretics and politicians, and a soft bundle of fragile papyrus wrapped in cloth and tied with a string.

"I will report back to my leader, Generalissimo Giuseppe Garibaldi, and I will bring this back to show him."

"But, no, I am sorry, *monsieur*, you cannot take anything from this room."

"Yes," Alisotti replied, pointing the gun at the man's head once again, "yes, I can."

And with that, he exited the Louvre Museum with the Paletti Notebook tucked under his arm.

After showing it to Garibaldi, Alisotti was instructed to return at once to Rome, and bring the Paletti Notebook with him.

VIENNA 2021

JULIUS MEINL GROCERY, VIENNA

April 9, 2021

Priest was anxious to reconnect with Alana and bring her up to speed on what they got from Noonan. Aggie was hungry. So they agreed to meet for lunch at the upscale grocer and deli Julius Meinl. After meandering the deli counters and colorful displays at Julius Meinl, they choose an assortment of appetizers and sandwiches, then relocated to the picnic tables in front of the store to enjoy the sunny weather.

Priest explained what little they had gotten from the interview with Noonan, and then launched into a translation that he hadn't even told Aggie about yet.

"I worked on this part of Fra Nizza's journal this morning before going to the hospital. I'm not sure what it means and whether it has much to do with the current location of the Paletti Notebook, but I thought I should read it to you."

> *Thanks to Benito Mussolini's mistress, Margherita Sarfatti, the Notebook didn't remain in Rome. Signora Sarfatti, a Jewish journalist and art critic, was familiar with the legend of the Paletti Notebook. She had never seen it and was reluctant to raise the point with* Il Duce, *but as the Nazi scourge spread across Europe, she became nervous about her own safety.*

When Mussolini joined Hitler's plan to exterminate the European Jews by publishing "The Manifesto of Race," Sarfatti concluded that she could no longer remain in Italy. Knowing that she had to disguise her intentions, she used her profession in art journalism to convince Mussolini that she needed to see the Paletti Notebook herself. He allowed that, which gave her a degree of freedom. But he didn't anticipate that she would take the collection and escape from Rome with it in her possession. She took the collection to the Abbey at Sant'Antimo outside of Montalcino but had to leave it there as she hurried out of the country. She settled in Argentina and was never heard from again.

That was when I came into possession of the Paletti Notebook.

"Aha!" exclaimed Aggie, to the subtle cheers of Priest. "That's how Nizza found it."

"Yeah, so we have closed the loop. He came to have the Notebook around 1938..." said Priest.

"Yeah, sure," interjected Aggie, "that tracks with the beginning of his journal. Remember, he said that at the very top."

"Right."

"And, thanks to this Margherita gal," Aggie said, "we can assume that the Notebook left Rome and ended up in Sant'Antimo, exactly as Nizza described it.

"Seems that way," said Priest. "I guess we need to pay a visit to the abbey."

"You think anybody will talk to us?" asked Alana.

"Well," Priest added with a smile, "that's up to you and your friend Rafaela, isn't it?"

ROME 1938

ROME

September 11, 1938

"DARLING," SAID MARGHERITA AS SHE PULLED THE STRAP OF her satin slip over her shoulder, "I trust that you will take care of me and my daughter, no matter what your wife says."

He leered at her as he sat on the foot of the bed, pulling his knee-high black boots on.

"Of course, I will," but the curl of his lips left her doubting his promise.

Benito Mussolini was dressing for combat, the kind of combat he knew best. Not the kind that involved guns and cannon, but the rhetorical one that pitted his wit and dynamism against other politicians who thought they could thwart his ambitions. He would be addressing another of the crowds that filled the squares to hear him speak, this time in the Piazza Barberini, and when he was done destroying his opponents with words, he would turn to his assistants and instruct them to find more permanent ways to destroy those who would question his rise to power.

Mussolini had spent years building the myth of *Il Duce*, occasionally infusing an otherwise impressive life story with fictional accounts that convinced the Italian people that he was destined to lead them. Biographers were even fooled initially by the grandiose stories he told of his early life, but later came to know the real story behind him.

He rose to power in the 1920s in part on the power of his oratory, giving fiery speeches to the gathered crowds who became enamored of him. His huge barrel chest, large jutting chin, and serious demeanor provided the image of a trailblazer, one the people were attracted to and whom they could trust.

Mussolini pushed nationalism and a return of the Italian culture to the center of attention in the world. He knew that proving Italy's exceptionalism in arts and history would be the best route to success and domination. Fascism rose to prominence in part due to his leadership, but also as an accident of timing. With Hitler's government pushing a xenophobic agenda, the tenets of Fascism – and the propaganda of Mussolini – fit right in.

He became the dictator of Italy in 1925 and, in parallel with the militaristic plan, he focused his attention on culture – arts, literature, cinema, and architecture – as symbols of Italy's greatness. The fact that he developed a close relationship with Margherita Sarfatti, an art critic and journalist, was a natural outgrowth of his attention to these matters. The fact that she was a Jew didn't dissuade him from taking her as his mistress, a not-well-hidden relationship that survived both of Mussolini's marriages.

Il Duce allied with Hitler and adopted many of the German's beliefs, except for one: Mussolini didn't believe initially in the inferiority of the Jewish people and resisted calls by Hitler for the elimination of that race. For this reason, Margherita felt safe with him, although she converted to Catholicism in 1926 as a back-up plan.

When Mussolini moved to his new residence at Villa Torlona in Rome that year, Margherita moved to a house on Via Rasella to be closer to him. She brought her daughter Fiammetta with her and trusted that her relationship with Italy's leader would protect both of them.

That was until July 14, 1938, when Mussolini published "The Manifesto of the Race" in *Il Giornale d'Italia,* his first public pronouncements concerning the Jewish people in which he condemned the intermarriage of the Jews with the Italian Aryan race. At first, Margherita viewed that as merely a government statement of prohibition, but she harbored fears that Mussolini would transform into a near-Hitler-like leader. She had heard stories of the atrocities in Germany and Poland already, and rumors of Hitler's plans for extermination, and any hint that her lover might follow the same path would be extremely dangerous for her.

"Yes, I'm sure you will," she said, putting an affirmative response to her question in Mussolini's mouth.

Still, she feared for her safety and knew how Mussolini had dispatched others who questioned him, so Margherita decided to develop a plan that would allay his suspicions but still allow her to get out of Rome. As an art critic and journalist, she told him that she wanted to search the environs of Rome for the rumored Paletti Notebook then present it to him as a gift, a unique cultural treasure that would fit right in with his plan to place Italian art at the center of everyone's attention.

He liked the plan and approved it, but this approach would also give her more freedom of movement. She knew stories of the Notebook had circulated for centuries and also believed that they led to Rome. Not certain where to look, Margherita had already spent months on her own under the auspices of her professional role as an art historian and so she narrowed the list of places that it might be. With Mussolini's approval of her plan, she had the added authority to search throughout private homes, collections, churches, and museums.

Margherita had failed to find the Notebook at several places so far, and next on the list was the Basilica di Santa Croce, the Basilica of the Holy Cross.

"This is not the most important thing we have," said the hunch-backed priest as Margherita accompanied him around the nave of the church. With a bent arthritic finger the old priest pointed toward a small chapel by the side and, taking Margherita by the hand, walked slowly toward it.

"Here," he said, "we have thorns from Jesus's crucifixion crown, a nail that was driven into Our Lord's feet, and here," he pointed with pride and admiration, "are pieces of the True Cross."

Margherita studied the relics for several moments, impressed but not moved by them. Then she returned to her question.

"I am looking for a collection of art, a leather satchel, very old," she said slowly, using her hands to denote the size of the Notebook that she was searching for. "It would contain old drawings and letters, and possibly something much older. On papyrus."

The priest smiled but didn't quite understand. He nodded his head but Margherita could tell that he didn't recognize the thing she was looking for.

"We have other relics here, too, *signora*," and he took her arm again to show her other reliquaries in the church.

"Thank you," she said, "but I am looking for something else. Something with great value to the leader of Rome, Signor Mussolini."

This made a momentary impression on the old priest but as a man of the cloth he didn't remain interested very long in anything that *Il Duce* would want.

"Do you know who Paletti is?" she asked.

"Oh, yes," the priest said brightening up. "The artist!"

"No, he wasn't an artist. But he collected art. Do you know his name?"

"Yes, but certainly he was an artist. We have some of his work right here!"

The priest led Margherita around the pews and chapels of the basilica, occasionally pointing out paintings that he attributed to Paletti, but with Margherita's knowledge of art she quickly dismissed his assertions in every case.

Shaking her head, she identified the true artist for each of these works, which discouraged the priest and he seemed close to giving up. Then he pointed one index finger in the air.

"I have it!" he said gleefully. Then he took Margherita by the hand once again and led her past the nave of the church to a small door at the far wall. They went through that door and descended a winding stone staircase. At one point, he reached up the wall in the darkened space and turned a switch up as lights illuminated in the pathway ahead of them.

At the bottom of the steps, he asked her to wait just a moment. He went to a cabinet set against the wall, raised the wooden lid, and extracted a key, then approached the door where he had Margherita waiting.

She laughed to herself at that.

"Why have a key if you keep it in such an obvious place?" she asked him.

"No one would care what we have down here," he responded with a smile.

The priest opened the door, then raised his hand to a round knob on the wall, twisting it clockwise and pausing a moment until the timer began ticking as expected. With that, the lights in the room turned on and Margherita could see that the room was filled with chests, trunks, books piled up on one another, and random boxes.

Her escort picked up one leatherbound folder, brushed off some dust from its surface and turned toward her.

"Here is the artist, Paletti," he said.

Margherita's heart skipped a beat. She gingerly took the folder from him and looked for a tabletop to lay it on. When she had done so, she unbuckled the strap, pulled back the flap, and pulled out a stack of papers inside it. Her eyes went wide as she saw drawings and sketches, unmistakably the work of Leonardo da Vinci. She saw a draft of a head, one which looked remarkably like the capstone of Michelangelo's famous *David* sculpture. There were letters with "Ces. Borgia." inscribed at the bottom, and neatly drawn lines of prose that read like portions of Machiavelli's *Il Principe – The Prince.*

Margherita knew that she held the Paletti Notebook in her hands, a centuries-old collection of the greatest artists and thinkers of the Renaissance. But there was one more part of the legend that she had to check.

Reaching inside the leather folio, she felt a cloth-covered bundle tied with a string. Pulling it out onto the table, she untied the string and let the cloth wrapping fall away. It was in a language that she couldn't understand but her training convinced her that it was Coptic verse.

"This must be the lost Gospel of Matthias," she whispered to herself. She kept her voice low but also spoke in English so that the priest wouldn't understand what she had found.

She reassembled the contents of the Paletti Notebook and rebuckled the strap holding it closed.

"*Il Duce* must have this," she said to convince the priest of her authority and power over such things. She didn't intend to give it to Mussolini, but she also knew the priest would never report it to the government. Instead, she would spirit this collection out of Rome and hide it on her way out of the country.

VIENNA 1988

HILLYER'S APARTMENT

April 9, 1988

Father Andrew Noonan had just heard the confession of a dying man, whose name was either Ira Hillyer or Karl Hilgendorf, depending on which story he believed. Hillyer was in the hospital suffering from gunshot wounds administered to him by a street gang in Vienna. Noonan wasn't convinced that this was a random shooting, but that's the story Hillyer was telling.

"We don't shoot people on the street," Noonan said emphatically.

"Not without cause," wheezed Hillyer. "They may think that they had a right to kill me and, perhaps, in the eyes of God, they did."

Noonan shook this off, not wanting to give any kind of approval to shooting. But he detected a note of remorse in the voice of his patient, this Ira Hillyer who had called for him to hear his confession and provide absolution for his sins.

Noonan had done as he was asked, listening with pain in his heart as the patient unburdened himself, telling tales of his service as a German officer during the war, of his killing people, taking women against their will, and stealing works of art from the Italian people, all by the authority of the Third Reich.

Noonan made the sign of the cross, blessed Hillyer and

commanded him to say a list of prayers as his penance for confessed sins. The priest hesitated asking whether Hillyer felt remorse; he had learned from past confessions that many of the Nazi officers resisted that question.

As for the last, and most egregious sin that Hillyer confessed – greater than the sin of changing his name from Karl Hilgendorf to hide from the authorities and escape prosecution – Noonan heard the dying man's description of a collection of art unlike anything he had ever imagined. Sketches, drawings, letters – all worth millions, all precious pieces of art history, all from the Renaissance in Italy – all still within Hillyer's control and possession. This last great thing startled Noonan and induced him to make the sign of the cross on his own chest as he heard Hillyer recount it.

"It is the lost Gospel of Matthias," said Hillyer. "Of that I am sure. I have studied it and the history of it, and I know now that this Coptic gospel is from Matthias, a first century man who befriended Jesus and wrote about His life in intimate detail."

Noonan had heard rumblings of such a thing throughout his priesthood, often told in terms of the heresies of the author, but he doubted the truth of the stories. Here, before him now, was a man confessing his sins on his deathbed, saying he not only has seen the Gospel of Matthias, but he has a copy of it, perhaps the only copy in existence.

The priest left Hillyer when the patient fell asleep. He had received clear instructions from the man as to the location of this great collection that he had described, and Noonan wanted to go to the place and see if what Hillyer described was really there.

Entering through the lobby of Hillyer's apartment building, the priest pulled back the collar of his coat to reveal to the desk attendant the stole he wore around his neck when performing the rites of the Church. Nodding to Noonan, the desk clerk let him in.

"Do you know where you are going, Father?" asked the clerk.

"Yes, I do," he said curtly, keeping the key that Hillyer had given him in his enclosed hand.

Noonan proceeded to the staircase and ascended the two floors to where Hillyer said he lived. Apartment 33 was there, just off the stairs, and the priest turned toward the door, looking over his shoulder to see if anyone was watching. Seeing no one in the hallway at that time, he quickly pushed the metal key into the lock and pushed the door inward.

It was a simple apartment, sparse furniture not unlike Noonan's own residence in the refectory. Single men tended to live with few embellishments in their quarters. He walked directly to a wall that fit the description given him by Hillyer and examined it for markings, trying to uncover any suggestion of a hidden area. Finding none, Noonan sat down on the chair facing the wall and considered what to do next.

VIENNA 2021

CASCADE BAR, VIENNA

April 9, 2021

"NOT A LOT OF HELP," SAID AGGIE.

He and Priest found a seat at the Cascade Bar after the interview with Father Noonan. Aggie ordered a beer; Priest a glass of red Bordeaux.

"No, really not," Priest replied. "What did we get from it? Noonan heard the guy's confession... of that, I'm pretty sure."

"Growing up Catholic," Aggie said with a smirk, "I can tell you that the priests will not talk about someone else's confession."

"So, if Noonan talked to Hillyer – and remember, we think that Hillyer had the Notebook and killed Gutman for it..."

"Wait," said Aggie, holding up his hand. "How did you get there? We were told that Gutman died suspiciously, but..."

"And that it happened not long after he and Hillyer had taken out a safe deposit box at DFR Wien."

"Okay," Aggie said nodding, "I get your point.

"So, if Hillyer killed Gutman," Aggie continued, "probably to take sole control of the safe box and its contents, then he – Hillyer – was gunned down by Nazi hunters and confessed to Father Noonan, isn't the priest our only way to connect the dots?"

"Yeah, I think so."

Priest's phone chirped and he saw it was Alana's name on the screen. Ever since the talk earlier in the day, he found conversing with her a little easier, so he quickly poked the receive button.

"Hey, Alana. What's going on?"

"If you mean, am I over it, no," she said, just to remind Priest not to take things too casually. "But, yes, Darren, we're okay."

"We have been discussing Noonan," Priest told her, "and how he might be involved. At least what he might know about Hillyer and why he killed Gutman, and then was killed himself. I think we need to interview him again. But we couldn't get much out of him when we interviewed him at the hospital."

"True. You boys aren't very persuasive with old, dying priests."

"Okay, so you have a lot of experience with old, dying priests?" Aggie quipped.

"No," Alana replied. "But perhaps he might yield to the soothing sounds of a woman's voice."

"Then, you can come with us back to see Noonan?" Priest asked.

"I recommend only me, or maybe you but not Aggie," she replied. "No offense, Aggie. We just don't want for it to seem like we're ganging up on him."

"Got it," Aggie replied. "I'll just sit here in the Cascade Bar and order another drink."

"Easy, fella," Priest said with a chuckle.

SISTERS OF MERCY HOSPITAL

April 9, 2021

Priest entered the hospital in the same manner as before, though this time with a badged cop by his side, He approached the desk and asked for permission to visit Father Andrew Noonan. The woman at the desk called over her shoulder again for assistance and a woman motioned them to come around to the other side of the desk, where she proceeded to guide them to the elevator lobby.

When they reached Noonan's room, the patient seemed worse than on the earlier visit. All the tubes and wires were the same, but Noonan's skin had taken on a slightly grayish pallor. His breathing, even with the help of the oxygen mask, was thinner, and his eyelids – still closed – had a bluish hue that was not indicative of good health.

"Father Noonan," Alana asked gently, touching him on the arm. "Father?" she said repeating herself.

He didn't rouse but just lay there still even with occasional light taps on his arm. Priest decided to not let it go, so he pulled up a chair for Alana and sat down on another one next to the bed.

"What do you plan to do?" she asked.

"I think we should stay, at least for a while, and see if he wakes up."

Alana looked over at the patient, stared at him for a moment, then settled back into the chair that Priest had set up for her.

They sat quietly for about a quarter of an hour; then suddenly Noonan opened his eyes. He didn't look over at his visitors – "probably doesn't know we're here" thought Priest – but stared at the ceiling for a moment. Priest and Alana stood and leaned over the bed, a movement that drew Noonan's attention. He rolled his head to the side and spotted Priest first, then lowered his gaze toward the foot of the bed and saw Alana standing next to him.

"Father, my name is Alana Weber. I am an inspector for the *Bundespolizei* here in Vienna. How are you feeling?"

No response from Noonan.

"This is Darren Priest," she continued, pointing to him, "and we would like to ask you a few questions. Is that alright?"

Still no response from Noonan.

"It has to do with a man named Ira Hillyer, but you may know him as Karl Hilgendorf. Do you recognize those names?"

Finally, a slight nod from Noonan.

"Thank you. We don't want to ask anything that is personal, intimate, or confidential, but we'd like to find out more about Mr. Hillyer – or Mr. Hilgendorf, if you prefer – so that we can find out what he may have done, what people were injured by his actions, and what his actions might portend for other people in the future.

"Is that okay?" asked Alana.

Noonan gave a slight nod.

"Yes," the patient responded. It was the first time that Priest had heard the man speak and, with an apparent opening created by Alana's method, he thought that they may be able to get something.

"Okay," Alana began. "Mr. Hillyer, Mr. Hilgendorf. You knew

him in 1988, when he was in the hospital being treated for gunshot wounds, correct?"

A nod.

"You administered last rites to him, correct?"

A nod.

"Did you speak with him before administering last rites?"

"Yes," Noonan whispered.

"What did you talk about?"

"Hillyer...asked me...to hear...his confession," he whispered weakly.

"And did you?"

A nod.

"Okay," Alana continued, proceeding carefully and with understanding. "We do not want to ask you anything about his confession. Although some of the questions we ask may seem to relate to, well, things he confessed to you. It is not our intention to cause you to violate the sanctity of the confessional, but we need to know whether Mr. Hillyer had information or knowledge of certain things that have great historical consequence."

A nod from Noonan.

"So, we won't ask about what things Hillyer, also known as Hilgendorf, might have done as an officer of the German army during World War II. We do not want to know about that. That is strictly between Hilgendorf, his confessor, and his God.

"We would like to ask about things that he might have possessed, rightly or wrongly. Of course," she said, pausing to find the right words, "that may at times seem to border on sins he confessed. For that, I am sorry. Let me explain what we're looking for and then you can decide whether we can continue. Okay?"

A nod from Noonan. He peered at her closely, seldom blinking, and not looking at Priest at all.

"Okay. We believe that Hilgendorf – can I just call him that?"

A nod from Noonan.

"Right. So, we believe that Hilgendorf might have had a

collection of art and other things. A satchel or notebook, perhaps in a leather case. He might have told you about this in the process of his confession."

She paused.

"I don't want to know about his confession, or whether he admitted to obtaining such a thing illegally. I just want to know whether Hilgendorf spoke of such a collection of art."

Noonan nodded and then pointed his left index finger at the wall. Priest didn't know what he was indicating, so he walked over there, pointing at the sideboard in the room, the window, the curtains, each one in turn and looking to Noonan for recognition. The old man shook his head at each thing Priest pointed at, until he laid his hand on Noonan's nylon suitcase. Priest tapped the bag several times and got nods in reply from Noonan. Rather than opening it himself, Priest brought the bag over to the patient's bed and laid it upon the blanket. He didn't want to rush the process and wanted to take every precaution to assure Noonan that he was respecting his privacy.

Noonan stretched out his fingers and said, "Open the bag... pull the zipper...open it."

Priest followed his instructions. Inside he found clothing and some wrinkled pages from a journal, and a leatherbound book with penned narratives included on the pages. He held them up for Noonan to see and got a nod of assent in reply.

Priest handed the pages to Noonan, but the patient pointed to Alana, as if to tell Priest to give them to her.

"I wrote these," Noonan said haltingly, pointing to the short stack of papers, then he stopped for a breath. "I wrote these...so I would have...a record...of what Karl Hilgendorf told me."

Priest looked at the pages and knew that these would prove invaluable. They were in German but neatly written, so he was sure that Alana could easily translate them.

"I also have this," Noonan said, gently tapping the bound journal. "Open it."

Priest did as he was told and saw on the first page a short

inscription signed by Fra Nizza. And he realized that he held in his hands the entire journal of the monk, the man who had researched and chronicled the path of the Paletti Notebook from its origins around 1500 to his own death in 1943.

The other pages that Noonan had written would likely provide the path of the Notebook from that year, 1943, until the present. It was an absolute treasure in this search for Paletti and his collection.

"You will find here...the information...you are looking for," Noonan added, then closed his eyes.

Priest and Alana retreated from the room, secure in Noonan granting them permission to take both his own diary and Nizza's journal.

"I'll bring this back to the precinct and get a translation on it immediately," she said.

Priest returned to the Marriott and found Aggie still at the Cascade Bar, as promised.

"I'd like a gin and tonic," Priest said to the bartender, sitting down next to Aggie.

"How'd it go?"

"Pretty good. Great, actually."

"Yeah?" Aggie said, sitting forward in his chair. "How great?"

"Alana got Noonan to talk and he showed us what he was keeping in his suitcase by the bed. Turns out that he had some diary notes of his own and – are you ready for this? – Fra Nizza's original journal."

"Shit! That's fantastic!" Aggie exclaimed. "Now what?"

"Alana's taking both back to the precinct to get a quick translation."

"I hope things continue to lead to Sant'Antimo," Aggie said, sipping from his beer. "It would be nice for the pieces to begin to fit together."

Priest nodded as the bartender delivered his gin and tonic.

After about an hour of light conversation – including Aggie asking Priest whether he should look up Benedetta Incisa when he returned to Rome – Priest's phone chirped. It was Alana.

"Here," she said as soon as he answered. "I have something. This is a translation from Noonan's diary.

During my career as a priest, I have answered every command that God gave me, and this has included many instances when I thought there was a personal or public danger. In particular, I have protected the sanctity of the confessional and refused to divulge knowledge of sins committed or planned...until now. I have come into possession of information that bears on matters of great concern, not only for the Church and the penitent who confided in me, but also for civilization as we know it.

Ira Hillyer was shot on the streets of Vienna one week ago. His attackers, Nazi hunters, had concluded that he was an officer in the German army during the war. His original name was Karl Hilgendorf, someone the hunters had charged with the killing of Jews and other war crimes. He was approached on a street, professed his name to be Ira Hillyer, but the men surrounded him and insisted that his name was actually Hilgendorf and that he was responsible for the crimes that they listed. When he tried to run away, he was shot. A passerby intervened before the attackers could put another bullet into him, and Hillyer was carried to the hospital where he lingered for a few days.

I know this, and more, because Herr Hillyer called me to his bedside to hear his confession and administer last rites. At that time, he confessed to his sins during the war, admitted that his true name was Karl Hilgendorf, and then proceeded to tell me about a great treasure that he had in his possession. He called it the Paletti Notebook, something that I had heard rumors of, but then he explained what it contained. In addition to the art of the great masters of the Renaissance from about five hundred years ago, Hillyer told me that the Notebook also contained an ancient text, something written in Coptic, allegedly a gospel written by a man named Matthias. This, too, I had heard of, but only as a mythical document, a heresy perpetrated by apostates to attack the Church and its teachings.

I had every reason to believe what Hillyer told me; he was after all, making his confession. But I doubted whether the contents of the folder were exactly what he insisted they were.

At the end of his confession and just before I administered last rites, Hillyer told me that he had hidden the Paletti Notebook in his apartment, and he described its exact location.

I performed the sacrament of Last Rites and left Hillyer that afternoon, but my curiosity drove me in the direction of his lodgings. I entered the apartment using the key that he had given me, approached the room and section of wall that he had described, and found nothing unusual in its construction. There was no door, no window, no special bookcase or other construction that would suggest an opening to a secret hiding place. I went over Hillyer's words again in my mind and confirmed that I was standing in the right place in front of the right wall.

Convinced that I was following his instructions correctly, I decided that I would have to open the wall. Such a bold decision is not within my usual manner, but by that time I had become convinced that the Paletti Notebook as he described it was hidden in there. Not finding a carpenter's tool or other device, I went to the kitchen and retrieved a butcher knife. Standing before the expanse of the blank wall, I struck the plaster with a downward motion not unlike the way an assailant stabs his victim. The thin layer of plaster erupted with my blow, scattering shards of white powdery chips onto the floor. Another assault by me and the knife, and a hole opened up. Another blow and another blow, and I had an opening that was about twenty by fifty centimeters, enough to allow me to peer inside the wall.

Of course it was dark in there and I saw nothing at first. I turned around looking for a flashlight or other device, spying only two decorative candles on the table behind me. Not being a smoker, I couldn't light them without matches, but Hillyer had conveniently stowed some in the kitchen as would anyone with a gas stove.

Returning to the hole I had made in the wall, I lifted one of the candles, lit its wick, and held it just outside the hole, leaning toward the darkness within. Shadows danced on the interior cavity of the wall as the flame flickered in my hand, so that I couldn't make out anything right away. But after a few seconds, as my vision adjusted to the darkness within, I could make out a bulge of something just inches below the opening I had created. Seeing that the object was too big to lift through the gap I had created, I attacked the wall again, this time with my hands, pulling large chunks of material away, mostly downward toward the thing I had seen inside the wall.

When the opening was large enough, I reached in and withdrew a very old leather satchel secured with a strap and buckle. Brushing off the dust that I had created with the destruction of the plaster wall, I laid the satchel on the table and opened it.

It was filled with old papers and parchment, drawings, letters, and what seemed to be preliminary artwork. Most of it was masterfully done, although some of the sketches seemed less perfect, some were even a bit revolting. I saw one sketch that I was unable to figure out, a convoluted mixture of curves, shading, and lines, until I realized that the outer parts of the drawing clearly depicted the spread legs of a female form.

I also found in the satchel a cloth-wrapped bundle which I opened. The string held it together but, once untied, the cloth fell to the side as if it suffered from many years in its current folded position. Inside the cloth I found sheets of ancient papyrus with lettering that I knew to be Coptic. I understood a bit of the language since we had studied original texts of Christian writers, but I could only barely make out the subject and author.

"Matthias" appeared near the top of the first page, along with various occurrences of the Coptic symbol for Jesus and "savior." In my studies, I had been told about – and warned about – the heresy that is represented in the rumored Gospel of Matthias, warned either because it was mythical or blasphemous, and this seemed to be what I was looking at.

I bound everything up again and decided that I would bring this thing, this Paletti Notebook to my friend and mentor, Abbot Roberto

Conti at San Marco abbey in Florence for safekeeping. I assumed that he would be most interested in the art, the letters, and the purported Gospel of Matthias, so I kept the journal written by Fra Nizza for myself.

A few days later, I arrived in Florence and went directly to San Marco. The abbot received me graciously but, before I could tell him the reason for my visit, he informed me that he was relocating to the abbey at Sant'Antimo, in the Tuscan countryside.

"We'll continue working on the translation," she said, "but I knew you'd like to hear that much."

"Yeah, thanks," Priest replied.

As Priest and Aggie rose to leave the lobby bar in the Marriott, Priest's phone chirped.

"Hello," he answered automatically, but then looked at the screen. It said "restricted," giving him a hint that he should be on guard.

"Do you have it yet?"

The voice was distinctive. Dr. Bordrick was calling, probably from Washington, and he made the call through a black box system to make it untraceable.

"Sure," Priest said, leading him on.

"Okay, then I want you to return home immediately," Bordrick said in his gravelly voice. Call me with your travel particulars and I will..."

"No, not really," Priest added.

"I said call me," emphatically.

"Yeah, I know. I meant that 'no,' I don't have the Notebook yet." He took a certain pleasure in teasing this man, someone whom he didn't like or trust anyway.

"Fuck!" came the reply over the phone. "Goddamn it, Priest, don't pull that shit with me. Do you have it or not?"

"Not yet, but people are getting killed over here," Priest added. Did you know that was going to happen?"

"Have you found the Notebook yet," Bordrick repeated, ignoring Priest's comment.

After a pause, Priest asked "Does your interest have anything to do with the encrypted message in the collection?"

"I want the Notebook," came the reply, but Bordrick didn't respond to the question about the encrypted message.

"We're getting closer," Priest said. "Do you mind giving us time to carry out this mission?"

"Yes, I do mind! You're not on a vacation or a tour of the museums of Europe. Get the damned Paletti Notebook! Now!"

A click indicated that the connection had been terminated. Priest couldn't decide whether he wanted to say more, or that he should be pleased just to get Bordrick's ire up.

"What was that about?" Aggie asked.

Priest had been careful not to mention Bordrick's name out loud so that Aggie and Alana might hear it. Although he had briefed them in on his assignment, plausible deniability might come in handy later.

After completing the call with Bordrick, Priest returned to their conversation.

"So, based on what Alana read to us, it seems like the Paletti Notebook might have been in Hilgendorf's apartment..." Priest began.

"Yeah, but back in 1988," Aggie added. "And it sounds like Noonan went after that thing with a vengeance. No way he left it there. I think we need to go see him again."

"Well, his notes say he took it to Abbot Conti at San Marco..." she said.

"And that Conti was moving to Sant'Antimo," Aggie added.

"Just as you said, Aggie. Perhaps we're going to Sant'Antimo," replied Priest. "And now with more reason."

After they returned to their rooms, Priest got another call from Alana.

"Is Aggie with you?" she asked.

"No. I'm in my room and I think he went back to his."

"Call him over. I think he'll want to hear this too, a further translation that we have. Call me when you're together."

Priest rang up Aggie and told him that Alana had more to read, and he came right over to Priest's room.

"Okay," Priest said to Alana when she answered. "We're together. I'll put you on speaker."

"Right. Here goes. It's additional pages from Noonan's diary.

I spoke at length to my friend, Abbot Conti while he remained at Abbazia San Marco in Florence. He was due to transfer soon to Sant'Antimo and I was fortunate to have found him before that event.

"I want to give you something of possibly great importance," I told him "and I beg you to keep it to yourself, with yourself, even if you move to Sant'Antimo."

He agreed but seemed at odds with the mystery surrounding this announcement. I told him what I had found, beginning with the declaration given to me by Ira Hillyer – a confession, actually – at which Abbot Conti crossed himself and seemed to regret hearing details of another man's sins given in the confessional. The rest of the story unfolded, including my attack on the wall in the man's apartment, at which the abbot smiled and appeared to be visualizing it in the recounting.

"And what became of Herr Hillyer?" he asked me.

"His request for Last Rites was very timely," I responded at first. Then, pausing, I informed the abbot that later on the day that I visited with Ira Hillyer, reports circulated that he had been smothered in his bed.

The abbot was alarmed at this report and asked more about it.

*I told him that there was a note attached to his hospital gown, on his chest, reading "*Ego sum ira Dei,*" and asked if he knew what that meant.*

Abbot Conti was well versed in Latin but did not want to offer a translation, pulling back a bit at the mention of it.

"It is Latin," I said in his stead, "and it means, 'I am the wrath of

God.'" With that in the open, Abbot Conti's expression changed and the frame of his mouth turned downward.

I pressed him for more and he told me about Arma Dei, *the cult of self-proclaimed "sainted soldiers" who had assumed the role of protectors of Church hierarchy. "They have been with us since the early Sixteenth Century," he said, "and apparently they are still here."*

I told the abbot that I wanted him to take this Paletti Notebook from me and hide it. When he protested, I pushed harder.

"I cannot possess it," I insisted, but then he said that he should not have it either. After some discussion and persuasion, he agreed, saying he would take it to the cloister at Sant'Antimo and hide it there.

I kept the journal that had been written by Fra Nizza and my own diary, but gave the ancient works to Abbot Conti to keep in a safe place in Sant'Antimo.

"So, that's it, then," Aggie said. The Paletti Notebook is in Sant'Antimo."

"At least as of 1988," Priest corrected. "We'll find out tomorrow when we visit Abbot Conti."

Turning his attention to Alana on the phone, he asked, "Can you make arrangements for our visit?"

"Yes, of course. I'll get Rafaela to set it up."

1516 BREWING COMPANY, VIENNA

April 9, 2021

In the cool of the evening, the three sleuths decided to repair to their favorite beer hall in Vienna. The selection of drinks and food at 1516 Brewing Company would have been enough, but the outside garden proved irresistible on this unseasonably warm day.

"I've got something here from the office," Alana said to Priest and Aggie. They were sitting at the outside tables in the beer garden.

"It's not good," she continued. "Seems there was a scuffle at the hospital right after we left. Hang on; let me read it first."

Priest looked on, waiting for more from Alana. Aggie sipped his beer.

After a moment, Alana slumped back into her chair.

"It's Noonan. He's dead."

"How?" asked Priest.

"You said the guy was in late-stage cancer," Aggie said hopefully. "Was that it?"

She looked at them for a moment.

"I don't think it was cancer," she began. "Some guys were found in Noonan's hospital room, three of them. Don't know how they got there. A nurse noticed that Noonan was writhing on the bed while one of the other men leaned over him, pushing a pillow onto his face. When she screamed, one of the other guys punched her, then the three ran. Noonan didn't survive. He was suffocated."

"Any description?" Priest asked.

"No, not really. We have a slip of a comment from one nurse..." she said.

"A slip?" asked Aggie.

"That means a glancing view, a short recall," Alana said, "nothing more. She said she saw a cruciform tattoo on one man's wrist. Their faces were covered."

"That sounds like the tattoo we saw on the guys who attacked us at DFR Wien," Aggie offered.

"Yeah," she replied, "that's what I was thinking."

"Why Noonan?" Priest asked, but he knew the answer.

"Yeah, why," replied Alana. Clearly it was because of their visit that afternoon.

"If *Arma Dei* was there to get information, I doubt that Father Noonan gave them very much," she noted. "He didn't even give us much."

"Except for the pages from his diary and Nizza's journal," said Priest, suddenly very pleased that he had salvaged those pages for their investigation. "Those tell us a lot, and *Arma Dei* won't get them from us."

"Let's hope they don't try," said Aggie, sipping his beer.

"Okay, let's move on," Priest said, producing another set of papers from his rucksack. "I have some more translation from Fra Nizza's journal."

It was in 1938 that I came into possession of the Paletti Notebook. I was a monk at Sant'Antimo and, as an historian, I was asked to read, then catalogue, and then control the contents of the collection. When it came to me, it was obvious that no one had opened the leather folder for many years, so the abbot didn't know what it truly contained. He expected me to deal with it, but over the years of being hidden from view, it was clear to me that the collection that Paletti had maintained had grown, although it was still relatively unknown to anyone.

I found all the things that I have described above in the few years that I was the custodian for this collection, but I want to be sure to include what happened to it after I received it.

I kept it at Sant'Antimo and conducted my research in Florence, Rome, and other places in order to make a complete accounting of where the Paletti Notebook had gone. In 1943, as I watched the world fall under the evil domination of Hitler's Nazi party, I became concerned for my welfare, for the welfare of my fellow friars, and for the protection of great and historical things like the art and letters that Paletti had collected.

By then, I had managed to translate some of the Coptic text and saw that this more ancient addition to the Paletti Notebook was likely the lost Gospel of Matthias. While I didn't believe what the man wrote two thousand years ago, I believe it was my responsibility to preserve it.

As the German army swept through Italy, terrorizing the local people and stealing the art of our country, I realized that I would have to move the Paletti Notebook to a safer place. Knowing that the German army was probably closing in on us and knowing that their aim is to confiscate great art and treasures from Italy, I felt the time had come for me to take action.

My friend, Emil Gutman, was in Vienna during that time, and so I resolved to bring the Notebook to him.

Emil is a kind and gentle man, but as a Jew he lives in fear every day that the Germans will come to collect him. Still, he wants to remain in Vienna as long as he can. So I knew, at least for a time, I could find him there.

I booked a seat on a train to take me to that city and deliver the Paletti collection to him. He was surprised by my visit and startled by what I was giving him, but he willingly accepted it. Emil should be remembered as a kind and loving soul, and I appreciate what he did for me on that day.

I also gave him notes on all of my research, and even these pages of my journal to put in with the collected works in the Paletti Notebook. I do not presume to offer the genius and brilliant art of the men whose work is captured there, but I want to preserve the history and chronology of the collection as I have been able to discern it.

"That's where it ends," he said, folding the papers and putting them back into the rucksack.

"We know that Emil Gutman was killed not long after the safe deposit box was registered," said Aggie.

"And from Gutman's note..." said Alana, "what was the date?"

"March 8, 1943," said Aggie.

"Good memory," noted Alana. "Gutman's note said that he was forced to give the things that Fra Nizza had given him, forced to give them to Ira Hillyer. And soon after Gutman was found strangled."

"So, in 1943, or thereabouts," Priest filled in, "the Paletti Notebook went from Fra Nizza at Sant'Antimo, to Emil Gutman in Vienna, and then to Hillyer."

"And when Hillyer was shot by the Nazi hunters in 1988, only Father Noonan knew about it," said Alana.

"And he told us he delivered it to Abbot Conti at San Marco in Florence, resulting in it being moved by Conti back to the abbey at Sant'Antimo," added Priest.

Draining his beer, Aggie announced, "I think I know where we're going next!"

But Alana was not so sure that would be their next stop. She had been watching the people at the tables around him. Only a handful of the chairs in the garden were filled, but there was a group of men on one side who weren't drinking and instead were paying too much attention to her, Priest, and Aggie.

"I think we should go inside, use the restrooms, and exit separately," she suggested.

"Why?" asked Aggie, but Priest came to the same conclusion. The table of four men near them, attentive to their conversation and appeared ready to act when called upon.

"Do you have any shadows?" Alana asked Priest, referring to

the guards often sent to protect him when he was traveling. "Meaning, could they be on our side?"

"I wasn't told I'd have any," he replied. "Besides, below the bulge in their jacket pockets I see a sheath on one guy, carrying a knife. Our guys don't pack knives."

"I suddenly have the urge to take a piss," announced Aggie, who got up and marched into the interior space of the beer bar.

"I'll go too," said Priest, "although I'd rather you go inside first, Alana."

"Still trying to protect me?" she asked.

"Yeah. Always."

"Yeah, well, I'm the one who's armed. You're not," she smiled back at him. "I suggest you go in now and I'll follow."

As Priest rose to go inside, one of the men stood to follow him. Anticipating this, Alana rose from her chair quickly, made it to the door first, and then dropped her napkin, forcing her to bend over and pick it up. She hoped that setting a barrier would slow the guy down; if not, she hoped that bending over and showing the tight form of her blue jeans might also help.

Each of them found separate doors to leave the bar and reconnected two blocks later.

"So, did everyone make it out okay?" she asked.

Smiles all around were her answer, but one block later there was a group of five men, all appearing very interested in the path that Alana, Priest, and Aggie were taking.

"Okay, this is getting weird," Aggie said.

Without slowing their pace, the threesome continued down Schellinggasse toward the hotel. Without giving it away, Alana reached into her pocket and pressed the panic button on her police phone. Within the three minutes it took her and her friends to reach the corner where the group of men stood, sirens were heard and patrol cars turned onto the street just in front of them.

"Wow, great timing!" exclaimed Aggie, but Priest just smiled.

He didn't notice Alana's action either but figured out what had happened.

"*Guten abend*," she said to the officers who emerged from the police cruiser, nodding in the direction of the men they had spotted, then steering her group around them.

"I've got to get one of those," quipped Priest.

"Yeah," she replied, "that and a Beretta."

They made it to Marriott Parkring without another incident. Alana called her parents who were still staying at her house and she asked them to watch Kia for her.

"I'm pulling an all-nighter," she told her mom. "We've got to get this case solved."

"Yeah, I'm sure," her mother replied, although both of them knew the all-nighter would not be spent at the police precinct.

Priest didn't want to continue to cart the photographs with him everywhere they went, so he had arranged for Stefan Haber to keep and protect them. Now that they needed them, Haber met them at the entrance to the hotel with a satchel containing the photographic evidence of the Paletti Notebook.

"*Danke schoen*," Priest said as he relieved Haber of the bag.

They rode the elevator to their floor, entered the room, and opened the satchel of photographs.

"Let's see what we have so far," Aggie said spreading the pictures out on the bed. "Bao Chinh is dead, Emil Gutman is dead, Fra Nizza is dead, Ira Hillyer is dead, and now so is Father Andrew Noonan. Any other casualties that I haven't catalogued?"

"Not in recent times," responded Alana, "unless you'd like to add the guy from the bank or the anonymous assailant from *Arma Dei* in the hallway outside this room."

"Nope," replied Priest. "But we have a lot of information. We haven't translated all the journal entries that there are pictures of..."

"Nor have we deciphered the coded German transcript..." added Alana.

"Yeah, we've got to get to that," Priest said to complete her thought. "I think it's fair to say that we've chased the Paletti Notebook all over Europe and back again, over four centuries. Do you think we know where it is now?"

"Not sure, really," opined Alana. "The last we heard it was at the Abbey Sant'Antimo. But as Aggie was quick to suggest some time back, that was over thirty years ago. Think it's still there?"

"Don't know, but I guess we can go and find out."

"And do you think our friends will join us?" asked Aggie.

"By friends," said Alana with a smile, "I suppose you mean the murderous bastards whose kill sheet continues to rise?"

Priest took a moment to remember Bao. With all the excitement, he had forgotten that his friend was killed for the very treasure that he was still looking for.

"And if these friends join us," added Aggie, "will we have to fight our way in, or out?"

"Probably," Alana said, and she gave Priest a long and serious look. He remembered her anger from earlier and knew that he had to make good on protecting her and making sure that she made it back to her daughter when it was over.

"I think it's time for bed," she announced suddenly. Aggie looked up, smiled, and got the message, leaving them promptly to return to his own room.

"Good night all," he said, "sweet dreams."

"We've got a flight at eight a.m. tomorrow," Priest reminded him.

"On a private government plane," Alana added. "Don't be late."

Aggie smiled and had to remind them, "Fine. At least I won't be up late tonight!" Then he pulled the door shut behind him.

Once they were alone, Alana busied herself with collecting

the photographs and storing them in the folder that they had been using. Priest watched her from a short distance, his hands by his sides, until she looked up.

"What?" she asked.

"Did you mean what you said?"

"About the private plane?" she teased.

"No, earlier. When we were at the Café Central."

"Oh, yeah. About killing you? I really meant it."

"No, the part before that."

Alana put her finger to her chin as if trying to remember.

"Let's see, before that. Hmmm."

"Alright, alright. I get it. You didn't mean it," Priest added, then he turned away as if finding something to do on the desk.

Alana stood still, the bed separating them, and a tear welled up in her eye.

"Yes," she said. "I did. Did you?"

"Yes."

Still with the separation of the bed, she asked plaintively, "Then what are we going to do about you living in the States and me living in Vienna?" The tear broke free and rolled down her cheek.

Priest circled the bed and came over to wrap her in his arms.

"We'll figure that out later. Just let's enjoy this moment for a while."

Kissing her softly on the lips, Priest sat them down on the edge of the bed. Then he brushed her long hair back from her shoulder and kissed her neck. Alana reached her hand around his head, drawing it closer and let out a little sob.

"What's wrong?" he asked quietly.

"Nothing. Nothing at all," she said with a smile.

SANT'ANTIMO 2021

ABBEY SANT'ANTIMO

April 10, 2021

The plane was on time; Aggie was late.

"Sleep well?" he asked, tossing his bag onto the plane.

"Yes, we did," Alana replied, "even without sleeping in like someone I know."

After a brief trip and a soft landing on an isolated airstrip in Tuscany, they were taxiing along a private runway not far from the abbey. Alana had made arrangements for a car with Rafaela who insisted on joining them.

"Just to protect your car?" Alana asked.

"Yes, but I thought it would be a good way to get some time with you."

"That's sweet," Alana added with a chuckle, "but I don't believe you. You're just prying into what we're doing."

"Yes, and that," came the reply.

They drove through the rolling hills of Tuscany, past vineyards and farmland, until they reached the ancient stone abbey of Sant'Antimo on the outskirts of Montalcino, situated on a raised plain and comprised of several wings to house the workers and monks at the abbey. At over one thousand years old, Sant'Antimo had enough history to fill several books, but at the present time it was only lightly used, principally by the Olivetan monks who maintained it, used it for their work, and conducted the liturgy in Gregorian chant several times a day.

A short man with graying hair met the Priest entourage at the entrance to the chapel that faced the parking lot.

"Hello, greetings!" he said cheerfully, bounding up to them. "I am so pleased that you would make the time to come to Sant'Antimo. But without any warning, I had no time to arrange for an official tour."

"Don't worry, padre," said Rafaela, who then addressed him in Italian and offered words of peace and comfort.

"For what reason do I owe this visit?" he asked, smiling, and looking at each of them in turn.

"It's actually very important business, padre," Priest said. "First, may I ask your name?"

"*Sì*, it is Father Roberto Conti. I am the abbot here at Abbazia Sant'Antimo. How can I help you?"

Priest expected to meet with him but wanted to be sure that there wasn't some intermediary at the gate who might slow down the process of their work.

"Thank you. I am..." and he wanted to use his Italian name, Armando Listrani. "I am Darren Priest from America. This is Inspector Alana Weber from the Austrian police in Vienna. This is Arnold Darwin, also from America."

Rafaela stepped forward, offered her police credentials, and introduced herself.

"Father," began Priest, but Rafaela cut him off, speaking rapidly in Italian and getting a raised eyebrow from the padre.

Priest looked at her and asked for a translation. Rafaela merely stated that she had told Conti that they were here on official Italian government business and that she would appreciate his cooperation.

"Okay," said Priest, turning to address Rafaela directly. "Let me be clear. I know we're on Italian soil, but we have been pursuing this thing throughout Europe, principally in Austria, and it contains significant, highly classified information that belongs to my government. You may think that it belongs to the Italian government, and I don't want to dispute that right now, but we will take the Paletti Notebook with us when we leave here."

"We'll see," was all Rafaela would say.

"Can we at least agree that we're on the same side for now?" Priest asked.

"Of course," Rafaela said. "What other side is there?"

"Well," Aggie added, "If you look over your shoulder, you'll see another side," and he hooked his thumb to indicate dust clouds from the road approaching the abbey.

"Looks like there may be more than one side pretty soon," Priest said.

Turning to Abbot Conti, Priest pressed him for details.

"Father, I'm sorry to rush this a bit, but it seems like we might have come competition soon and things might get ugly."

Conti's eyes went wide as he considered what he should do to protect himself and his abbey.

"Do you know Father Andrew Noonan?"

"Yes, but why?"

"Father Noonan told us to come to see you. He was very helpful in our quest, and he said that you would be too."

Conti looked from one face to another, as if he didn't quite trust anyone.

"Where is Father Noonan?" he asked.

"Father," Alana said, lightly touching the abbot's arm with her hand, "I am sorry to say but Father Noonan has passed away. Just recently."

"But he wanted to help us find something of great value," added Priest, "something that he knew you could help us get."

As the cars came closer, Aggie waved his hand in a circle, trying to speed things up.

"Come on. Let's move it along a little faster," he said, looking over his shoulder at the approaching cars.

Conti's hair stood on end and his face flushed with fear.

"We better hurry it up, Darren," said Aggie, pointing to the cars approaching the abbey in great haste. "By the way, I can't say as I know why, but there's another contingent coming to join the party, a few cars a bit behind them. They're big black Suburbans. Isn't that funny," he said with a chuckle. "They look just like the ones the CIA uses."

"Okay, everybody," Alana said, spreading her arms wide and pushing the small group forward as if she was herding sheep. "I think it's time to get inside."

Conti obeyed but was obviously in distress. As they jogged into the nave of the church, Priest continued pelting him with questions.

"Father Noonan told us that he gave you something, a great collection of art and papers, back in 1988. Do you remember that?"

At a slow jog, Conti looked up at Priest and nodded.

"Okay. He gave it to you back then. Where did you put it?"

Conti looked at Priest again but didn't say anything.

They entered through the massive wooden doors that gave way to the inside of the church proper at Sant'Antimo. Once inside, they stopped to let Conti catch his breath. Physical exercise didn't seem to be part of the regimen observed by Olivetan monks as he leaned down and pressed his hands against his knees, taking in huge gulps of air.

"Father, this is important," Priest pressed. "Father Noonan gave you something that most people call the Paletti Notebook. Isn't that correct?"

Conti looked up at Priest from his crumpled position. Reluctantly, he nodded.

"Okay, quickly, father, we need to know where it is," Priest asked.

"Yeah, real quickly," said Aggie. "They've arrived and are just outside the door. Maybe we need to not only know where the Notebook is, but we need to get there now. Now!"

Priest took Conti by the elbow while Alana and Rafaela drew

their sidearms. Aggie had no responsibility other than to follow Priest and avoid getting shot.

The *thwack* of bullets ricocheting off old stone walls helped quicken their pace. Alana got off a few rounds but decided that escape was more important, so she focused on keeping up with Priest, Aggie, and the abbot. Two more rounds were discharged from close by and, looking back, Alana could see that Rafaela had stopped, taken refuge behind a column, and was covering them while they escaped. Not to be left out, Alana turned back, squeezed in between a wall and an altar piece, and discharged three rounds in the direction of the attackers, hitting one in the leg and making the other two pause long enough to take cover.

While Rafaela and Alana held their positions and let the others move back into a safer position, a sudden burst of automatic fire came from just outside the entrance to the church. The first attacking force was already inside, so it couldn't be them. Alana peered around the round stone façade of the column and saw some very American looking men in black suits taking down the original attacking force from behind.

Sensing an opportunity, Alana and Rafaela looked at each other, nodded, and raced toward the sanctuary of the back room where Conti had led Priest and Aggie. Once inside, they counted heads, seeing that everyone had made it, and shut the door. All around them were rows and shelves of old books, pressed together as if they had been collected over centuries and bursting for more space.

"We are in the scriptorium," Conti said. "Where the monks used to come to copy the books and writings of many years ago. It is safe here."

Yeah, sure, thought Priest. Except that the door through which they entered the scriptorium was the only one in the room. Not so safe. No escape.

"There's not another door," he said to Conti.

"Yes, there is," came the reply, and Conti pointed to a huge bookcase that lined one wall. "It was put here only because we had so many books," he said of the massive piece of furniture, "It is not a permanent fixture," he commented, tapping the wooden structure. "We can move it and then there is a way out."

"Okay, that's a relief," Aggie said. "But let's not forget why we came here, and why we are risking our lives today."

"Right," added Priest. Then, turning to Conti, he continued his questioning from before.

"Father Conti, we are here for the Paletti Notebook."

And just as the words came out of his mouth, gunfire exploded in the outer room. It had been quiet for a time, convincing Priest that the CIA-looking guys had overwhelmed the original attackers. But now there was more and it was coming from a different direction.

"Let's speed this up a bit, padre," Priest shouted. "Do you have the Paletti Notebook or not?"

Conti looked at him sheepishly. From his training Priest knew the answer was yes but he also sensed a great reluctance from the abbot to talk about it.

"Seriously, padre. We're all going to die here. Today. Right now. Unless you cooperate."

Conti looked at Rafaela, the only Italian in the group. She nodded to him and he turned back to Priest. Just as he was about to speak, his mouth open to frame the words, an explosion ripped a hole in the wall on the side of the scriptorium opposite of where the gun battle had been going on.

Priest looked through the craggy opening in the stone wall and saw about a half dozen more men running toward the opening.

"Looks like we've got more troops from *Arma Dei* to contend with here," deadpanned Aggie. "They're coming in from the front and now back here," he said, indicating the hole blasted through the exterior wall of the scriptorium.

"And I'm pretty sure we have an unexpected visit from the CIA too," said Priest, thinking hard and fast about how to organize this.

He needed to get the Paletti Notebook, now that Conti's reticence had convinced him that it was here, and then he needed to get everyone out of the church alive. First things first, he thought.

"Father, give me the Paletti Notebook. Now!!"

Conti turned away and leaned into the bookcase that covered the other doorway out. Straining to move it, which of course was too much for his little frame, he made it clear that he needed help. Alana and Rafaela kept their gunfire trained on the opening blasted through the wall while Priest and Aggie put their shoulders into the bookcase, pushing it slowly to the side. The wood creaked and groaned as it scraped against the floorboards but, in a few seconds, when they had moved it about four feet, Conti stopped. His heart was pounding and he was trying to catch his breath, but with a finger pointed downward, he indicated the floor under the bookcase.

Priest and Aggie quickly pried back the floorboards as gunfire crackled behind them. Once opened, the hole below the floor showed that it contained only one thing: a leather satchel bound by a strap and buckle. The two men looked at each other, exchanged a quick smile of amazement, and lifted the treasure from its hiding place.

There was only a little time but Priest had to know that they had found what he was looking for. Under the serenade of bullets bouncing off the stone walls, he pulled back the strap and opened the leather folio. Inside, he immediately recognized the actual drawings and documents that they had been staring at in photographic form for days. Aggie looked at him with a look of glee, and then Priest reached back in and retrieved a cloth-wrapped stack tied with a string. He was afraid to damage it or waste any more time, but he had to know that this was the real Gospel of Matthias.

"Are you finished yet?" yelled Alana. "I'm getting a little tired over here. Wanna switch places?"

Priest untied the string and let the cloth fall to the side. The yellowed, brittle sheets of papyrus stared back at him, covered with unreadable symbols that he had already been schooled to think of as Coptic.

"This is impossible!" muttered Aggie.

"No, it's not," Priest replied. "But getting out of here might be."

"Come on," he yelled to Alana and Rafaela. "We're ready to go."

"What about Father Conti," the Italian cop asked.

"We'll bring him with us," Priest responded.

The original assailants came in the front of the church and they were attacked from behind by what seemed to be American agents of some form. Whichever team had survived that battle would be waiting for them at the door they used to enter the scriptorium.

The other contingent of what seemed to be *Arma Dei* had blown a hole through the outside of the wall, so escaping through that portal might be problematic. But Conti had said there was another door, one which they had just cleared by moving the large bookcase.

"Where does this go?" Priest asked Conti.

"Into a side room, and then into the cloister."

"Let's go!" Priest said.

"You don't want to go out in the direction of your American agents?" Rafaela yelled.

"First of all," Priest shouted, "we don't know they're our agents. And secondly, even if they are CIA, we don't know if they're going to be friendly. Our best bet is to escape and let these three teams fight it out themselves."

He tucked the Paletti Notebook under his arm and approached the door that Conti had indicated. Looking through a tiny window in the door, he could see that their car was parked less than one hundred feet away.

"Here's the plan," he said quietly. "We're going to run like hell and head for that car. Rafaela, do you have more than that one sidearm you're carrying?"

"I have a Beretta as well as this one," she replied, and without asking why, she handed it to Priest.

"I'm first," Priest said, "then Conti, then Alana comes after us, then Aggie, finishing up with Rafaela. That spreads the weapons at positions one, three, and five."

"I don't think I can run that fast," Conti said with fear clearly showing in his voice.

"Padre," Aggie warned him, "you better run like the devil himself is chasing you."

"Because he will be," said Priest. "Ready? Let's roll."

Priest pushed the door open. It was slightly to the right of where the *Arma Dei* force had breached the wall, so he had a slight advantage of surprise. When he ran out he was able to catch some of them uncovered on their flank and he took three of them down quickly.

Conti wouldn't go at first until Alana pushed him through the door. Once in the open with a rain of bullets all around him, the old padre picked up speed and ran right behind Priest. Alana was next and she ran with ease, discharging her Beretta in a steady stream at the opposing forces, dropping one more that Priest had missed.

Next was Aggie. He was faster than Priest and made a dash for the car. Still, he caught a round in his thigh which almost dropped him. Priest looked back when he heard Aggie scream, but he didn't retreat to help him. He knew that Aggie would have to make this on his own if they were going to survive.

Rafaela, deprived of one of her weapons, was still a force to be reckoned with. She used the semi-automatic feature of her Beretta to lay down a barrage of bullets and kept the attackers pinned down until all of them could make it to the car. In a final moment, she switched her weapon to her left hand and pulled the car starter from her right pocket, clicking it several times to unlock the doors.

Priest was already there, taking cover behind the fender and Conti caught up completely out of breath. Priest pushed the abbot down to the ground to take cover and Alana was right behind them. As Aggie and Rafaela caught up, they all dove into the car and buried themselves in the floorboards. Rafaela clicked the remote starter, fired the engine and sped out of the area in a cloud of dust.

Priest leaned out the window but instead of firing on their assailants, he took aim at the two cars they had arrived in. He took a breath and aimed carefully, putting one slug into each gas tank which erupted in fantastic explosions that rocked the cars and made the ground shudder.

Behind them, they could still hear the rat-a-tat of gunfire and assumed that the various teams were still fighting for their survival.

But Priest, Alana, Aggie, and Rafaela had found and rescued the Paletti Notebook, so that was all they came for. Abbot Conti was in the car with them and they would have to decide when and how to return him, but no one was thinking about that just yet.

Alana was in the back seat treating Aggie's wound when Priest looked over his shoulder at her. She seemed okay but then he noticed a growing blood stain on her shoulder.

"Alana, what happened? Are you okay?" he asked.

"Yeah, I'm fine. Why?"

"Why is your shoulder bleeding?"

She pulled the fabric of her shirt aside, ripping one of the buttons to get at it, and saw what Priest was looking at.

"I guess I didn't know I was hit," she said calmly. Abbot Conti looked at her wound and passed out. "It's not bad, I see the scrape, probably a surface hit. Not a puncture." And added, "Don't worry, Darren."

But all he could think about was their conversation in the Café Central when she had admonished him for not telling her what she was risking on this mission.

Rafaela continued to maintain speed on the dirt road departing Sant'Antimo. She was headed for Montalcino and the medical assistance they would need there.

Aggie and Alana were being treated for their wounds and getting patched up. Abbot Conti was treated for stress, given some prescription relief, and released. Rafaela was busy on her phone, calling in the event and the damage to Sant'Antimo, and offering to fill out a complete report when she returned in the morning.

Priest was spent. He just sat there with Rafaela holding the Paletti Notebook firmly in his lap.

When Alana and Aggie emerged from the treatment rooms, they gathered together to leave the hospital.

"You're pretty good with that Beretta," Rafaela said to Priest. "I'm guessing that didn't come accidentally."

"No. Not accidentally."

Alana knew of his training and his marksmanship rating, but she had never seen him use a gun. Nice time to perform, she thought.

As they got to the car, Rafaela told them about the conversation she had with her precinct.

"Not everything, I assume," Alana asked.

"Not everything," Rafaela assured her. "I only told them that I had been involved in a firefight to save a priest's life," and she and Alana had a chuckle over the double meaning. "I didn't tell them which priest, or about the Paletti Notebook."

"Good thing," Priest said.

"Wait," Rafaela insisted. "You can't take that," she said pointing to the leather folder on his lap.

"I'm afraid I must," Priest responded.

"It is the property of the Italian government, and the Italian people."

"That's actually questionable," interjected Alana. "The Paletti

Notebook has been in Vienna for over seventy years. Perhaps it is the property of the Austrian government."

"I'm happy that you two want to fight over this," Priest said, "but I have very clear instructions to bring it back with me to the States."

Aggie stood aside and smiled at the three-way bickering.

"I represent the Italian government," Rafaela insisted, "and I say it will stay here."

"Well, I represent the Austrian government," said Alana, "and I say it comes with me."

"Nice, ladies," Priest said still holding firmly onto the Paletti Notebook, "but I represent the American government – which you would all like to stay in good graces with – and I say it comes with me."

Alana and Rafaela looked at him, then back at each other.

"What if I made you a deal," Alana said, addressing Rafaela.

"What's that?"

"You can get an original drawing from Leonardo da Vinci for your collection. Just choose one from the Notebook."

"That sounds like a bribe," Rafaela said, but she softened the accusation with a smile. "Besides, I don't have a collection."

"But what a wonderful way to start one," her friend replied.

"What's in it for you?" Rafaela asked her.

Alana looked at Priest and then back at her friend.

"Let's just say a long-term commitment."

WASHINGTON 2021

DULLES AIRPORT

April 11, 2021

The plane from Vienna arrived at Dulles Airport right around four p.m. and Priest and Aggie deplaned along with the other passengers, riding the people-mover to the international reception terminal and customs desk. They used their Global Entry passes to get past the long lines of tourists, processing through the incoming lines in only a few minutes, then gathered their luggage from the rotating rack.

While he stood waiting for his bags, Priest thought back to Alana, their argument and its resolution, how his mission might have caused her death, and how she still forgave him – still believed in him – and he had to fight back tears. There was so much he wanted to say to her, so much that they had to discuss and resolve, and this quick trip back to the States was delaying him from doing that.

Alana remained in Vienna, as she should have. Her daughter Kia would need her mother and their reunion would give Alana strength. Priest had to fight back the urge to turn around and board another plane right then to go back to Austria.

But first, he had a mission to complete. He had precious cargo that he was instructed to deliver and, once he had done that, he had the freedom to find Alana and – what? – propose?

The thought wasn't far from his mind. It had been on his mind for two years, since they first met, and through all the trips across the pond to spend time together. Maybe now was the moment when he had to resolve that.

Once Priest and Aggie got beyond customs and bag claim, they walked the long corridor that separated arriving international passengers from the waiting area, then passed through the double doors into the throngs of people greeting relatives, friends, and lovers.

None of those were waiting for Priest and Aggie.

A short man in a black overcoat approached them.

"Hello, Priest," Bordrick said. "Welcome home," although his voice didn't convey a welcoming attitude.

"Yep," was Priest's laconic reply.

Bordrick didn't look at Aggie but focused his attention on the rucksack slung over Priest's shoulder.

"Is that it?" the man asked.

There were two black-suited men standing behind Bordrick. Priest figured they were either CIA or special agents assigned to Bordrick.

"What?" Priest asked.

"Don't pull that shit with me again, Priest. Do you have the Notebook?"

"Yep. I have it right here," he said, tapping the bag over his shoulder.

"Give it to me."

"Who are you going to give it to?" Priest asked, while Aggie stood by and admired the debate.

"None of your fucking business," Bordrick said. "Give it to me."

"I plan to visit President Pendleton later this week," Priest said. "Should I tell him that I gave this to you?"

"You're not going to see Pendleton this week, and if you don't give me the Paletti Notebook now, the only thing you'll see is the inside of a Federal prison."

"Not likely," replied Priest.

He slung the rucksack off his shoulder, pulling it in front of him and unzipping it. Reaching inside, Priest pulled a weathered leather folio out of the rucksack and reached out to one of the agents standing next to Bordrick.

"Here. Protect this," he said to the man.

"Goddamn it," Bordrick blurted out. "Give it to me!"

Bordrick grabbed the leather folio and took it from Priest, tucking it under his arm and turning to leave. Then he stopped and turned back to Priest.

"You're a fucking idiot, Priest. If I wanted to, I could have you in chains."

Priest just smiled. Bordrick then spun on his heels and stomped out of the reception area of Dulles Airport.

"Nice company you keep," Aggie said.

"Yep."

Then Priest pulled out his phone and called Alana. It would be late at night but he knew she'd be expecting his call.

"Where did you put the photographs of the Notebook?"

"In a safe place," she replied.

"Good. Stay safe yourself until I get back there. I don't think this is over yet. We need someone to break that encrypted text. Maybe we need to make that priority number one."

He paused, then added, "One more thing, Alana," he said turning to Aggie so that his friend could hear the conversation. "I love you."

Clicking off on the phone, Priest looked at Aggie.

"How about a beer?" he asked. "I know a great place in Georgetown."

ABOUT THE AUTHOR

Dick Rosano's columns have appeared for many years in The Washington Post and other national publications. His series of novels set in Italy capture the beauty of the country, the flavors of the cuisine, and the history and traditions of the people. He has traveled the world, but Italy is his ancestral home, and the insights he lends to his books bring the characters to life, the cities and countryside into focus, and the culture into high relief.

Whether it's the historical drama that played out in The Sicily Chronicles, *the political dramas of* The Vienna Connection *and* The Etruscan Connection, *the workings of a family winery in* A Death in Tuscany, *the azure sky and Mediterranean vistas in* A Love Lost in Positano, *the intrigue in* Hunting Truffles, *or the bitter conflict of Nazi occupation in* The Secret Altamura, *Rosano puts the life and times of Italy into your hands, capturing the culture and color of the country's history.*

To learn more about Dick Rosano and discover more Next Chapter authors, visit our website at www.nextchapter.pub.

OTHER BOOKS BY DICK ROSANO

Islands of Fire: The Sicily Chronicles, Part I—An historical novel that captures the settlement of the island of Sicily from ancient times to the Roman era, including the wayfaring invasions and battles fought for domination of the land.

Crossroads of the Mediterranean: The Sicily Chronicles, Part II—An historical novel that captures the progress of habitation on the island of Sicily, from the period of Julius Caesar to the present day, including invasions by Greeks, Romans, Goths, Carthaginians, Byzantines, Fatimids, Swabians, Angevins, and many more over the centuries.

The Vienna Connection—Darren Priest's hitch in military intelligence is behind him as he plies his new trade as a writer. But when high-ranking officials call up, he realizes that "some things you can't unvolunteer for."

The Etruscan Connection – Darren Priest is called upon to unravel a mysterious death of an archeologist working on an Etruscan dig in Tuscany. His search unearths the history of the Lydian Kingdom and its links to Italy and the Roman Empire as he tracks down a series of murders meant to hide the true meaning of the dig.

A *Death in Tuscany*—A young man mourns the suspicious death of his grandfather while preparing to take the reins of his family's winery in Tuscany.

The Secret of Altamura: Nazi Crimes, Italian Treasure—Secrets hidden from the Nazis in 1943 are still sought by an art collector in modern days. But evil stalks all those who try to reveal it.

Hunting Truffles—The slain bodies of truffle hunters show up, but the truffle harvest itself has been stolen.

Wine Heritage: The Story of Italian American Vintners—Centuries of Italian immigration to America laid the groundwork for the American wine revolution of the 20th century.

OTHER BOOKS BY D.P. ROSANO

A Love Lost in Positano—A war-weary State Department translator falls for a woman under the blue skies of the Mediterranean, then she disappears.

Vivaldi's Girls—The young red-haired prodigy could make women swoon with the sweeping grandeur of his violin performances—even more so after he traded in his priest's robes for the dashing attire of a rich and notorious celebrity.

To Rome, With Love—Some memories are never forgotten. As Tamara discovers the charms of Rome in the arms of her first love, the sights, food, and wine sweep her away.